I0591355

THE MOM IDENTITY

THE MOM IDENTITY

CASE FILES OF AN URBAN WITCH™ BOOK TWO

MARTHA CARR

MICHAEL ANDERLE

DISRUPTIVE IMAGINATION

This book is a work of fiction. All of the characters, organizations, and events portrayed in this novel are either products of the author's imagination or are used fictitiously. Sometimes both.

Copyright © 2021 LMBPN Publishing
Cover by Fantasy Book Design
Cover copyright © LMBPN Publishing
A Michael Anderle Production

LMBPN Publishing supports the right to free expression and the value of copyright. The purpose of copyright is to encourage writers and artists to produce the creative works that enrich our culture.

The distribution of this book without permission is a theft of the author's intellectual property. If you would like permission to use material from the book (other than for review purposes), please contact support@lmbpn.com. Thank you for your support of the author's rights.

LMBPN Publishing
PMB 196, 2540 South Maryland Pkwy
Las Vegas, NV 89109

First US edition, March, 2021
Version 1.02, Ocotober 2021
ebook ISBN: 978-1-64971-622-4
Print ISBN: 978-1-64971-632-3

The Oriceran Universe (and what happens within / characters / situations / worlds) are Copyright © 2017-21 by Martha Carr and LMBPN Publishing.

THE MOM IDENTITY TEAM

Thanks to the JIT Readers
Dave Hicks
Diane L. Smith
Dorothy Lloyd
Wendy L Bonell
Jackey Hankard-Brodie
Angel LaVey
Jeff Goode

If we've missed anyone, please let us know!

Editor
Skyhunter Editing Team

From Martha

To everyone who still believes in magic and all the possibilities that holds.

To all the readers who make this entire ride so much fun.

To Louie, Jackie, and so many wonderful friends who remind me all the time of what really matters and how wonderful life can be in any given moment.

From Michael

*To Family, Friends and
Those Who Love
To Read.
May We All Enjoy Grace
To Live The Life We Are
Called.*

CHAPTER ONE

Lucy and Jackie stepped out from behind North Broadway Bridge's supports, onto the concrete embankment running down to the Los Angeles River. They both had their wands raised, and Lucy held up the protective amulet that acted as her identity badge.

"Silver Griffins," she said. "Put your weapons down and step away from the manatee."

The smugglers standing by the riverbank did the opposite. Hidden from the mundane world above by the bridge, two gnomes and a nereid turned to face Lucy and Jackie. One of the gnomes carried a handgun, while the other one and the nereid raised their hands, magic shining around their fingers. The nereid's power shone blue and green, the natural colors of a sea nymph, while the gnome's was a glistening black like tar. Behind them, a manatee lay on the edge of the river, a spell holding a film of warm water around its body other than its head. Two crates had been strapped to its back with military-style webbing, while a third lay waiting to be loaded.

"Get back, or I'll blow you both away!" the gnome with the handgun said. He held the gun sideways as if he'd been watching too many gangster movies, a stance that matched his baggy t-shirt and low-slung pants. Lucy had never seen anyone try so hard to get away from their roots.

"Dilabor." Lucy waved her wand.

The gnome pulled the trigger a second too late. As his finger tightened, the ammo clip dropped out of his gun, the hammer fell off, and the barrel clattered to the ground.

"Water rage and thunder round," the nereid chanted, waving slender, seaweed-draped arms, "hurl my enemies to the ground."

A pillar of water rose from the river and rushed at the two Silver Griffins.

"Evaporo!" Jackie shouted.

Fiery light blazed from her wand, briefly turning her blond bob red. There was a ferocious *hiss* as the heat collided with the water and a blast of hot air as the liquid turned into steam. A cloud swirled around them, hiding everything from view.

"Quick, before they get away." Lucy ran forward.

She reached the gnome as he was throwing away the useless pistol grip. He swung a fist at her, but she caught it, twisted his wrist around, and shot out a foot, kicking his legs out from under him. He fell to the ground and groaned. Another quick spell tightly wrapped him in chains.

Jackie advanced on the nereid with her wand raised, the two shooting spell after spell as they countered and intercepted each other's magic. There were bursts of steam and blocks of ice, ripples of power in the air, and sudden moments of silence as obliterated spells swallowed the energy around them.

"You have no authority over me," the nereid declared as she backed toward the river. "I am a mistress of the ocean, not bound by the laws of the land."

"The laws of magic apply to everyone," Jackie retorted. "This sure looks like a magical moment to me."

The nereid swung her arm around, and long strands of seaweed shot out, entangling Jackie's wand arm. As Jackie tried to break free, the nereid stepped closer, and the seaweed crept up around Jackie's throat, cutting off her next attempt at a spell.

"Can't... breathe..." she gasped as she clawed at the seaweed, its slippery tendrils sliding from her grasp.

"Disseco!" Lucy swung her wand. As she did, a blade of air formed at its tip and sliced through the seaweed. Severed from their source, the tendrils around Jackie went limp and fell to the ground, hitting the concrete with a spattering sound.

"No!" The nereid sent more seaweed from her other arm, but Lucy was ready. The grasping plants slid off a magical barricade and tangled around themselves. As they withdrew, Jackie slammed into the nereid shoulder-first, and the two of them fell to the ground with Jackie pinning the magical to the rough concrete.

"I've got this," she said. "Go after the other guy."

Lucy ran down to the water's edge, where the remaining gnome was pushing the befuddled looking manatee into the river. The creature made a noise of protest and flapped a flipper uselessly in the air.

"Last warning," Lucy called. "Step away from the manatee."

"You have no right." The gnome pointed his hand at her, dark magic shimmering around his fingers. "I'm an honest merchant engaged in family business."

"Honest merchants don't bring magical artifacts through illegal portals or smuggle them down the coast while they think no one is looking."

"It's cheaper to carry cargo by manatee than by rail. Everyone knows that."

"Manatees don't live on this coast. How can that be cheaper?"

"He's an immigrant. You gonna get racist on me now?"

As he talked, the gnome was trying to shove the manatee down the last few feet of concrete into the water. Managing the beast clearly hadn't been his role in the plan since he could barely shift it, despite straining and grunting with exertion. The manatee tried to push back and looked at Lucy with pleading eyes.

She launched chains at the gnome, but he shot back a blast of magical tar that brought them down before they could reach him, then dodged a freezing spell. In retaliation, he summoned a blast of fire that singed the side of Lucy's Black Canary t-shirt.

"You little wanker!" she exclaimed as she saw the damage to the shirt, her English accent stronger in the moment of stress.

"There's more where that came from," the gnome growled as flames danced between his fingers.

Lucy tightened her grip on the uneven handle of her

wand. As if from nowhere, a thought came to her: what did a stranded manatee dream of?

"Somniabunt revelare," she chanted.

It wasn't a spell she'd ever been taught, and she knew as she cast it that it wouldn't quite match what her wand was hinting at, but it was near enough. Suddenly, ocean water surrounded the gnome, the manatee, and her.

As she and the gnome gasped for breath, the manatee flexed its tail. Back in a familiar environment, it knew how to protect itself. The tail hit the gnome hard in the back, knocking him over.

The ocean lasted only a few seconds. Then they were back beneath the bridge, soaking wet and with the gnome lying face down on the concrete. Before he could get up, Lucy was on him, pressing a knee into his back while she slapped on a pair of magically reinforced handcuffs.

"Thanks for the assist," she told the manatee. "You're a real sweetheart."

Jackie emerged from the last of the dissipating steam, looked at Lucy, and laughed. "What happened to you?"

Lucy tucked a soggy strand of hair behind her ear. "A little experimental magic. Sometimes I think this new wand has a mind of its own."

"At least it's on your side." Jackie helped haul the gnome to his feet. "Or at least it didn't side with this guy."

They cuffed the captives together in a huddle on the bank, then Jackie called for assistance while Lucy opened the crates. Inside was everything they had expected: glowing crystals, bags of rune stones, magical amulets, and a couple of small grimoires.

"You have some real cheek, sunshine," Lucy looked at

the ocean-soaked gnome, "skimming this sort of loot off a mobster like Zero. You're lucky we're the ones who caught you because he wouldn't have sent you anywhere as nice as Trevilsom Prison."

"Haven't you heard?" the gnome said. "Zero's dead. This was up for grabs."

"Oh, I know about Zero. It was my family and me who took him down, with some help from friends of ours." Lucy crouched in front of the gnome and tapped his nose with the tip of her wand. "My eight-year-old daughter spoiled Zero's magic at the height of his power. What on earth makes you think a two-bit tosser like you could get away from me?"

The gnome trembled, fearful eyes fixed on the wand. "You…you took down Zero?"

"What can I say? Taking down LA's most powerful gangster is just another Tuesday to me. You might as well confess now, because you're going to in the end."

"We did it!" the other gnome said in a voice of panic. "We were going to take the crystals to—"

"Shut up Rudy, you idiot," the wet gnome snarled. "Don't say nothing until our lawyer's here."

"But I'm a—"

"I said shut up."

Jackie returned, long legs taking the walk along the river bank in swift, bouncing strides. "Wagon's on its way. I called a guy from the Heal the Bay Aquarium to help with the manatee."

"How long are they going to be?" Lucy glanced at her watch. "I need to get going if I can."

"Me too, but one of us needs to keep an eye on today's

catch."

"Well, what do you need to get away for?"

"Coffee date. And you?"

"Meeting with my manager."

"So you're going to argue that Applegate should take precedence over my—"

"Don't even finish that sentence." Lucy laughed.

"Hey, I was gonna say love life. If your mind went somewhere bad, that's your problem."

"We could guard ourselves," the nereid said hopefully. "I promise I won't try to escape."

"I've heard how much your kind value promises to landlubbers," Lucy said. "Don't think I'll take my chances." She looked at Jackie. "Rock paper scissors for it?"

"All right."

Fortunately for Lucy, she'd learned to predict which choices her friend would make. Her rock blunted Jackie's scissors, and two minutes later she emerged from under the bridge, leaving the crime scene behind. She headed up to Baker Street, where her electric Rivian SUV was parked. She was unlocking it when another vehicle caught her eye, a familiar black van with an eagle painted on the side.

"Subtle and stylish," she muttered to herself while rolling her eyes.

There was no one in the van, but as she approached, she saw a figure skulking between a pair of bins across the street. She walked over, offering a wave and a smile full of friendliness that she didn't really feel.

"It's Level Three," she said. "What's a mid-league bounty hunter like you doing in a run-down place like this?"

Ringo Fuller straightened his wraparound shades and

stepped out from between the bins. He flexed his arms, muscles moving in an exaggerated way beneath his tight black t-shirt.

"That's none of your business, Agent 485," he said. "It's a free country, and last I checked, even the magical laws didn't stop me from going wherever I needed to be to catch criminals."

"True, true." Lucy's smile widened. "Wait, you weren't after a bunch of smugglers today, were you? Like, maybe a couple of short blokes meeting a nereid down by the river? Anyone left over from Zero's crew probably has a bounty on them, and if you catch them carrying out a crime, there's usually a bonus. Shame if you missed out on that."

"I don't know what you're talking about," Fuller said.

His shades hid his expression, but Lucy liked to think that there was disappointment there.

"Wouldn't be the first time I beat you to the target," she said. "Won't be the last. If you want to see what you missed, Jackie has them trussed up under the bridge."

"I have things I need to do." Fuller pulled out his keys and headed for his van. "Agent 782 can entertain herself."

"If that were true, she wouldn't go on so many dates. You go do your important business that you definitely didn't just make up."

Lucy waved as the van headed off down the street, then climbed into her Rivian. Bad guys captured, smug bounty hunter thwarted, and she would still be on time to grab a cuppa before she had to get back to HQ. It was another beautiful day in LA.

CHAPTER TWO

Ellis Ellis, Silver Griffin Agent 399, walked out of LAX onto West Century Boulevard. He strode along in his oversized red sneakers, glad to be off the plane and able to stretch his legs. There were advantages to being a traveling Griffin agent, like seeing new sights and always having an excuse not to go to bad parties, but there were some giant downsides as well, and being crammed up for hours inside a flying tin can was one of them.

The Uber he'd called was already waiting for him in the street.

"East Florence Avenue, right?" the driver asked as Ellis climbed into the back, slinging his duffel bag down on the seat next to him. He could come back for his luggage later if he needed to. With any luck, he'd catch his target today and be straight back out of town.

"That's right," he said. "As close to the Walgreens as you can get."

The driver laughed. "Walgreens parking lot then?"

"That would be perfect."

While the driver took them through the bustle of afternoon traffic, Ellis reached up his sleeve to check that his wand was readily available, settled snugly in its quick draw holster, then felt inside his jacket to check that his amulet was in place. He was pretty sure the target didn't know he was coming, but a con woman had to live by her wits, a magical one doubly so, and he wasn't going to take any chances.

"You here on business?" the driver asked, taking in Ellis's charcoal gray suit. Then he registered the narrow tie in a bright red that matched Ellis's sneakers. "Or are you a musician? You have that look, with the little beard and all."

Ellis stroked his goatee and laughed.

"That's mighty kind of you, but I ain't any kind of entertainer. I'm just here for work."

"What sort of work?"

"Insurance salesman. Don't suppose I could interest you in a life insurance policy?"

"Nah, dude. I'm all good."

Ellis smiled. That was the beauty of the insurance cover story. It was dull enough that no one wanted to ask more, and most people would shut up once they heard it, in case you tried to keep selling them something.

The car pulled up to the Walgreens. Ellis grabbed his duffel, said goodbye to the driver, and hopped out. Then he pulled out his phone and called up his fake app.

To call it a fake app wasn't completely true. It was a real app. It simply didn't do anything real for itself. Instead, it was something like a magical receiver, tuned to a frequency Ellis had set. Whatever spell he was concentrating on, some reflection of its content would show up on the screen. These days, folks practically expected you to be staring at a phone screen all the time. That made it a hundred times less conspicuous than having a magical display hovering in the air in front of you and far less awkward to explain than staring blankly into space while you looked at data no one else could see.

This time, the app showed the results of a tracking spell that Ellis had been weaving for months as he gathered information on his target and what she'd been up to. He'd slowly kept feeding into this spell while he chased other criminals, until the pieces started to form a coherent whole: known aliases, past crimes, bits of description, habits, and ways of speaking. Of course, half of the information he had on her would be untrue since that was the way she worked, but he'd written the spell himself, and it was smart enough to take that into account.

Now, at last—months after she escaped a holding cell— it had pinned a magical trace on Meredith Womack. Specifically, it had traced her to this Walgreens, on a schedule that said she was working there.

Ellis walked into the store and looked around. Assorted customers roamed the aisles, perusing shelves full of painkillers, bandages, and shampoo. Near the back was a photo processing place—who used those anymore?—next to the pharmacy counter. A few staff were around, working the counters, stocking shelves, and offering advice to customers. None of them looked like the woman he was after, but that didn't mean anything. Womack was a master of disguise, both mundane and magical, without which she would have been sent to Trevilsom years ago.

Eyes flitting from his phone to the room around him,

Ellis made his way slowly down the aisles. He made sure to spend time looking at the shelves as if searching for something while he scrutinized the store's other occupants. The app said that she was nearby, but it was having trouble pinning her down. That was the trouble with fuzzy magic. The results got sloppy in a high-magic setting, and there were few cities on Earth with as much magical activity going on as LA.

"Can I help you with something?" A redhead young woman in a store uniform walked up to Ellis with a smile on her face.

"Sure." Ellis took a second to consider which lie would work best on her and decided to go for something with a hint of drama. "Please don't look around because you might spook them, but I'm looking for someone, and I hoped you might help."

"Looking for someone?" The young woman raised an eyebrow. "That sounds kinda suspicious to me. I think maybe I should get my manager."

"It's not a problem if you want to do that, but it might work better if you didn't." Ellis pulled a card from his pocket and handed it to her. "Edward Jones, insurance investigator. I'm searching for a woman who might be going by the name of Meredith Womack, looks kinda like this."

His long finger tapped the phone's screen, and a mug shot came up.

"Did she cheat on a claim?" the young woman asked while looking at the photo.

"Far from it." Ellis smiled. "I'm here with good news for her. A great aunt passed away, bless her soul, and left behind a sizable life insurance policy. If I've found the right woman at last, then Mrs. Archibald's spirit can finally rest in peace, knowing that her family's cared for."

"This isn't how insurance companies usually work, is it?" The redhead frowned and stared at him suspiciously. "I thought you were all about trying to avoid paying up."

"That's what sets us aside at Texas Corporate and Mutual. Our clients pay that little bit more to know that we'll go the extra mile. They want the comfort of knowing that their policy does what it should, to take care of those they love. Insurance, ma'am, is like any other game: you get what you pay for, and if you don't mind my saying so, some of your big city firms, well, they ain't worth one shiny dime of the cut-rate you pay them."

"Huh." The young woman squinted at the photo. "May I?"

"Sure." Ellis handed her the phone, and she held it up, zooming in for a better view of the woman with her long dark hair, round face, and wide brown eyes. "That could be Molly Webster. She turned up a couple of months ago, working here part-time. Quit suddenly yesterday, said she'd got an offer of work elsewhere, but something about the way she said it sounded off, you know? Like, she wouldn't say what the job was, and she was buying travel sickness meds." She handed back the phone. "Are you sure she's not in trouble?"

"Not with me. Don't suppose you know where she lives or anything about what she does when she ain't stacking these here shelves?"

"Far as I know, she lived local. I remember her saying she'd looked at an apartment over a shop in Inglewood, but

I don't know what shop or if she even took the apartment in the end. I know she didn't invite me for any house-warming."

"Well, thank you for your time. If anything occurs to you or any of your colleagues, could you give me a call? My number's on the card, email too."

"Sure thing." The woman smiled, then leaned in to whisper, "A word of advice? Next time you're trying to blend in, maybe don't be a dude browsing in the tampon aisle."

Ellis laughed. He hadn't even noticed what he was doing.

"Mighty kind of you." He headed out to the parking lot.

Once he was gone, the redhead walked to the back of the store, where her manager worked the checkout.

"Hey Walt, is it all right if I take my break?"

The manager looked around, then nodded. "Sure thing. Just don't be too long."

The redhead grabbed her bag, walked out through the back of the store, and took a moment to look around for the so-called insurance investigator. Everything seemed to be clear, so she hurried away past the Buy Low, down East Beach Avenue, before turning left up Edgewood and taking the long way around to a Starbucks half a mile from the shop. It wasn't the safest choice, given who else regularly made use of Starbucks, but that was part of the appeal. Silver Griffins were a pretty smug lot, and it seldom occurred to them to look right under their noses.

In the Starbucks bathroom, she stripped off her uniform, then the ginger wig, and took out the green contact lenses that went with it. She'd got everything she wanted from her time at the Walgreens anyway, so while it was always a shame to abandon a good cover story, this one was no great loss. One less identity to maintain meant more time free to follow her main plan, which was finally getting into gear. The location was set, the marks were ready, and she'd assembled all the resources she needed to start.

Dressed in bright shorts and a tourist's souvenir t-shirt, with a wide-brimmed hat and sunglasses to hide her face, Meredith Womack stepped out of the Starbucks and back onto the streets of LA. She pulled out her phone and attached a tiny handheld device, one she'd hidden between her fingers the whole time she held the Silver Griffin's phone. A copy of his data sprang up on her screen, and she smiled. In some ways, it was good that he had almost caught her. Now she could find out exactly what he knew and how he had used that information.

With any luck, he would conclude that his target had bolted and that his best bet was to leave LA. Then she would be free to get on with her real work, the big plan she'd been building up to for years.

This was her moment. In years to come, criminals would speak the name of Meredith Womack with respect, maybe even with awe. With any luck, law enforcement would forget that it was a name they had ever heard.

In the Walgreens parking lot, Ellis summoned an Uber to take him back to the airport. Most of the cars nearby were busy, so he would have to wait ten minutes. With time to kill, he switched back to the fake magic app.

Something was wrong. The connection between his signal and the app had been disrupted as if some other device or magic had gotten between them. He called up the app's logs and saw a spike in data traffic where nothing should have been, only a couple of minutes before. Something had happened in the store.

Something had happened with that girl.

He strode back in and looked around. She was nowhere to be seen.

"Excuse me, sir," he said, flashing a cop-like badge at the manager. You could get a long way with a silver disk and a serious voice. "The redhead young woman who was here a few moments ago, do you know where she is?"

"On her break." The manager jerked a thumb toward the back room. "Go find her if you want."

"Thank you kindly."

Ellis strode into the break room at the back of the store. The room was empty, and a locker in the corner hung open, as did the back door. Maybe she had gone out for a smoke.

As he stepped out the door, he knew that he wasn't going to find her, just like he knew that this time tomorrow, the store would be looking for a new employee. He laughed, half at the absurdity of it all, half in admiration at Meredith Womack. Despite his efforts, she'd seen him coming, and now she was in the wind. If she hadn't gotten greedy and messed with his phone, he never would have known. He would have taken that bait about travel sickness meds and headed right back out of town.

However, now he knew. She was here, in LA, and she was staying. His tracking spell wouldn't get him any further, but there was more to detective work than tricks and gadgets.

It was time to call in the locals.

CHAPTER THREE

Lucy pulled her Wonder Woman travel cup from the glove box, picked up a paper bag, and headed into the Starbucks.

"Usual?" the barista asked when she reached the front of the queue.

"Please." Lucy wondered if it was her face that made her memorable or whether it was the superhero cups. Did every Silver Griffin get recognized in every Starbucks on their patch? They all went into the shops often enough. What did the baristas think? Presumably, the same magic that hid the station doors kept staff from noticing the repeat customers who vanished into the back. Without something like that, the whole cover could fall apart. Or were the baristas in on it?

By the time she got to the end of that thought, her tea was being held out to her. She gave it a good stir, got rid of the teabag, and added milk. A sip of that flavor immediately reminded her of home. You couldn't get Yorkshire Tea for love nor money in LA, but this was good enough to make her think of home.

She headed for the back of the coffee shop. Near the toilets, surrounded by a faint chocolate scent, she slid the wand from her back pocket, tapped the wall, and walked through.

Beyond, a set of metal stairs wound down in a well-lit spiral. Her footsteps sent out hollow *clangs* as she descended, the bustle of the magical underground rising to meet her. She turned off before she reached the main station and used her wand to get through a restricted turnstile, down a narrower corridor and another stairwell, to a specialist station.

A small platform, clean and bare, sat next to a single track. A shiny blue train car sat on the rails, gleaming in the glow of a row of brass lamps. Lucy held out her wand as she stepped onto the platform. A small box on the ceiling above her turned with a whir, magic-mechanical sensors shifting to evaluate the new arrival.

"Agent 485," she announced. "Heading in for a meeting."

"Welcome, Agent Lucy Heron," said a smooth baritone voice. "Please take a seat. Your train will depart shortly."

The door of the train slid silently open, and Lucy stepped inside. Two leather benches faced each other across the car, one of them occupied by a pair of suited gnomes. Lucy took the other one, setting down her paper bag beside her, and sat drinking her tea while the train rushed off down a darkened tunnel. While she contemplated the merits of a good cuppa, the gnomes talked about the odds on an upcoming baseball game.

"What do you think?" One of them looked up at Lucy.

"I think I prefer cricket," she said. "Got to love a sport with tea breaks."

The gnomes turned back to talking among themselves, and a minute later they arrived at the stop for Silver Griffins HQ. Lucy got off first and headed over to the station keeper's office, a small wooden booth between the platform's exit tunnels. A gnome in a navy blue uniform with shiny brass buttons smiled at her as he pulled up the wooden-framed window at the front of the booth.

"Afternoon, Normandy," Lucy said.

"Good afternoon, Agent Heron." The gnome tapped the brim of his cap. "How are you doing?"

"Great, thanks. And you?"

"Looking forward to the weekend." Normandy nodded at the gnomes from the train as they walked past. "I've started taking pottery classes. This week, I'm going to make a vase."

"Is that from your class?" Lucy pointed at the brightly colored, slightly misshapen bowl sitting on Normandy's desk.

"Isn't it fine?" He held it up for her to see. "All my work."

"Well, here's something to go in it." Lucy handed him the paper bag.

"Ooh, chocolate chip," Normandy licked his lips as he stared at the cookies. "Thank you very much, Agent Heron."

"My pleasure."

Lucy headed down a tunnel and up a spiral of metal stairs that ran through the hillside above the station. At the top, her wand opened a door, and she emerged into a darkened corridor. Excited chatter emerged from a doorway a few feet away as tourists waited in the Griffith Observatory Planetarium for the next show to start. It never stopped amazing Lucy that this was where she worked, even if she seldom had the chance to make the most of it.

She walked out to the central rotunda, past curious kids and contented-looking parents who were enjoying the spectacle of the place, then along the exhibit hall, past models of planets and bright images of outer space. Another tap of her wand took her through a small door hidden in the wall, while a haze of magic distracted visitors from noticing her disappearance.

In the reception room of the Silver Griffins' headquarters, a young wizard was sitting behind a mahogany desk. "ID please."

"Of course." Lucy held up her Wonder Woman cup.

The receptionist raised an eyebrow. "Your other ID?"

"It works in Starbucks."

"So does calling a medium coffee tall, but I'm not falling for that here."

"Fine."

Lucy waved her wand over a sensor. A light blinked green on the desk, and the receptionist nodded.

"In you go, Agent Heron."

Roger Applegate was waiting for Lucy when she got to his office. The regional manager was impeccably dressed as always, his three-piece suit distracting from the fact that he was red-faced, slightly overweight, and heading out the far side of middle age. Although old-fashioned smart wasn't Lucy's dress style, she could appreciate the good it did some people.

"You look like you've had a run-in with a bonfire." Applegate gestured at a seat.

"Oh, yeah." Lucy looked down at the singed section of her t-shirt. She should have thought to cover that up. At least it didn't reveal anything indecent, only a couple of inches down the side of her belly. "One of the lads we were arresting had a touch of fire magic."

"I assume that justice was served?"

"Yes, sir. I left Jackie to guard them until the arrest wagon arrives."

"Splendid. One more victory for the good guys." Applegate reached across the desk to hand Lucy a bulging cardboard folder. "Now I have another one for you. A string of thefts of magical artifacts that we think might be linked."

Lucy opened the folder and skimmed through the papers.

"Most of these aren't on my turf, sir. Shouldn't someone else handle the case?"

"They're scattered across town, so it's not really anybody's area. I thought your interest in art and history might be useful in looking for connections between the artifacts. Plus…" Applegate leaned back in his chair. "Well, your family spotted the pattern in the Zero case. I thought this might be a chance to tap into their talents again, as we discussed."

"I'll have to check with Charlie," Lucy said firmly. "We said we wouldn't get the kids involved without agreeing to it first."

"Of course. Your family, your rules." Applegate smiled at her. "Think of it as an opportunity, not an order. If you want Team Heron to tackle this one, you can do that. If not, it's over to you, agent."

"Thanks, sir. Will that be all?"

"No, one other thing." Applegate picked up the receiver on his desk phone and prodded a button. "Sam, could you send Agent Petrie in, please?"

Lucy tensed. She didn't mind picking up whatever cases Applegate flung her way. She was happy to get her family involved if they could help with the investigation. Teaming up with Kelly Petrie? That wasn't a place she wanted to go.

Kelly walked in, smiling brightly from behind her perfect makeup, her pantsuit almost as smart as Applegate's. She glanced at Lucy's burned shirt, and that helpful smile almost twitched into laughter.

"Can I help with something, sir?" She beamed the full wattage of her attention onto Applegate.

"Actually, I'm going to help you ladies. Or rather, the department is." Applegate picked up a pair of thick ring binders off his desk and passed one to each of them. The binders were identical, their glossy blue covers decorated with stock photos of brightly smiling people in suits. "You've both shown an interest in promotion, and you have the fieldwork experience, but leadership is a whole other ball game. To help you crack that part, we've signed you up for a management training course."

"Oh." Lucy stared at the folder, trying to work out how she would fit training alongside her job, the kids, and all the other things in her life. Sure, this was useful, in theory, but in practice…

"Thank you so much, sir," Kelly said. "I'm sure that Lucy appreciates the opportunity too, even if it doesn't look that way right now."

Lucy stifled the urge to glare at Kelly.

"Absolutely. I'm sure this'll be grand. When does it start?"

"Right now!" Applegate laughed. "Well, this week, but you'll want to get started on the reading, I'm sure. On that basis, I won't keep you any longer. Get to it, ladies, do this department proud."

With the case folder and the ring binder stuffed under one arm, clutching the remains of her tea in the other hand, Lucy followed Kelly out of the office. The door swung shut behind them, and they stood together, staring at the thick binders full of unexpected homework.

"There go my free evenings," Lucy said.

"I suppose you'll abandon the hiring committee, then," Kelly said. "Leaving the rest of us to pick up the slack at school."

Lucy froze for a second. With the business of the day, she had forgotten the other thing she was doing with Kelly.

"I'll still be there," she said. "I chose to join the PTA, and I chose to join that committee. I stand by my commitments. Besides, it's not only your kids at that school. I want to make sure that Ashley gets the best education she can."

Knowing that Kelly was involved made her doubly determined to help make the right choice. Kelly would probably pick the teacher who dressed best or stuck closest to the rules or did the best job of kissing up to her. The kids deserved someone creative who would think of new ways to engage them, not someone who stuck with hierarchies and old-fashioned thinking.

"Good," Kelly said, without conviction. "This is serious business, and you'd better treat it that way."

"I'll be fine, as long as you don't pull any cheap magical tricks again."

"I don't know what you mean."

"Sabotaging my contribution to the bake sale?"

"I did no such thing."

"Yeah, right."

They stood glaring at each other.

"It seems we're going to be spending a lot of time together." Kelly tapped her binder. "Between the course, the committee, and work."

"Don't remind me. Next thing you know, we'll be double-dating."

"What a delightful idea."

"Huh?"

"I've only met Charlie in passing, and I'm sure Max would love to meet you both. It would give us an opportunity to iron out our differences."

Lucy stared at Kelly. Was she serious? This had to be some sort of elaborate windup. Or perhaps it was a scheme, a way for Kelly to gather dirt on Lucy and her family, to undermine their position with the Griffins. Either way, an evening out together sounded like some kind of hell.

Or perhaps Lucy herself was being unkind. They worked together, both here and at the school. Would it be such a bad thing if they tried to get along, if not for their sake, for everybody else's?

"Sure," she said. "Let's arrange something for next week."

Kelly smiled stiffly, leaving Lucy to wonder if the whole

point had been for her to say no. If so, then she'd won this round by accident.

"Great. I'll message you." She stalked away, leaving Lucy alone with a heap of paperwork and a cup of lukewarm tea.

She was very glad she had the tea.

CHAPTER FOUR

Meredith Womack stood at the front of the room, a teacher in front of her class. Not any sort of teacher she had ever encountered growing up, but that was the point. She was going to teach these people how to make proper use of their skills.

Behind her, faded inspirational posters still hung from the walls, remnants of when this had been the office of a failed tech startup. One was about how you should teach a man to fish, another about taking each day as it came. Womack was incredibly glad she hadn't been here when the previous occupants were still in business. That sort of management bullshit would drive a woman insane.

"All right, boys and girls," she said. "What did you learn from the presentation?"

A couple of dozen eager faces stared at the TV screen. They were a mixed band of magicals, including witches, wizards, gnomes, elves, a dwarf, and even a Willen. None of them was more than twenty years old, and the younger ones were at the bottom end of their teens—young minds, ready to be molded by her. Womack smiled at the thought of what she was going to achieve.

On the screen, an image from the Walgreens security camera was on pause. It showed Womack interacting with the Silver Griffin in the suit before he left the shop. Womack had rewound to this point to remind the class of how close she had come to the enemy and got away free. It was important to let them know who was boss.

A gnome raised her hand. "Is it something about the art of illusion?"

"Sure, you can learn that if you want," Womack said. "But it's not what I'm getting at."

This time it was a wizard with a mullet who spoke. "That people are idiots, and we can take them for a ride."

"True, but not the point either."

"Is there no lesson at all?" The Willen twitched her rodent nose. "Because this sure looks pointless to me."

"Wish I'd thought of that." Womack laughed. "'Cause you're right, not everything in life has a point, especially not things like the Silver Griffins. No, there's a real lesson here."

The class looked at her. Their expressions were blank except for a few who were starting to look irritated.

"Only use your magic when you need to." Womack held up her ginger wig. "If the safe's unlocked, don't bother blowing it open. If the crowd is distracted already, don't cast the glittery light show. If you can hide from the Griffins with a cheap wig and a uniform, don't bother morphing your face."

"This is bullshit," the Willen declared. "You said we were signing up for a magic crime school, and now you're telling us not to use magic? Seems like we're the ones being conned."

There were mutters of agreement.

"I'm not saying you should never use your magic. I'm saying save it for when it's needed. That way you'll have more power for what's important." Womack pulled out a deck of cards and gestured to the Willen. "Snivvery, right? Come stand across this table from me, and the rest of you gather around so you can see."

Chairs scraped across the floor, and the students formed a loose ring, watching as their teacher extracted three cards from the deck, one of them the queen of hearts. Womack put the cards face down, then started moving them rapidly back and forth, switching and shuffling.

"Hide the lady, oldest con on the street. So, which card is the queen?"

"None of them," Snivvery said, arms folded across her chest, her face full of disdain. "She's in your hand."

"Wrong." Womack flipped over the cards. All three were queens of hearts. Snivvery frowned, and the other students laughed. "There's probably a way to do that without magic, just like there's a way to open a safe without magic, but I don't know it. I use magic for the parts I don't know how to do any other way. That's why I save my magic when I can, so I can pull that off."

Snivvery grabbed the deck of cards, shuffled the three queens back in, then drew three cards, and started another game of chase the lady. Cards slid deftly across each other, and Womack barely saw the moments when the switches happened, but she did see them. Her pupil was gifted, not a genius. At the end, Snivvery flipped the cards, and once again, all three queens of hearts were on show. A few of the other students applauded. The rest watched their teacher warily.

"I can do that without magic," Snivvery said. "Which means you've taught me nothing so far."

"Okay, what are you going to do with your rigged deck when the cops grab you?"

"What rigged deck?" Snivvery held up her hands, showing nothing there.

"Accendat secreto." Womack waved a wand that hadn't been in her hand a moment before.

Smoke and flames burst from the pocket of Snivvery's jacket, which she tore off and stamped on until the flames went out.

"That rigged deck," Womack said. "Better no evidence than hidden evidence they might find."

Now her students looked impressed, all except the scowling Snivvery.

Womack grabbed a box from the corner of the room and slammed it down on the table. The contents *clanked*.

"Locks," she said. "How many of you can pick one already?" A few hands rose. "Well, now you'll learn to do it with magic, for those times when your other tools are missing. Everyone grab a lock and find a desk to work at. Try any spells you know already that you think might help. First one to finish gets the prize of looking smug."

The class spread out, each working on their lock. They started out eagerly, using levitation and movement spells to try to shift the pins and cylinder inside each lock, but Womack had carefully picked out quality locks, ones that wouldn't give way easily. Frustrated, some of the students started applying heat or brute force, trying to melt or crush their way through.

Snivvery just stood over hers, arms folded, looking from the lock to her teacher and then back down at the lock.

"Not even trying?" Womack asked.

Snivvery shrugged. "Give me ten minutes, and I could pick this thing by hand, but I know locks well enough to know I don't have the magic for it. That makes me think this is another of your bullshit lessons. You said to save our magic, so I'm saving it."

"Well done." Womack smiled, for her sake rather than for Snivvery, although the Willen was welcome to take it as approval. Smart students who bucked against authority would be useful later, in a different way from the simple, obedient ones. Snivvery could turn into a real asset if Womack played her right. "You win today's star prize, being the first one to learn a new spell."

Womack pulled out her wand again, a slim rod of black wood bound in dull iron. Something dark and plain that wouldn't catch the light. She held another lock in her hand and pointed the wand at it.

"Resigno," she said softly. Magic flowed from her wand into the lock, as soft and slow as syrup running off a spoon. A series of *tiny* clicks followed, and the lock opened.

"You going to teach me that," Snivvery asked, "or stand there looking smug?"

Womack talked her through the spell, the strands of magic it pulled on, how to draw it together and direct it. Soon, Snivvery had the lock *clacking* open at a wave of her hand.

"I'm going to teach that to the others," Womack said. "While I'm busy, work out what I haven't explained."

"You are so full of shit." Snivvery shook her head, but her expression now was less frustrated and more intrigued.

"You learn better by working things out for yourself. Try it."

While Womack gathered the others around her and explained the spell once more, Snivvery took her lock to the corner of the room. She waved her hand back and forth across the mechanism, running the spell forward and backward. The lock clicked open and shut, open and shut, faster and faster. She was good at this, it hadn't taken her more than a few seconds in the first place once she learned the spell, so there must be something else that Womack wanted.

Click, clack, click, clack, went the lock.

The room was full of that sound now, as other students practiced the spell. *Click, clack.* A chorus of bolts snapping back and forth in locks. A noise distracting her from her thoughts.

That was it, the noise.

Snivvery strode up to the front of the room, where Womack sat with her feet up on her desk, drinking a bottle of beer and flicking through a glossy catalog, about as far from the image of a teacher as Snivvery could imagine.

"Got it." Snivvery dropped her lock on the desk with a *thud*, right next to Womack's boots. The rest of the class went quiet, looking up to see what the drama was.

"Got what?" Womack sipped her beer.

"The thing you're not teaching us." Snivvery held her

34

paw out over the lock. "That we need to practice being quiet."

She whispered the spell, the word so soft even she could barely hear it. The magic emerged, but she held it back, only letting it flow a little at a time, easing its way into the lock over slow seconds. One by one, the pins moved, none of them making a sound, and the bolt slid back so softly it didn't break the silence of the room.

"Snivvery wins today's grand prize." Womack handed another beer to the Willen. "The chance to put her feet up and watch the rest of you work. Now follow her lead and see if you can get those locks open without a sound."

Some people laughed, others groaned, but they all got back to work with renewed intensity.

"It's not only about the silence, of course," Womack said as Snivvery sat next to her. "It's also easier not to leave evidence if you do things slowly and with care. Plus, this is useful practice in nuance for some of what we'll deal with later."

"I guess you're not just conning us when you say you know how to teach."

"Not just conning you, no, but never trust a criminal who pretends they're not running some scam."

"What's yours?"

"That would be telling." Womack waggled her eyebrows. "Remember, learn by working it out."

Snivvery sipped her beer. "There are times when we'll need to do stuff quick, not subtle."

"Oh, I know, and that's a lesson for another day. For now…"

Womack drained the last of her beer, tossed the bottle

into a recycling bin, then stood and banged on the table. Once again, her students turned their attention to her.

"Time to give you all your homework," she announced.

This time, the groans and protests were all for comedic effect. Every student in the room was eager to put their new skills to use and to prove that they were the ones who deserved to be at the front of the class, drinking beer and putting their feet up.

"Eskible and Flint's *Catalog of Magical Tools and Ingredients*." Womack waved her glossy brochure. "I'm going to give each of you a page with an item circled." She tore out a page and handed it to Snivvery, then started walking around the class, her footsteps accompanied by ripping noises. "As a test of your reconnaissance and burglary skills, you will steal the circled item from somewhere in this city. Teamwork is allowed, but you must all use your magical skills as part of the exercise. Bonus points for thefts from unusual places. Needless to say, you won't get many marks if the Griffins catch you."

That got another laugh.

"In addition," she said as she returned to her desk, "each of you should steal one other item from the same page of the catalog and come up with an explanation for why it's useful either to this school or to your future crimes. The whole class will judge whose answer is best.

"Class dismissed. Go forth and steal."

CHAPTER FIVE

Charlie Heron ran a hand through his mop of blond hair, distractedly turning a minor mess into a wild tangle that pointed in every direction. "Over here, Buddy," he called.

Buddy the dachshund turned from sniffing at the roots of a lemon tree and dashed across the family's yard, tongue hanging out, eager to please his master.

"Good boy," Charlie praised. "Let's try this again now that you're not distracted by butterflies. Roll over."

He waved a hand, using the same signal that the trainer had used in the YouTube video. If Buddy understood, he didn't show it. Instead, he tried to leap up and catch Charlie's hand. Unfortunately for Buddy, his legs weren't as long as when he'd been a bloodhound, and that hand stayed tantalizingly out of reach.

"Like this," Charlie prompted. He lay down on the lawn and rolled onto his back. "Can you do that?"

Buddy climbed onto Charlie's chest and licked his face. Charlie laughed, patted Buddy's head, and tried to wipe off the affectionate slobber.

"What you doing, Dad?"

Charlie looked up past the dog to see his twelve-year-old son Dylan emerging from the house, a cookie in his hand. Three-year-old Eddie followed him and had already reduced his cookie to a smear of crumbs across his dinosaur t-shirt.

"I'm teaching Buddy to do tricks." Charlie pushed the dog off him and got to his feet. "Steve at work said he's teaching his dog to fetch beer and snacks."

"Buddy can fetch snacks?"

"Right now, he can't even play dead, so don't expect him to bring you a donut any time soon. Speaking of which…"

"Mom said we could have a cookie each," Dylan said. "Ask her if you want. She's gone down the tunnels to take one to Ashley."

"Okay." Charlie turned his attention back to Buddy. "Now, remember what we were just saying? Roll over!"

He made a gesture again, and this time Buddy seemed to take the hint. He dropped to his belly, then rolled onto his back, little legs waggling in the air.

"Me too!" Eddie dropped to the ground next to Buddy. He waved his arms and legs in the air, giggling. Then there was a shimmer of magic and Eddie turned into a fluffy white terrier. The two dogs yapped and rolled around in unison, Buddy getting more excited by the moment.

"It's so much easier getting computers to do what you want," Charlie said. "Maybe I'm not cut out for this."

"What sorts of tricks could he learn?" Dylan watched Buddy thoughtfully.

"All sorts of things, if I can work out how to program

him right. Fetching, chasing, posing in different ways, maybe bringing me my slippers."

"Could he find things that are missing?"

"Sure, if he can sniff them out."

"And tell people where to go?"

"I guess."

"Cool."

"All right, Buddy, let's do this again..."

Charlie started Buddy on his training regime once more, running back and forth across the yard while Dylan watched, quietly contemplating the possibilities of a well-trained dog in a magical world.

Ashley Heron sat in the heart of the underground tunnel network she and her brothers had built. In front of her, a bank of monitors showed video feeds from all across LA.

"I've been following those suspicious dwarves for an hour." The voice coming in was a whisper from a twelve-year-old girl in Pasadena. "Looks like they've finally met someone."

On the screen, a group of bearded dwarves gathered around a single elf in a trench coat, his ears hidden beneath his long hair. One of the dwarves held out a canvas bag, and the elf pulled out a stone, which he held up to examine. An angular rune on the stone's surface glowed with magical power.

"Forged rune stones, just like we thought," the girl whispered. "Should I get closer for a better look?"

"No," Ashley said. "Stay back, stay safe, and see where the elf goes. Once we know that, we can tell the real Griffins where to find him."

"We are real Griffins," said another voice indignantly, a ten-year-old boy from West Hollywood. "You busted Zero, remember?"

"And that ring of bike thieves," someone else added.

"And—"

"The Silver Griffins, then," Ashley said. "Or the adult Griffins."

"The boring Griffins, more like," the boy said and made a farting sound. "I'd much rather be a Mini Griffin."

Ashley made a face. She liked that her network of kids was so committed to the cause of fighting crime, but sometimes she wished she had more control over them. She understood that there was something awkward about her, an eight-year-old, telling older kids what to do, an awkwardness they only avoided because the others appreciated what she did. That kept her from answering back sometimes. Still, she didn't like it when anyone was less than enthusiastic about the Silver Griffins. After all, that was who her mom worked for, and in theory, she and the rest of the family could be called on to work for them too. The whole network of Mini Griffins might end up helping their adult counterparts one of these days.

"The Silver Griffins are great," the girl in Pasadena hissed. "They helped my mom out when those gnomes tried to steal her car. You take that boring comment back, Tommy, or I'll come round and kick your backside."

"You don't know where I live!"

"I tracked these dudes down. I can find a numbskull like you."

"Guys," Ashley interjected, "we're supposed to be on the same team, remember? The team supporting the Silver Griffins?"

"Sorry," the boy mumbled. "They're not boring. I still think we're the best."

"Totally," several voices said.

Footsteps sounded in the tunnels behind Ashley.

"Someone's coming," she said. "AFK for the next five."

She took off her headset, pushed her chair back, and turned to see her mom walk in.

"Hey, sweetheart." Lucy handed Ashley a glass of milk and a plate with a cookie on it. "How's the world of super-secret adventures going?"

"Can't tell you. Then it wouldn't be a secret."

"But you will tell me, right? I mean, if you find anything serious."

"Of course, mom. I'm a kid, not an idiot."

"You are *definitely* not an idiot. In fact, you might be as far from an idiot as anyone ever gets." Lucy kissed her daughter on the forehead, then ran a hand across her dark, neatly tied black hair. "Speaking of which, would you like to help me work something out?"

"Something Silver Griffins?" Ashley's eyes lit up.

"Exactly."

Lucy stuck a thumb drive into Ashley's computer. They waited while specially adapted software did a virus scan, then a set of files popped up on the screen.

"These are all the thefts in a new case I've been given,"

Lucy said. "Dates, times, locations, what was taken and from who. I'm looking for a pattern. Think you can work your magic?"

"I don't do magic." Ashley's expression was serious as she set aside the half-eaten cookie and grabbed her keyboard. "That's Dylan."

"I didn't mean that sort of magic, sweetheart. It's a metaphor."

"Oh." Ashley fired up one of her analytical programs and copied the data into it. "I don't like metaphors. They make things messy. Analysis is all about tidying up, putting things in their proper place so that you can see how they fit together."

"If you say so."

While the program churned through the data, a machine emerged from one of the tunnels running into the room. The information-gathering robot scurried along on eight mechanical legs as it hurried to Ashley's side, then held out a small tub of dirt on the end of a telescopic arm.

"Thank you, Octo," Ashley said. "Leave the sample in the chemistry lab, please."

The robot retracted its arm and hurried away.

"You have a chemistry lab now?" Lucy asked.

"Of course. It's good for checking biological samples as well as inorganic ones, like what sort of grass seeds are on someone's shoes, or whether hairs come from a dog or a cat."

"Wow." Lucy smiled in amazement. Her daughter never stopped impressing her.

The computer had finished sifting through the data and

presented the results in a spider diagram of clustered information and connecting lines. Lucy still hadn't got used to how this worked and struggled to make sense of it.

"That's interesting," Ashley said.

"What is?"

"Most of these artifacts and ingredients are good for security spells. If someone wanted to create the most burglar-proof building in LA, these are the things they would start with."

"So, I'm looking for someone with valuables to protect?"

"Yeah, I think so."

"Except anyone with wealth worth protecting can afford to buy the things they need to protect it. Theft is an unnecessary risk."

"Oh, yeah." Ashley smiled. "You're so smart, mom."

"Coming from you, that's quite a compliment. You said *most* of the thefts were about security, but what are the rest?"

"A case of rottenwart root and a batch of golem clay. I don't know what those are for, and two data points aren't enough for the program to identify a connection."

"Dummies."

"Huh?"

"When I did my Silver Griffin field magic training, the dummies were made using rottenwart. I remember because of the stink whenever we broke one. You need golem clay for animated magical constructs."

"Someone's stealing dummy parts?"

"Maybe." Lucy glanced at her watch. "I need to go cook

dinner. If you have any other insights, you can tell me then."

"Here you go." Lucy spooned stir fry and noodles onto Eddie's plate, then set the pan down on the table. "The rest of you, help yourselves."

Dylan dived in first, piling the food on his plate.

"You sure eat a lot for such a skinny kid." Charlie winked.

"That's rich coming from you." Lucy prodded her husband with a chopstick.

"What's the saying, takes one to know one?" Charlie loaded up his plate to the point of overflowing. "Besides, I've had a busy day."

"Been working hard at the office, my little installation wizard?"

"Been working hard trying to teach our dog new tricks. Turns out he might be too old."

"Buddy's not old," Ashley contradicted in a matter-of-fact voice.

"It's a saying," Dylan said. "You can't teach an old dog new tricks. Right, Mom?"

"That's right."

"Old dog!" The air around Eddie shimmered, and instead of a little boy, a hairy spaniel sat at the dinner table, ears drooping into his food.

"No magic at the table." Charlie pointed at the jar on the counter.

Eddie turned back, sighed dramatically, and got down from his seat. He took a colored slip of paper off the counter, scrawled an "E" on it in felt tip, and stuffed it into the jar.

"That's a lot of your markers in there," Lucy said. "Looks like you'll be cleaning the house until you're Al's age."

Eddie's mouth hung open in shock as he pictured their retired neighbor and tried to work out how many chores Al added up to. That was a lot of missed opportunities to watch cartoons.

"Quiz time!" Charlie announced. "Who has the first question today?"

"Ooh, me," Dylan said. "Which king of England had to be ransomed by his younger brother, John?"

Lucy raised her hand.

"Hang on," Charlie said. "Being English feels like cheating for this one."

"It wasn't cheating for you lot to be American last week when he'd been reading that biography of Lincoln."

"You still knew more answers than me."

"I know." Eddie stuck up his hand.

The others all looked at each other. Eddie's enthusiasm always outstripped his knowledge, but the answers were often entertaining.

"Okay, what was his name?" Dylan expected to hear about King Superman or Professor SpongeBob the First.

"King Richard." Eddie looked pleased with himself.

"Well done." Lucy clapped, and everyone else joined in. "How did you know that, sweetheart?"

"He was a lion," Eddie said. The air around him shimmered, and a diminutive lion shook the beginnings of a mane.

"He's been watching Disney again, hasn't he?" Lucy asked.

"Turns out it's educational." Charlie gave the lion a meaningful look. "Quizzes are no excuse. Magic jar."

CHAPTER SIX

Leontine stood in the doorway of a closed-down shop, watching the bustle of Chinatown go by. A trickle of sweat dribbled from under his baseball cap and down the side of his face. The Arpak shifted from one foot to the other and flapped his long coat, trying to let more air in.

"Are you all right?" Twylan asked. The aviator shades that hid the magic glowing in her eyes also hid half her expression, but her concern was clear enough.

"I'm too hot," Leontine said. "I get that I have to keep my wings hidden, but there must be a better way of doing it than this coat."

"The better way would have been for you to stay in the tunnels."

"And leave the rest of you out here without my protection?"

"Have some faith. The Underfoot Brigade can take care of ourselves."

Leontine shook his head. "I still think it's a stupid name."

Twylan laughed, a sound as soft and musical as her words.

"You agreed that we should all decide on the name together, and you knew that the other kids were younger than us."

"Still, it makes us sound like something out of a cartoon."

"It could be worse. Half the ideas they came up with had the word 'fart' in them."

Another of the Underfoots, an elf named Siltor, walked up to them, his features hidden beneath a hoodie. "'Sup?"

"Stop trying to sound like a gangster," Leontine growled. "You end up sounding like an idiot."

"At least I'm not the one acting like a jerk," Siltor retorted.

"Boys," Twylan said, "is this any way to behave?"

The other two teens reluctantly shook their heads.

"Good. Now, what did you see, Siltor?"

"Same guy who was robbing homeless dudes last week. He thinks Kix is a beggar, and now he's following her this way."

Kix, an Underfoot Brigade gnome, walked down the street toward them. Down in the tunnels, she took pride in her appearance. She scoured the thrift stores for the best clothes she could find on the tiny budget they had and altered them to fit her squat physique. Today, she had turned her eye for clothes in a different direction, becoming the scruffiest, most down-and-out hobo Twylan had ever seen. She shuffled along the pavement in torn and tattered army surplus, a battered cardboard cup in her hand, change rattling in the bottom. Mismatched flip flops trailed from grimy feet. Behind her came another figure, full human height, wearing a sleeveless black hoodie and a predatory expression on his face.

"All right," Leontine said. "This is it. Good luck, Brigade."

He strode down the street and into an alley mouth. A minute later, Kix reached the same point and headed into the alley, followed by her stalker.

Twylan and Siltor followed into the alley. As they went, Siltor slid a couple of wooden disks from his pocket, the blunted equivalent of throwing stars.

In the alley, Kix stopped halfway down, putting on a great act of coughing. She'd heard the footsteps following her, as they'd planned, and now she needed to give the guy time to act.

It didn't take long.

"Hey you." A hand descended on her shoulder, fingers as fat and pink as hot dogs. He pulled her viciously around. She looked up into a square, snarling face framed by the ragged edges of a mullet. "Gimme your money."

Kix looked up at the guy. It didn't take her much effort to look very scared. The attacker was twice as tall as her and nearly twice as wide. The missing sleeves of his hoodie showed off muscles that, while not bodybuilder impressive, were a lot more bulging than those of a tunnel-living gnome. He wasn't much older than her, but that didn't stop her from shaking.

"I didn't do it," she said, eyes going wide. This was the plan: act panicked, keep him busy, wait for the others to arrive. As plans went, it had seemed a lot more appealing a couple of hours ago.

"I said gimme your money." The attacker grabbed her cup and peered at the change inside. "Is that all you got?"

Kix nodded frantically.

"Bullshit." With one hand, the guy lifted her off her feet, then pulled his fist back.

"Stop that right now," Twylan said.

She stood a few feet away, Siltor next to her. They both looked determined, but much as Kix admired her friends, they seemed a lot less tough compared to this thug.

"We know what you've been doing," Twylan said. "Beating up homeless people and stealing from them. It stops now."

The attacker snorted. He dropped Kix and turned to face Twylan, knuckles clicking as he wrapped one hand into a fist. "You gonna make me, girly?"

"Yes, we are."

Siltor's hand flicked out, and the disks hurtled through the air. One struck the thug in his shoulder, and he howled as his arm went limp. Another hit him in the forehead, and he staggered back. Then Twylan leapt at him while Kix grabbed his ankle. Limbs flailed, bodies tangled, and they were on the ground, Twylan pinning one of the guy's arms while Kix sat on his chest.

"Now." Twylan paused to catch her breath. "It's time to talk about—"

"Flamma!" Light flashed from the guy's hand. Twylan twisted aside in time to avoid being hit by a ball of fire.

The guy threw Kix off and leapt to his feet. Fire blazed from both his hands.

"Think you're so clever, huh?" He raised his hands. "I'll burn you all to a crisp."

"Sonum aquarum!" Water flew from Twylan's hands, hitting the fire as it flew across the alley. Steam hissed and billowed.

"Like that, huh?" The thug viciously grinned. "All right, let's see what you're made of."

Siltor threw more disks, but a shield of flames flashed up, turning them to ash. Then those flames rushed out, and it was all Twylan could do to counter one part of them and keep her friends safe.

"Hey, asshole." Leontine soared through the air, his crippled wing flapping extra hard to keep up with the healthy one. He veered left and right as fireballs hurtled at him, lost his balance, and crashed down in a heap of garbage, his body awkwardly twisting as he landed.

"Leontine!" Twylan dashed toward him, but more fireballs cut off her path. She swung around, and the aviators fell from her face, revealing the raw power that crackled from her eyes.

"Whoa." The thug stared at her open-mouthed. "What's wrong with you?"

"Me? What's wrong with you, beating up innocent people for pocket change?"

Her voice rose in anger, and the magic flared, leaving dark streaks across her cheeks. Lightning flashed through the alley, bright and wild, completely out of control. When it had passed, the guy stood untouched, but at least so did the members of the Underfoot Brigade.

"Nice trick," the guy said. "But I don't reckon you have another one of those in you."

Twylan leaned against the wall, her legs weak and arms trembling. It was years since she'd flared like that.

Normally these days she had her power under control, not enough to hide it but at least enough to govern what she spent. Now she was exhausted, depowered, and still facing this guy with fire flaring from his hands.

With a cry of anger, Siltor and Kix charged across the alleyway. This time, the guy didn't even bother with his magic. He swung a fist, knocking Siltor back, and kicked Kix hard. But if he thought he would deal with her that easily, he hadn't faced a tenacious gnome before. She wrapped herself around his leg and clung on tight, trying to drag him down.

"Get him, Siltor!" she shouted.

The elf flung himself at the thug, fists swinging. The guy ducked one punch, blocked another, and grabbed Siltor's wrist while he tried to shake Kix off. There was a *crunch*, and Siltor yelped in pain as he was wrenched around, his arm up behind his back.

"Get the hell off them." Leontine growled like an angry beast as he dragged himself to his feet. Blood trickled from a cut on his forehead and he held his left arm protectively close to his chest, but he looked as fierce as the others had ever seen him.

"You're tenacious. I'll give you that," the thug said. "That ain't enough."

Siltor's hoodie burst into flames, and he cried out again in panic.

"Sonum aquarum!" Twylan dug deep, drawing out what magic remained. Water flew from her fingers, a fine spray instead of the usual blast, just enough to quench the fire.

Kix flew across the alley as the guy finally shook her off. Before he could follow up, Leontine was on him. He punched and kicked, forcing the thug onto the defensive, driving him back toward the wall. Grunts and *thuds* echoed around the alley.

"Why you little..." The guy swung a kick and Leontine dodged back. It was the gap the guy needed. He slammed into Leontine shoulder-first, flinging him to the ground next to the curled-up ball of Kix and the bedraggled form of Siltor, who whimpered as he ran a finger over his burned skin.

The thug grinned ferally. "Thought you could play at heroes, huh?" He raised a finger and fire flared from it, narrowing to the shape of a knife. "I'll show you what heroes are made of, inside and out."

"Hey, jerk."

The guy turned in surprise at the voice only inches behind him.

Twylan swung a punch. It wasn't a powerful blow loaded with magic or years of combat training. It *was* her type of strike: focused, targeted, and powered by the desperate desire to protect her friends. It smashed into his jaw. There was a spray of teeth, and he staggered back.

"You little—"

Twylan raised her hands and drew on the last of her power. Lightning leapt between her fingers.

"Still want to mess with me?" she whispered.

The guy looked at her, then down at her friends, who were dragging themselves to their feet despite all their injuries.

"You didn't win," the guy said. "I ain't fighting anymore."

"Oh, we won," Twylan said. "If we ever see you messing

with anyone in this part of town, we'll do it all over again. Now get out of here."

The guy glared at her in impotent fury, then turned and ran away.

At last, Twylan let herself sink exhausted to the ground.

"Dude's tougher than he looks." Siltor peeled off pieces of burned hoodie. "My skin really hurts."

"I have a spell that can help," Twylan said. "Give me five minutes."

"You're going to need more than that." Leontine winced as he ran a hand over his shoulder. "We all are."

"We did win though, right?" Kix asked. "I didn't imagine that?"

"We didn't lose," Leontine said. "But I'd hardly call it a win."

Twylan laid a hand on his arm, stopping him a moment before he would have hit the wall. The anger that fueled him could be great when he channeled it into protecting the Brigade, but sometimes it needed to be put away.

"Does this mean it was a bad idea?" Kix asked. "Looking after the neighborhood, I mean?"

"We can do it," Twylan said. "We need to learn more first. More spells. More fighting skills. More about tactics and how you win a fight."

"I know my top combat lesson for today." Siltor winced as he stood. "Don't let anyone set you on fire."

"Great insight, master," Leontine said. "How do I sign up for your dojo?"

They helped each other to their feet, then pulled up the nearest manhole cover and climbed down, one at a time. Soon, they were walking through abandoned tunnels, back to their underground home. Twylan ambled, taking things easy while she waited for her strength to return. The others would need her magic soon enough to tend their wounds and distract them from their pain. Then there would be the long discussion about what to do next and what this half-failed effort meant for the Underfoot Brigade's future.

Leontine fell back to keep her company, his long strides slowing so she could keep up.

"You think we over-reached today?" the Arpak asked, quietly enough to prevent the others hearing. "Did I make a mistake suggesting it?"

"No," Twylan said. "The idea was good. We just didn't know he was a wizard. Next time, we'll be ready."

"How? We don't have a fight instructor or some expert witch to teach us spells. All we have is a bunch of kids living in the dark."

"We have friends." Twylan squeezed his arm. "If they can't help, no one can."

CHAPTER SEVEN

"Those are the only two things they took?" Lucy looked around the store. "A hand of glory and a bottled tangle vine?"

"Not a real hand of glory," the wizard behind the counter said sternly. "I would never stock a thing like that, no matter whose hand it was. This isn't the Dark Ages."

"Sorry, of course, a wax substitute hand of glory."

"That's right. No human, magical, or even animal parts go into making our hands. They're all-natural, vegan, and organically sourced to the highest modern standards, like everything in this store. It's what makes us unique."

Lucy looked around the store. She wasn't sure that unique was the word she would have used. The bottles, sacks, and refillable tubs looked a lot like the ones she'd seen in organic food stores, especially the ones that focused on reducing packaging. Maybe it was a more unusual niche among magic store owners, but she wouldn't have known. The Griffins bought most of the supplies she needed, and when she and Charlie needed something for

Dylan, she usually ordered it off the Internet. No, as far as she could tell, this was an ordinary magic store, masquerading as a whole foods outlet.

The store might not be unique, but it did have charm. The scents of spices filled the air, chimes rang out in the breeze from the fan, and gentle New Age music played from speakers by the counter. If she closed her eyes, she could imagine that she was at a yoga afternoon with Jackie and Sarah, about to begin a mindfulness exercise.

There was no time for mindfulness now. She had to wrap this up and get to school.

"Were they your most valuable items?" she asked.

"The hand is up there. Good substitutes like that don't come cheap. The tangle vine wasn't the most expensive thing on its shelf."

"Have you had any arguments with anyone lately? Any competitors or dissatisfied customers who might have done this for revenge?"

"Broken in and stolen two odd items? That's not much of a revenge."

"Just checking the possibilities."

The wizard shrugged. "I have competitors, but no one who would benefit much from this. They could do me more damage with a good marketing campaign."

"Okay. Thanks for your time. I'll let you know if I find anything."

Lucy walked out of the shop, away from the scents of candles and spices, into the not-so-fresh air of a Los Angeles afternoon. She didn't normally come this far west for work, but the theft matched the pattern of the ones she was after, sort of. It was specific, magically focused, and done using spells. The store's lock had almost certainly been picked using magic, and someone had dispelled the alarm wards, so they weren't simply using mundane approaches or mundane targets. The difference was that those previous thefts had been more subtle with the wards penetrated rather than dispelled, meaning that some of the thefts went unnoticed for days. This one, small as it was, had been impossible to miss.

Was it the same people getting sloppier, or merely a similar MO?

Lucy got into her Rivian and started the engine. Quieter than the other cars around it, the electric SUV pulled out into traffic, and she headed back toward Echo Park. Her mind was still on the case, trying to work out how the new thefts fitted the pattern Ashley had found. A hand of glory was supposed to keep people asleep. Historically it was a thieves' tool, so it didn't sit well with making security or training dummies. Maybe the tangle vine could be used in a security system of some sort, but there were more obvious choices.

Contemplating those questions carried her to Ashley's school. She parked, grabbed a plastic box full of muffins off the passenger seat, and headed into the building. Bright, cheerful artwork filled the walls, some of it the work of the elementary school kids, some of it posters designed to entertain and educate them. The sense of fun and color made Lucy smile and forget the cares of a Silver Griffin.

"Hi, Mrs. Heron." One of the school's admin staff, busy rearranging a display, took a moment to smile and wave at Lucy.

"Hi, Annie," Lucy said. "Do you want a hand with that?"

She put her box down and held up the corner of a big sheet of paper while the admin stapled it to a display board.

"Thanks, that was a lot easier with two." Annie gestured down a corridor. "You're here for the hiring committee, right? They're in the sports hall."

Lucy picked up her box and headed down the corridor. It was strange being here after the kids had all left for the day. Quiet didn't suit the corridors, which were normally bustling with life, and Lucy's footsteps echoed oddly back at her.

A couple of tables were set up in the sports hall, with chairs behind them for the hiring committee. A single lonely seat faced them from a position in the middle of the room.

"Hi, Lucy." Mary Holmes, Ashley's class teacher, waved at Lucy as she approached the last empty seat behind the tables. Kelly Petrie occupied one of the other chairs while Principal Reyes had taken up a central position, directly facing the interviewees' chair. Lucy was used to seeing him in shirtsleeves, his hands covered in poster paint or dough, or perhaps carrying an armful of basketballs. It was strange to see him sharply suited, looking more like an executive than the school's familiar head.

"Nice to see that you've dressed for the occasion." Kelly looked down the table at Lucy. The scorn in her voice was mostly hidden, presumably for the principal's sake, but Lucy had spent enough time around Kelly to know when the other woman was mocking her.

She looked down at her pantsuit with the blue blouse. It was one of the smarter outfits in her wardrobe and had been a lot less comfortable for a day's work than her usual jeans and t-shirt. Sure, it wasn't as well-fitted as Kelly's suit, but she felt like she'd made the effort.

She also appeared to have acquired cookie crumbs at some point in the day. She hastily brushed those off her lapel, then took the lid off her box and pushed it down the table.

"Muffins to help see us through," she said.

"Ooh, I shouldn't." Mary's hand hovered over the box.

"I certainly will," Reyes said. "Thank you, Lucy."

Annie the admin popped her head into the hall. "The first interviewee is ready when you are."

"Please bring her in." Reyes set aside his muffin.

The door opened, and a woman walked in. Her suit, like Lucy's, leaned more toward the practical than the refined, and she wore sturdy boots rather than anything with a heel. Lucy smiled in happy surprise as she recognized the face above it all: Heather Fields, chief of the Tolderai, an ancient tribe of woodland witches.

"Afternoon." Heather nodded to the panel as she took her seat. There was a flicker of recognition as she spotted Lucy, but she didn't say anything to give away their connection. Secrecy was the way of the Tolderai.

"Thank you for meeting with us, Miss Fields," Reyes said. "And thank you for the example lesson earlier. The children really seemed to enjoy themselves."

Heather smiled. "Who doesn't like planting seeds?"

Lucy wished that she had been around for the lesson and those given by the other candidates. It would have been good to see them in action, especially Heather. If there was one topic she was confident that a Tolderai could teach, it was biology.

"I thought the lesson was a little light on theory." Kelly frowned as she looked over some notes. "While it's important to engage the children, the whole purpose of that is to bestow knowledge. Which specific parts of the curriculum were you trying to address, between the mud and the watering cans?"

"Um…" Heather licked her lips, and Lucy worried that she was lost for words already. "My broad focus was the life cycle of plants, but I think your curriculum contains…"

She started talking about learning objectives, the life of plants, and some scientific terminology Lucy suspected was well beyond what the kids needed here. As she talked, Heather's confidence grew, especially when discussing the plants themselves. Seeing that Kelly was furiously scribbling notes, Lucy made one of her own: "Good on science, knows her stuff."

"Okay, let's talk pedagogy," Reyes said. "How would you adapt, say, a math lesson so that it could cater to both high achieving and low achieving children?"

"Hands-on exercises for the kids who don't get it," Heather said. "Sometimes it's easier to make sense of an idea if you have something to hold on to."

"And for the high achievers?"

"More difficult exercises, working with bigger numbers or the next idea coming up. Then get them to think about practical applications."

The questions kept coming. Reyes had given each committee member a few to ask, and they were allowed to add their own. Heather didn't look comfortable sitting there in a suit under all their scrutiny, and she shifted awkwardly in her seat, but all her answers seemed good to Lucy. There was something very appealing about the thought of having a Tolderai on the staff, someone who could connect the kids to nature and keep a quiet eye out for magical threats.

"I can't help noticing your lack of experience as a teacher," Kelly said. "This would be your first job in a school. Why do you want this job, and why do you think you're suited to it?"

Heather squirmed and looked down at her hands.

"I know I've not been in schools before," she said, "but I've spent a lot of time teaching kids about the woodlands and nature at outdoor sites. I've seen what gets them excited and how you can teach them things that really matter. I want to do more of that."

"You understand that you won't only be teaching the things that matter to you, like trees and flowers. You'll be teaching the whole curriculum."

"I can do that."

"One more question." Lucy smiled, hoping to take off some of the pressure. "What excites you about teaching?"

Heather smiled back, beaming with relief. "It's a chance to make a difference, you know? Who wouldn't want that?"

"Thank you, Ms. Fields," Reyes said. "We'll call you when we've made a decision."

Once Heather was gone, the next candidate came in. She was a sharply dressed woman with a bright smile and a decade's experience in other city schools. With a sinking heart, Lucy realized what stiff competition Heather faced.

Three more candidates and two hours of questions

later, the committee sat alone at last in the sports hall, looking over their notes and devouring the remaining raspberry muffins.

"Well, what do you think?" Reyes asked.

"That last one, Banks, would be my first choice," Kelly said before anyone else had a chance to gather their thoughts. "He has excellent qualifications, twenty years of relevant experience, and he presents himself well."

"You didn't think he was a bit stuffy?" Lucy asked, remembering the stiff tone Mr. Banks had shown in answering their questions.

"Formality can be good. Children benefit from structure."

"They benefit from creativity as well, and I thought Heather Fields would be good for that. She had so many good ideas about using nature to connect learning to real life, to make it come alive for the kids."

"Didn't you see the way she answered the questions? How is she going to handle a classroom of children if she can't face us? While I understand that she's worked with kids, I don't think that's at all equivalent to classroom experience."

"It could be better if she has fresh ideas."

"I liked her hands-on approach," Reyes said, "but she was very focused on a narrow part of the curriculum. If she could bring her big ideas to other subjects, maybe she's worth a shot, but I'm not sure. Mary, what do you think?"

Mary Holmes hesitated, then shrugged.

"I'm of two minds as well," she said. "You can't teach someone to be passionate about teaching, and she has that, but she would have a lot of catching up to do in some subjects."

"Banks is clearly the better candidate," Kelly said.

"On paper, I agree," Reyes said. "But Fields did have something about her..." He tapped a pen against the desk, then stood. "We don't have to decide today. Let's think about this, and we can discuss it later in the week."

As they walked out, Lucy shot a glance at Kelly. Was she deliberately trying to annoy Lucy or just to hire the most old-fashioned, uninspiring teacher? It seemed that they were destined to disagree on this, like everything else.

CHAPTER EIGHT

Ellis stepped out of the train carriage and into the station under the Silver Griffins' LA HQ. It was a charming station, with a quaintly old-fashioned air to it, from the analog clock to the mosaic on the wall to the station keeper in his little wooden booth. Airports, with their mediocre food, their generic decorations, and their identikit modern architecture full of branded stores, were part of the downside of travel as far as Ellis was concerned. A place like this, somewhere with a sense of history, made up for a lot. It made travel terminals worthwhile.

He walked up to the counter and held up his wand. "Howdy. Ellis Ellis, Agent 399. I'm here to see the regional manager, Agent Applegate."

"Good to see you again, Agent Ellis," Normandy said. "Are you in LA for long?"

"I hope not." Ellis was quietly impressed that the gnome remembered him. It wasn't like he rocked up to this counter every week. "Nothing against your fine city. I have other places I need to be."

"An agent's life is a busy one, eh?" Normandy tapped the brim of his cap. "Well, I won't keep you. Take the left-hand tunnel and take care once you're in the Observatory. We don't want the public seeing anything they shouldn't."

"You got it. Nice bowl, by the way."

"Oh, thank you! Do you know much about pottery?"

"Nope, but I admire any man who makes things for himself. Catch you later, station master."

Ellis strode down the tunnel, then up a flight of winding stairs. At the top, he stepped through a door into a darkened corridor. Through the doorway to the planetarium, he saw people gazing in admiration at a big old light show while some physicist talked about the planets' rotation. Maybe he should come back later and check that out. Make the most of being in LA. For now, he had an appointment.

Ellis walked through the Griffith Observatory past a school party and a cluster of excited tourists. A tall blonde attendant smiled at him, and he smiled back, wishing he had time to ask her about the pendulum swinging from the ceiling or one of the other displays. One more reason to come back when he had time to spare.

He found the secret door at the end of the exhibit hall and tapped it with his wand, then stepped through into the Silver Griffins' reception.

"Can I help?" said the smart young wizard behind the desk.

"Agent 399, Ellis." He waved his wand over a sensor on the desk, and a light went from red to blue.

"Ah yes, for a meeting with Agent Applegate." The wizard glanced at the screen in front of him, tapped a couple of keys, then smiled up at Ellis. "Take a seat. Someone will be with you in a minute."

Ellis settled onto a sofa by the door and looked around. He'd been to every Silver Griffins office in North America and several overseas, which made him as close as a person could get to a connoisseur. This one was slick and modern, with swaths of office space visible through glass partitions. Pigeons fluttered above the desks, carrying messages for agents out in the world, and admin gnomes hurried back and forth with bundles of papers in their arms. Wizards and witches sat peering at computers, drinking coffee, talking about cases, and occasionally practicing spells. He'd seldom set foot in this place before, but the familiar setup felt as much like home as anything did to him.

"Agent Ellis?" An androgynous, suited figure with short dark hair stood in the doorway. "Agent Applegate will see you now."

Ellis followed along corridors and past desks to a corner office. Inside, a red-faced guy in a three-piece suit sat peering at a cardboard folder like it was the start of an intricate puzzle.

"Agent 399 Ellis for you, sir," the assistant said.

"Thank you, Sam, you can leave us to it." Applegate set the folder aside with a look of relief and stretched out his hand. "Ellis, eh? Have we met before?"

"Just a time or two, sir." Ellis shook hands and sat. "When I've transported witnesses in over local lines."

"Oh yes, you're the agency's top traveling man."

"One of them, sir. I can't say as I'm the best."

"Well, you're certainly the most memorable," Applegate

said, despite apparently having forgotten him until a minute before.

Ellis had met plenty of Applegates in his time. The guy might or might not be a great wizard, he might or might not be a skilled investigator, but he had that special set of skills that saw a man rise through the managerial ranks, skills like a firm handshake and the ability to bluff his way through any encounter.

"So, what brings you to LA this time?" Applegate asked.

"I'm chasing a fugitive," Ellis said. "I hoped to get some local help."

"A fugitive, eh? Does he keep talking about a one-armed man?"

Ellis raised an eyebrow. "Can't say as I follow you there, sir."

"Before your time, I suppose." Applegate sighed and laid a hand on his belly. "Time may be the great teacher, but sometimes I'm left feeling like everyone else skipped a class. So anyway, this fugitive of yours?"

"Meredith Womack, witch and con artist." Ellis waved his wand and Womack's rap sheet appeared in the air between them, glowing letters listing a string of magical violations up and down the East Coast. "I followed her as far as LA, but she's shaken me off. I hoped you good folks could help me out, bring your local knowledge and resources to bear."

"Of course!" Applegate stroked his chin thoughtfully as he read the rap sheet, then he hit a button on his desk phone. "Sam, is Agent Kowal around?"

"Yes, sir."

"Could you send her in, please?"

Applegate smiled at Ellis.

"You'll like Jackie," he said. "She's smart, and she gets things done."

The door burst open, and a woman strode in. She was tall with short blonde hair, and wore jeans, a sports jacket, and a highly polished pair of black boots.

"You wanted me, sir?"

"Agent Jackie Kowal, this is Agent...er...is Ellis your first or last name?"

"Both," Ellis replied.

"What, like Prince?" Jackie's expression was scathing.

"Only if he called himself Prince Prince."

"One of your parents must have really hated you."

"Agent Kowal." Applegate shot her a warning look.

"Just joking." She threw her hands up in the air. "Happy to meet you, Ellis Ellis."

"Jackie, you've dealt with fraud cases before, right?"

"Sure, I guess. There were those imitation wands last year and the guy who claimed to be some long-lost lord of the gnomes."

"Then you can help Agent Ellis with his case. The two of you can be partners until he knows his way around, or the case is wrapped."

"You want me to babysit some new guy, on top of everything else? Isn't it Thompson's turn for something like this, or Chavez maybe?"

"Nonsense, you're the perfect choice." Applegate picked up his cardboard folder, looking pleased with himself at a situation resolved. "Well, go on, get out there and fight crime."

Jackie left the office, Ellis trailing her, and went back to her desk.

"I have cases of my own to deal with, you know," she said.

"I'm sure you do."

"I don't need some tourist getting under my feet while I'm working."

"I ain't planning on getting under anybody's feet."

"They never do." Jackie looked down. "At least you have solid shoes, even if they are too flashy."

"Some folks call them stylish."

"Some folks are idiots." Jackie pocketed her wand and her phone, then walked away from the desk. "Come on. I need to visit the armory."

Ellis followed her deeper into the Griffins' lair, explaining his case along the way. As they walked down a narrow corridor, a messenger pigeon flapped past too close, its wings buffeting Ellis's hair.

"So where do you want to start searching for your fugitive?" Jackie asked.

"I don't know," Ellis replied. "I'm new in town, remember."

"Well, who are her LA associates?"

"I don't know."

"So, what's she doing here?"

"I don't know that either."

Jackie stopped walking and stared at him. "Do you know anything, or are you expecting me to pull a clue out of my LA ass for you?"

"I know what her previous crimes looked like. I reckon we go through those, see if you can see what opportunities

LA might offer for a witch like her, and we take it from there."

"Sounds like a lot of work."

"It's not gonna be easy, I agree. If it was, I wouldn't be using up your time, would I?"

"I don't know what you'd be doing." Jackie set off down the corridor again. "Until ten minutes ago, I wasn't expected to care."

A set of stairs carried them down through a thick layer of concrete to the Special Equipment and Weaponry department. Jackie waved her wand and armored doors thick enough to stop a tank slid open. Beyond them, a magical net hung in the air.

"Guess you need to keep folks out of here, huh?" Ellis asked.

"More like we need to keep the weapons in."

The doors *clanged* shut behind them. At another wave of Jackie's wand, the net parted, breaking up into glowing strands, and they walked through.

"Wait there!" a man's voice called from around the scuffed and scarred corner of the corridor.

There was a *whooshing* sound, a flash of light, and a spray of water slammed into the wall in front of them. It stopped after a moment, and the remaining liquid flowed away down a drain.

"All right, you can come in now."

They emerged into a large, echoing chamber with concrete walls and a series of targets set up at the far end. Heavy metal music emerged from a speaker somewhere up above.

"Welcome to the Range," Jackie said. "Try not to get blown up or turned into a frog."

A wizard with close-cropped ginger hair and a flapping lab coat turned to greet them. Behind him, a soaking wet lab assistant lay blinking on the floor, chunks of ice and unconscious imps scattered around him.

"What in tarnation?" Ellis asked.

"We're experimenting with new booby traps," the ginger wizard said. "Nigel's my test subject, aren't you, Nigel?"

The lab assistant staggered to his feet, trembling with cold. "Y-y-y-yes Mr. Jenkins."

"Ellis, this is Toliver Jenkins, head of Special Equipment and Weapons," Jackie said. "Toliver, this is Ellis, some random guy from out of town."

"Cool." Jenkins scratched his head. "Was I supposed to have something ready for you?"

"The ballistics report on that wand we found in the harbor? You were going to tell me if it was the one used to turn a playground into quicksand."

"Right, yes, let me go find it…"

Jenkins strode off, the dripping Nigel following him. One by one, the imps woke up and picked themselves up off the floor.

"I get it. You've made your point." Ellis looked pointedly at Jackie. "You have an important case to follow, and you don't have time to look after me. You're going to drag me around on every errand on your list until I work out that I'd be better off chasing Meredith Womack on my own."

"I didn't say that." Jackie looked away.

"And you ain't gonna say it, on account of how your

boss gave you an order. But here's the thing, this isn't just some two-bit con-woman I'm chasing. She doesn't trick rich folks out of their jewelry or hedge funds out of their fully insured shares. She tricks genies out of their promises, wizards out of their power, dwarfs out of their ancient ancestral axes. She scoops up magic like it's candy, then heads for the hills, leaving anger and instability in her wake. Whatever she's doing in LA, it isn't gonna be good for LA, so it's as much in your interest as in mine to sort it out."

Jackie sighed. "Fine. We'll get out there and start turning your lack of clues into some sort of lead. Good thing for you I can work miracles when needed. First, I really do need this report. Yours isn't the only important case in town."

CHAPTER NINE

Lucy and Dylan sat in the window seats of an ice cream parlor, watching the traffic go past on Sunset Boulevard.

"Do all Silver Griffin investigations involve sundaes?" Dylan scooped up a spoonful of chocolaty goodness that dripped with caramel sauce. "Because if they do, I know what I want to be when I grow up."

"Not every one, but it's a good excuse to sit here." Lucy ate a spoonful of strawberry and vanilla, taking a moment to appreciate the finer things in life. "I thought I'd blend in better if I brought you with me. Some people think it's weird for an adult to sit eating ice cream on her own."

"Really?" Dylan scratched his head with the less sticky end of the spoon. "When I'm an adult, I'm gonna do things like this all the time."

"I raised you so well."

Lucy scooped a big spoonful of cream of her sundae and ate it all in one go.

"A real-life stakeout." Dylan grinned. "This is so cool. How will we know if they might be the thieves?"

"We're looking for people targeting the magic shop hidden behind that barber's place." She nodded across the street. "So the first thing is to see who's skulking around there, then see if any of them look unusual. Some magicals are good at disguising themselves, but others give the game away if you know what you're looking for."

"Like a big beard because they're a dwarf?"

"Yep, exactly that sort of thing."

Dylan narrowed his eyes, watching the passers-by with suspicion. It was like reading a *Where's Waldo?* book, except that instead of a brightly striped shirt he was looking for hidden wings or the suspicious bulge that might mean someone was carrying a wand.

"How do you know that they're going to rob that store?" Dylan asked.

"I don't know for sure, but there aren't a huge number of magic stores in LA, and Ashley said this was one of the ones most likely to be hit."

"If Ashley says that, it's a sure thing."

Lucy smiled. It felt good knowing that her kids had each other's backs. Growing up as an only child, she'd never had that bond, and she was pleased that she'd raised her kids well enough to find a strong, positive connection. Of course, it might not last into their teens, but she would deal with that problem when she got to it.

"What about that guy?" Dylan pointed with his spoon. "Short, big beard, maybe he's a dwarf…"

"Not quite short enough for a dwarf. Just a biker, I think, or maybe a Tolkien fan who really likes leather."

"Tall guy with long hair covering his ears?"

"You're right, that's an elf, but he seems to be passing through."

"This is harder than I expected and not so exciting. I thought we'd be chasing bad guys by now."

Lucy laughed. "Ninety percent of my work is re-reading evidence or waiting for someone else to act."

"Maybe I don't want to be a Silver Griffin after all. Ice cream for boredom is a tough deal."

Dylan finished off his sundae, then ran a finger around the inside of the glass to make sure he'd got it all.

"Do we need another one of these, so we'll still blend in?" he asked hopefully.

"Nice try, sweetheart, but you've had quite enough sugar already. Besides, I think we have our suspect."

"Where?"

"You have to promise you won't stare, okay? That would give the game away."

"I promise."

"All right. There's a bloke with a mullet and a black sleeveless t-shirt standing on the pavement by the traffic light. You see him?"

"It's called a sidewalk, mom. Pavement is the name of a band only dad listens to."

"Where do you think that name comes from?"

"I don't know, some magical country overseas where they let criminals get away because they're arguing about words?"

"Actually, we're waiting on purpose to see what the suspect does."

The answer to that question turned out to be not much.

The man stood by the traffic lights, peering up Mohawk Street, his hands thrust into his pockets.

"Why is he a suspect?" Dylan asked.

"Back of his jeans."

"Oh, he's carrying a wand!"

"And not very subtly, although I suppose it looks like a stick to most people."

After a few minutes, someone else walked up to the mullet-wearing wizard, someone short, with their face hidden by a cap and sunglasses.

"Suspect number two," Lucy said. "Now they're heading off. Time to see what they're up to."

Leaving the remains of her sundae behind, Lucy headed out of the ice cream store. Dylan followed, his hand reaching for his pocket.

"Don't do that, sweetheart," Lucy said. "It'll give you away."

"Thanks, mom." Dylan could feel his heart beating. This was one of the most exciting things he'd ever done, following his mom on an actual Silver Griffin case. His friends were going to be so jealous.

They waited at the side of the road for the lights to change and let them across. Fortunately, the suspects hadn't gone far. They walked past the barber, then stopped. Each of them made a gesture in the air, then they walked through a door and disappeared from view.

"What was that?" Dylan asked.

"Simple revelation spell," Lucy said. "It uncovers things that are hidden from mundane people, but magicals are supposed to be able to find. You can't have a magic shop right out in the open, but there's not much point in running one if your customers can never find it."

Lucy and Dylan crossed the street, walked a little way up Mohawk, and stopped on the same spot where the suspects had been.

"Can you see it?" Lucy asked.

Dylan tilted his head on one side, then the other, his dark wavy hair flopping back and forth. What was he missing?

Then he saw it. A line running down the gap between two buildings, each of them painted with murals. The gap was so slim it almost wasn't there at all, yet somehow it seemed like there was more going on, as if he was looking at a screen sideways, its whole image reduced to a slender, flickering shaft of light.

"There's another store there," he said. "Except that there sort of isn't."

"That's it. Now, follow my lead..." She made a small circle with her hand. "Revelare."

"Revelare." Dylan imitated the gesture.

Suddenly, there was another building crammed in between the two murals. It had a narrow front with a metal security door across an older, wooden one. A sign above the doorway read, "UNDERMOUNTAIN AND SONS MAGICAL SUPPLIES."

"Come on, quick," Lucy said. "We don't want people to wonder what we're looking at."

She opened the doors, waved Dylan inside, then followed him. As the doors closed behind her, there was a ripple of magic, and the world settled back into place.

Inside, the shop was old and dusty, with uneven wooden floorboards and rickety shelves. Gas lamps cast distorted shadows across shelves full of bottles, jars, and boxes.

"Wow, is this a proper wandering store?" Dylan asked. "I've heard about places like this, stores that are more like magic animals than buildings. My book says that they teleport from city to city, carrying a weight of ancient power with them."

"It used to be one of those," Lucy said quietly, "but the Undermountains settled down in LA decades ago. This shop is on the maps, for now at least."

One thing was missing from the shop, and it was the thing that never missed the sound of newly arrived customers—Tobias Undermountain himself.

Lucy raised a finger to her lips and pointed at the back of the store. Behind the counter, a door stood ajar, and voices were emerging

"I told you already, open the safe," said someone in a low voice tinged with a lisp.

"I'd like to help, really I would, but there's an elemental time lock. I can only open the safe at certain times of the day."

"What's the point in that?"

"To stop things like this from happening."

"Yeah, well, you find a way to unlock it, or I'll set your beard on fire."

"Hey, Hank?" This was a third voice, higher than the other two.

"What did I tell you about using names?"

"Sorry, sorry. Look, can't we use the spell she taught us? I mean, that's the whole point, right?"

"Go on then, try it, but you're wasting your time. She's only taught us the basics."

Lucy and Dylan drew their wands and crept toward the door. When they got close, they peered through into a storeroom. Like the rest of the shop, it looked like it had traveled from another age, with its rows of barrels, stacks of wooden crates, and a massive iron safe under a barred window in the back wall.

A gnome was standing by the safe, her hands hovering over its lock. She'd abandoned the baseball cap and sunglasses that had disguised her in the human world on the floor so she could press her ear against the safe. Tobias Undermountain, the shop's dwarf proprietor, stood beside the vault with his back against the wall and his hands in the air, eyes wide with fear. Facing him was the wizard with the mullet, his wand still in his back pocket, fire flaring between his fingers.

Lucy stepped through the doorway, wand outstretched. "Silver Griffins. Hands in the air and put that fire out."

The gnome's hands flew up. Her partner in crime turned, hands rising slowly, but the flames still danced around his fingers.

"What if I don't?" he said. He tried to make it sound like a growl, but he was missing his front teeth, and it was hard to sound menacing when half the words came out with a lisp.

"Then we'll find out how tough you are with the other teeth missing."

"Don't be a dumbass, Hank," the gnome said. "This isn't worth risking Trevilsom for."

"You think they won't send us to Trevilsom for robbing

this place?" Hank rolled his eyes. "We're what they built that place for."

He flexed his fingers, and there was a bright flash. Temporarily blinded, Lucy staggered back, clutching her eyes. She heard a *thud*, then footsteps, and a sizzling sound like steak on a grill.

After a few seconds, her vision returned. Hank and the gnome were on top of the safe. He was using his fire to melt the bars over the window while the gnome watched Lucy, hands raised.

"Villains are found. Now let them be bound." Lucy gave a flick of her wrist and a rope shot from the end of her wand. As it reached the criminals, it bounced off an invisible barrier running out from the gnome's hands.

"Fugere greges!" Dylan waved his wand and boxes hurtled off the shelves. Flying in sideways, one of them got past the barrier and hit the gnome in her shoulder.

"Ow!" She clutched her arm, and the air rippled as her barrier collapsed.

There was a *clang* as the last of the bars fell from the window, then a crash of breaking glass.

"Come on." Hank scrambled through the window.

Lucy fired her ropes again, and Dylan sent a spray of tangling vines to join them. They grabbed hold of the gnome as she was halfway out the window. Rope and vines together started dragging her back in while she squirmed and tried to kick them off.

"Hank!" she howled, clinging to the window frame.

Fire flashed again. The ends of ropes and vines fell away as ash. A heavy hand reached through the window, grabbed the gnome, and hauled her out.

"Should we go after them?" Dylan ran over to the safe.

"Not yet, sweetheart." Lucy crouched beside Tobias Undermountain. The dwarf was breathing hard, his face pale, and the bottom half of his beard was missing. What remained was blackened all along the lower edge.

"Such a tragedy," he whimpered. "Such a loss."

"You're safe now," Lucy said. "What did they get away with?"

Undermountain looked up at her. "Pardon?"

"The thieves, what did they steal?"

"Nothing, they never got into the safe."

"But you were talking about..."

"My beard," the dwarf wailed, tears welling in the corners of his eyes. "Those monsters destroyed my beautiful beard!"

CHAPTER TEN

The dummy stood in the middle of the room, looking like a vandalized reject from a department store display. It had been a mannequin originally, and that still provided most of its shape, but smears of golem clay and clumps of magical herbs littered its smooth surface, the stuff through which animating power flowed. Magical runes glowed through the fabric of the jeans and t-shirt Womack had dressed her creation in. It wasn't elegant, but it was a lot cheaper than building an automaton from scratch, and it was more than adequate for the lesson it needed to teach.

"Who's up next?" she asked.

The class had gathered around the sides of the room, some of them in the little cliques that had already started to form. A posse of younger kids who had found each other for the sake of self-protection, the gamblers and hackers who thought they were smarter than the rest with their hipster clothes and their expressions of cool indifference, Hank and his gang of thugs. There were loners too, the likes of Snivvery watching everyone else with disdain.

Like every little detail of people's behavior, this was something Womack could use to manipulate them when she needed to, even if she didn't know what it would be for yet.

Right now, she was focused on teaching them. After all, that was what they were paying her for, as well as the thing she needed to complete her master plan.

An elf stepped forward. She was one of the ones who normally robbed tourists down by the Bay and confident in her gifts as a pickpocket. Womack figured that the elf had waited this long so some others could fail first, making her look more impressive by comparison when she passed the test.

The elf walked across the room, not straight toward the dummy like some others, but approaching at an angle. Along the way, she pretended to wave at someone up ahead, then turned from that, her movements naturally flowing as she passed two feet from the dummy. Her hand flicked out, magic sparked from the tips of her fingers, and the wallet lifted out of the dummy's back pocket.

One of the dummy's hands shot out, grabbing the wallet from the air. The other hand swung at the elf, who leapt back far enough not to get slapped. As she glared at the mannequin, there was a ripple of laughter around the room, and a few of the previous contenders rubbed their reddened cheeks.

"Better than some," Womack said. "You still need to be more careful. If the dummy feels what you're doing, you can be sure a real mark will."

"This is stupid," the elf said. "If I'm going to pick a pocket, I'll get them looking the other way first."

"The point here is to work without that distraction, to

lift the wallet without any hint of what's going on. Remember, magic is for those times when mundane skills won't do." Womack looked at Snivvery. "Come on, your turn."

The Willen peeled herself away from the wall, and her rat-like nose twitched. She walked toward the dummy, stopped two feet away, and bowed.

"Good evening, ma'am, I'll be your pickpocket for this evening."

That drew another laugh from her fellow students, and it told Womack something else. For all of Snivvery's attempts to act aloof, she cared how the others responded to her. She wanted to be in charge here.

The Willen flexed her hand, and the wallet started to move, sliding slowly up from that back pocket. Snivvery stood, easily within range to get slapped, while the spell did its work. Inch by inch the wallet rose, and the whole room held its breath. Had the dummy tensed? Was it about to attack?

The wallet slid out and lifted away. The dummy didn't move an inch. Snivvery bowed, then returned to her place against the wall. "Now none of your wallets are safe."

This time the laughter was more nervous. Learning together and thieving together meant that the students were starting to bond, but it was a long way from that to trusting one another, and rightly so.

"All right." Womack rolled the dummy over to a corner of the room. "Time to see your homework assignments. Everybody put your loot out in front of you and the catalog page to show what you were after."

Rustling and chatter filled the room as students opened their bags and pulled out what they'd stolen. Womack's eyes lit up. Everything she needed to keep the school going was here, and a lot more besides.

Or almost everything.

"Hank, Lotty." Womack stood in front of the mullet-haired wizard and his gnome sidekick. Neither of them had produced the goods. "Are you holding out on me? Is this why you've been uncharacteristically quiet?"

"We nearly did it," Lotty said. "We found a store that had what we were after, and we did our recon work, but then—"

"Shut up, Lotty," Hank said. His voice was still low, but there was a hiss to it, something not quite right around the "s" sound.

"Oh, no, you don't get to shut up now." Womack grinned. "A failure is a valuable learning opportunity. We'll get to the winners eventually. I want to hear from the losers first."

"I'm not a loser." Hank glared. It was hard to take his anger seriously though, because as he spoke, he lost his composure, revealing the gap where his front teeth had been.

"Tell us what happened."

"No."

"If you want to stay in this class, then you will tell, in detail, right now."

Hank scowled, and his hands twitched at his sides. For a moment, Womack wondered if she was going to lose him.

"We went into the shop when it was empty, and we got the owner into the back," Hank said. "The safe was too tough for us to crack with the spells we got so far, so we were gonna make him open it."

"Not the sort of work I had in mind," Womack said, "but it's good that you played to your strengths."

"Since when is bullheaded thuggery a strength?" Snivvery asked, her voice full of mockery.

Fire appeared in Hank's hand as he glared at the Willen.

"Ignore her," Womack said. "Your grade depends on what you tell me."

Hank scowled, but he kept talking.

"We'd almost got the guy doing what we wanted, but then these Silver Griffins came in."

Womack tensed. This could simply be a coincidence. Silver Griffins got everywhere if you weren't careful. Still, if there was a connection, she needed to know.

"These Silver Griffins, was one of them a blond guy in a suit?" she asked. "Red sneakers and tie, looks full of himself?"

"No." Hank shook his head.

Womack relaxed a little, but she knew that she had more than one hunter after her. "Then what did they look like?"

"Lady in her thirties, jeans and t-shirt, hair tied back."

"That's only one. You said Silver Griffins, plural."

"It doesn't matter," Hank said.

"Lotty?" Womack turned to the gnome.

"A kid." Lotty's face flushed with embarrassment. "The other one was a kid, maybe twelve years old."

"Hahahahaha!" Snivvery flung her head back and howled with laughter. "Hank got his teeth knocked out by a tweenager."

"Shut up!" Hank yelled. "That was different. That was someone else."

"Oh, so a kid beat you up, and someone else knocked your teeth out? What a tough guy!"

With a roar, Hank leapt across the room. He swung a fist at Snivvery, who jumped out of the way, still laughing.

"What's next? You gonna get caught stealing candy from a kindergarten?"

Hank chased after Snivvery, who scampered around the room, sometimes on four paws and sometimes on two, constantly out of reach. Hank's frustration was bottomless, his patience almost nonexistent. He raised his hand, summoned a fireball, and flung it at the Willen, who dodged aside. The fireball missed and hit the dummy, which burst into flames.

Womack pulled out her wand and pointed at Hank and Snivvery. "Vocare pluvia!"

Clouds appeared above both students and rain poured forth, drenching Snivvery's spirits and quenching the flames that flickered between Hank's fingers. Both stopped and stared at their teacher.

"Are you done wasting all our time?" Womack snapped.

The two of them looked at each other with narrowed eyes, then looked back at her.

"I'm done," Hank said. "This little weasel's too cowardly to stop and fight."

"I was getting bored already," Snivvery said.

"Whatever." Womack dismissed the rain clouds. The two recalcitrant students remained soaked. "Now, Hank, you will finish telling your story, and Snivvery, you will shut up if you want to stay in this class."

Hank described the confrontation in Undermountain's storeroom, the magic used by both sides, and how he and Lotty had escaped.

"You're sure they didn't follow you?" Womack glanced at the exits, pondering her best escape route if the Griffins turned up now.

"I told you, we left them in the store."

"There's no chance they placed any sort of tracker on you?"

"They didn't even touch us. Right Lotty?"

Lotty nodded. "We did everything right. Split up after, went different ways, doubled back to watch for anyone after us. No way they could have followed us here."

That was something, at least. Womack chewed on her lip while she considered what the incident meant.

"Sounds like you got unlucky," she said at last. "It happens. What matters is how you deal with it, and how I'm going to deal with it is by improving security here, which will, of course, affect your homework assignments."

The class groaned, but she could see the excitement in their eyes. Every one of them except Hank and Lotty had pulled off a theft for her. It had been thrilling, it had been satisfying, and in that way, it had bound them a little closer to her. When she sent them out for the next round of robberies—back to security artifacts, an unfortunate setback to her plans—it would only reinforce their status as her minions. Always keep the con in mind.

Still, it would be good to reinforce those positive feelings before she sent them out again.

"Pair off," she instructed. "I want each of you to tell the other one how you did your theft and grade each other for style and results. Then work together to figure out how both of you could do it better next time."

She'd read about this one on a teaching website. Getting students to mark each other's work made them feel more important and reinforced the lessons they had learned. It saved the teacher time while making the students feel better about themselves. Teaching really was just one big con, designed to trick people into learning.

She was going to need something different for Lotty and Hank though. Hank in particular looked dispirited, and she couldn't afford to lose his loyalty. Not yet. Not when he might tell someone else what she was up to and when they might come to muscle in on her plan. She needed to be stronger before she revealed this place to the world.

"That was an impressive display of fire magic, Hank," she said. "I didn't see you use your wand."

"My great-grandpa was a Fire Elf."

"You inherited some of his powers?"

"Uh-huh. I can do some stuff with raw magic. Only need the wand when it ain't about fire."

"Were the muscles his, as well?" She touched his bicep lightly for a moment, enough to reinforce what his ego wanted to believe.

"These are all mine." He grinned.

"Impressive. Lotty, it sounds like you kept yourself calm in a difficult situation earlier. Well done."

"Thanks." Lotty blushed. "I, uh, I've never done anything like that before, facing a Silver Griffin."

"Really? I would never have known."

Of course, she had known. It was amazing that Lotty

had got through even one encounter like this without being arrested. The girl screamed liability, but she was friends with Hank, so she needed to stay in the school too.

"You got a homework assignment for us?" Hank waggled his eyebrows. "Something special, maybe?"

"I certainly have." Womack laid a hand on each of their shoulders, then turned them to face across the room, where smoke was still trailing from the class dummy. "You killed my teaching tool. I need you to steal the replacement parts for me."

CHAPTER ELEVEN

A flock of tiny black cats floated in the air, mewling and waving their paws. Beneath them, a dozen kids dressed in party hats laughed and pointed, delighted by the cats and wondering what the slender clown at the front of the room would do next. The only people who knew that something was amiss, apart from Lucy, were the birthday boy's parents. The father had caught one of the cats and was staring at it in growing bewilderment.

"You said that you're a colleague of Chirpy the Magic Clown?" the mother asked as she led Lucy into the room.

"Yeah, exactly," Lucy said. "I'm his glamorous assistant. Should have been here at the start, but I got caught in traffic."

"Oh." The woman's expression showed that Lucy would have to make a bit more effort if she wanted to count as "glamorous" in this neighborhood. "Well, here he is."

The clown looked at Lucy, and his face fell. There was an elf underneath that face paint, the pointed tips of his ears hidden by the bright red wig. It was amazing to see the jobs the magicals would take to get by on Earth and endlessly disappointing to see how often they thought they could get away with using a little magic.

"I can clear this up myself," Chirpy said. "I just need a few minutes."

"Too late for that, sunshine." Lucy drew her wand.

"Is this part of the show?" The husband looked up from the confused cat. His wife shrugged.

"Never was, never will be," Lucy chanted.

The humans froze, their expressions blank.

"What were you trying to do?" Lucy asked as she started grabbing cats out of the air.

"I tried to summon flying bats," Chirpy said, "but I had a slip of the tongue. How did you get here so quick?"

"I was in the neighborhood, and I saw a cat flying out the window. Seemed like the sort of thing the Silver Griffins should deal with."

"Please, don't send me to Trevilsom. I'm too pretty for prison."

"You're not going to Trevilsom, not unless you do something that really gets on my nerves. But we don't have long before this lot wake up, so we need to catch these kittens fast."

They rushed around the room, using magic and their hands to scoop up the purring balls of fur and stuff them into one of the clown's bags. Once the air was clear of flying felines, Lucy shoved Chirpy out the front door and into his clown car.

"No more using magic," she warned. "Even if you're going to pretend that it's all fake. There's too much risk of something going wrong."

"Sorry," the clown mumbled.

"Now get out of here before they wake up and wonder where the past half-hour went."

Lucy watched the clown's car disappear from view, then returned to her Rivian. She was about to climb in when she noticed a familiar figure walking down the street.

"Level Three." She waved at him. "What brings you 'round these parts?"

Ringo Fuller hunched defensively, and his brow wrinkled above his wraparound shades.

"Number 485," he said. "Never a pleasure to see you, always a chore."

"What's put you in such a perky mood?"

"Nothing. I've got nothing I need to talk to the Griffins about, so unless there's something you need my skills for, I'm gonna keep walking."

He strode on, army boots pounding the sidewalk, backpack bouncing against his back. Lucy watched him go with mounting curiosity. Even by Fuller's standards, that had been brusque, and that made her suspicious. It was a good idea for bounty hunters to stay on the right side of the Silver Griffins, to get information from them and possibly help if things went wrong. The two might not have the most friendly relationship, but he would normally at least take the time to exchange barbs. Which meant that either he was very busy, or he was up to something he shouldn't be.

Lucy looked up and down the street. There was no sign of Fuller's van. That made her even more suspicious. He usually brought the van as close as he could to his targets, so he could easily bundle them into the back.

She waited until he'd gone around the corner, then locked the Rivian and hurried after him on foot.

Fuller was standing halfway down the next street with his phone pressed to his ear. He was too far away for Lucy to hear what he was saying, but she doubted that part mattered. The phone call, real or fake, was an excuse to stand there while he watched a house opposite. He was casing the place.

Lucy ducked back out of sight, pulled her phone from her pocket, and brought up an app. It was one that Ashley had created for her, which connected to the Silver Griffins' database as well as publicly available records found on the magical web. It let her easily check for known magical connections to a person or place, whether it was a Silver Griffins arrest warrant, a social media profile, or some other listing. Nothing came up for this house. If there was someone here with a magical connection, the only reason why Fuller should be interested, then they were keeping clean and keeping to themselves. People like that shouldn't be of interest to bounty hunters.

When Lucy looked around the corner again, Fuller was crossing the street. There weren't many people around, but there were enough parked cars for her to follow him while staying out of sight. As he turned his head, she ducked behind an old Toyota with rust around its wheel wells. Peeking past the bumper, she saw him carry on, walking down the side of the house. He hadn't seen her.

Lucy paused for a moment. Fuller wasn't technically a suspect of any sort, and there were cases she should be dealing with. Still, if she hadn't followed the leads that came to her, she wouldn't have stopped the clown's kitten fiasco.

She crossed the street and hurried to the house Fuller had been watching.

It seemed like an ordinary house, a pale rancher with a lawn out front and an empty driveway. The curtains were halfway drawn, making it hard to judge if anyone was home or not. Bushes were rustling next to the fence, and she figured that Ringo must have gone through them, down the side of the house.

As she followed him closer, Lucy felt a tingle in the air. There was magic here, though it hadn't been obvious at first. She checked that no one was around, then drew her wand and waved it.

"Revelare."

Wards, sigils, and magical currents glowed for a moment in the air, then faded back to invisibility. They were all over the house: invisible bars on the windows, alarms on the door, anti-climbing spells up the walls, even something like an elemental land mine in the flower bed. The place had more magical protection than a dwarf bank.

Now that she was thinking about security, Lucy noticed the other features. Security cameras covered every angle of approach. A fake alarm box showed a blinking light, a real one was better hidden on a different wall, and there were spikes and anti-burglar paint along the top of the fence. Whoever Ringo was after, they really didn't want to be caught.

She pushed her way through the bushes, down the side of the house. As she emerged into the back yard, Ringo was at the kitchen door, his wand pointing at the lock. Paint covered the lenses of the closest cameras, and a black wooden box lay on the ground next to him, its magic deadening any sound.

"Revelare," Lucy whispered. Again, the magic in the area became briefly visible to her. There were alarm wards here too, but Fuller had broken those closest to him. He was systematically working his way through the house's defenses.

She crept up behind him, into a soundless space where even the songs of nearby birds disappeared. Then she tapped him on the shoulder. He leapt up with a start, his mouth opening and closing for what she assumed was a string of curses, their sound stifled by the magical box. At last, Fuller realized that his words were lost. He reached over and slammed it shut.

"What are you doing here?" he snapped.

"I was going to ask you the same thing." Lucy pointed at the house. "Is there a fugitive in here the Griffins don't know about?"

"That's none of your business."

"On the contrary, that's the definition of my business. Who are you after, Fuller?"

"Who says I'm after anyone?"

"Revelare."

This time she put more power into the spell. Every piece of magic on the house glowed like a set of Christmas lights. "Ordinary magicals don't make their homes this secure. No one would waste time and power setting spells like this on an empty house."

"I wouldn't know."

"Yet you're trying to break in?"

Fuller took a step back and raised his hands. "You can't prove that."

"I literally just caught you doing it. So, either there's a target in here worth catching, or you've taken up a life of crime. Which is it?"

"I've got nothing to say to you."

"I'm not trying to kill-steal here, Fuller." Lucy rolled her eyes in exasperation. "If you have a legitimate target, I can help. We get them off the streets together, and you get your bounty. Everyone wins."

He stuffed the anti-sound box into his bag. Lucy glimpsed rope, spray paint, and other equipment in there. A bulge in the pocket of Ringo's cargo pants told her he was packing a pistol as well as a wand. The guy had come prepared, but for what?

"I've got nothing to say to you," he declared once more and strode away.

"Half a second, sunshine." Lucy grabbed him by the arm. "If you don't have a legitimate target here, it looks like you were using magic to commit a burglary instead, or maybe even a kidnapping. Do you want to talk to me about that idea?

Fuller shook her off.

"If you have a case, arrest me. Otherwise, I'm out of here."

He stormed off around the side of the house, pushing through the bushes.

Lucy waited a minute, then went after him. He was right, she didn't have anything to arrest him for, but maybe if she followed him, she could work out what was going on. Then they could revisit the whole arrest question.

Except that, when she emerged in front of the house, Fuller was gone. She dashed down the driveway and onto the sidewalk, looking all around. However, for once, Ringo Fuller got his magic right. He'd disappeared into thin air.

CHAPTER TWELVE

Ashley walked down the ramp into the section of tunnels where the Underfoot Brigade had their home. It was a little nerve-wracking, leaving her tunnels behind and stepping out into the wider world underneath LA, down dark passages and abandoned spaces, where anything could be hiding. She felt proud of herself for having made the trip.

It helped that Octo was with her. The robot scuttled along, spider-like, on its retractable metal legs, its sensors and antennae gleaming in the light of its headlights. The information it gathered would be useful to her later when she drew up a map of the greater tunnel system, and it had some defensive measures if they ran into trouble.

Octo's headlights switched off as they emerged into the Underfoot lair. A mixture of fires and electric bulbs illuminated the space, along with some fairy lights across one of the shelters, giving the whole place a welcoming glow. It wasn't as carefully constructed as Ashley's tunnels, in part because the Brigade didn't have the resources she did. Still, a lot of work and love had gone into making a home down here in the darkness, somewhere that the city's rejected magical teens could safely live. The love and labor showed.

"Hello?" Ashley called. There wasn't a doorbell she could ring or a door she could knock on, but she felt like she was entering someone's home, and she shouldn't do that unannounced.

"Hello?" someone shouted back.

"It's me, Ashley. Um, is it okay if I come in?"

"Of course."

Footsteps echoed around the tunnel as someone walked toward her. She decided to wait until she could see who it was. That seemed politer somehow than walking in before she'd seen her hosts. As the footsteps came closer, she saw that it was Twylan, magic shining like lightning from her eyes.

"It's lovely to see you," the older girl said. "You really can come in."

Twylan hugged Ashley, then led her down the cavernous tunnel. Octo clicked along behind, swaying slightly under the weight of the bags Ashley had brought.

"Mom said I could only come if I brought some food for you guys." Ashley pointed at the shopping bags. "There's boring stuff she picked in there, like noodles and sauce, but I made sure there were cookies and chips too."

"That's really kind of your mom. Please say thank you from all of us."

They stopped outside one of the shacks, which had a pipe protruding from its roof. There, they unloaded the bags from Octo, who rose several inches as they removed the weight. The robot didn't have a face, but the tilt of its body seemed far more relaxed.

"Where are the others?" Ashley asked.

She had expected the place to be bustling, having seen how many of the teens there were, but no one seemed to be around, and all she could hear was a single voice in the distance.

"School," Twylan said. "You want to see?"

They walked past the Underfoot Brigade's homemade houses, built from mismatched construction materials and plastic sheeting, filled with abandoned furniture scavenged off the sidewalks of LA, and Ashley felt increasingly impressed. On no budget at all, these kids had built a home as cozy as her tunnels. While she wouldn't have given up her lab or her computer room for anything, she could happily have lived in a place like this.

Off the tunnel to one side was a large chamber. Ashley couldn't work out what it had been for originally, but now it was filled with benches and plastic seats, neatly laid out in rows, and the Brigade sat on them. At the front of the chamber, Leontine stood behind a table with his wings spread wide behind him. He was reading from a textbook, and Ashley recognized it as one that Dylan had lent out from their library.

"This has a list of spells used to catch people," Leontine was saying. "Like, to stop them getting away. Who can tell me some of them?"

He looked out expectantly across the class.

Near the front, someone raised a hand. "That one with the chains?"

"Sure, but what's the name of the spell with the chains?"

"Um, I don't know, something about fetters?"

"Does anyone know the chant for it?"

No one responded.

"Or what elements it calls on?" Leontine's voice was growing louder and higher as he got frustrated. "Come on. You must know something. I've been talking about this stuff for, like, an hour."

"That's why we're bored." Kix, a gnome girl in a sparkling top, waved her hands in the air. "Like, I know school isn't supposed to be the most fun, but this is just..."

She sighed dramatically and slumped in her seat.

"Yeah, Leontine, this is the worst," someone called.

"Why are we doing this anyway?"

"You know why!" Leontine slammed the book shut. "We need to learn about magic and monsters and all these other things. It's the only way we can be safe. It's the only way we can look after ourselves."

"Well, I'm not learning anything."

"Me neither."

"That's why you need to listen!"

"But it's sooooo boring!"

"You bunch of moaning, ungrateful—"

"Let's take a break." Twylan clamped a hand over Leontine's mouth. "When we come back, Siltor is going to tell us about the types of elves."

"I am?" Siltor looked at her in confusion.

"You are." Twylan smiled. "Until then, everyone get a drink and a rest."

The class dispersed, chattering among themselves, leaving only Leontine, Twylan, and Ashley.

"None of this is working." Leontine slammed his fist down on the table. "They won't listen."

"I know," Twylan said in a soothing voice. "Give it time. None of us are used to being in school, remember."

"It's a little different at my school," Ashley said. "I mean, not just that we don't have lessons in a tunnel. Ms. Holmes only talks for a little, then she gives us something to do, and we talk about it again afterward."

"See?" Twylan smiled. "We need something like that. Practical exercises to stop the others getting bored."

"Like what?" Leontine scowled at them.

"Like practicing the spells you talked about," Ashley said.

"They can't practice it because they don't know it. And they don't know it because they won't listen."

"Maybe if you explain it differently?"

"How do I do that, huh?" Leontine glared at her. "Come on, smarty pants."

"I, um..." Ashley shrugged. "I don't know either. Things make sense to me. When I try to explain them to other people, they usually look confused or bored."

"Well, then maybe you could take my place. Apparently everyone's bored already."

Twylan pulled a candy bar from her pocket and handed it to Leontine.

"Here, you know you get grumpier when you're hungry." She sat near the front of the classroom, the text-book in her lap, and leafed through it. "There's so much here, and it could all be useful. Maybe if we teach a little bit at a time..."

Leontine, chewing on the candy, sat down next to her, and Ashley joined them. If it had been her, she could have learned by reading that book. In fact, she had read that book already, cover to cover. Telling them that probably wouldn't help.

"I heard that there are places where teachers go to learn how to teach," she said. "Maybe one of you could go there."

"Yeah, right." Leontine flexed his wings, then looked pointedly at Twylan's glowing eyes.

"Leontine." For the first time, Twylan's tone didn't sound so soft. "It was a good idea, even if it won't work for us. I think you should say sorry to Ashley."

"Sorry," Leontine muttered.

"I'm going to go out there and get them to practice the spell. Maybe we can still learn something today."

Twylan walked out, then called the Brigade around her. A few minutes later, the tunnel filled with the sound of rattling chains and cries of alarm. Ashley peered out into chaos.

"At least they're practicing," she said.

"Are they learning anything?" Leontine asked.

"Um…"

"That's what I thought."

Leontine sighed and rested his head in his hands. "It sounded like such a good plan, sharing what was in the book."

A length of rope snaked into the schoolroom and flopped down on the floor. A moment later, Kix rushed in, gathering the rope as she went.

"That one half-worked." She smiled sheepishly at Leontine.

"Hey, that's better than I was doing," he said. "Well done."

The gnome smiled and hurried out.

"So you came to see our school?" Leontine asked.

"Not really," Ashley admitted. "I brought groceries from my mom, but mostly I came to see you."

Leontine blinked. "Me? Why?"

Ashley opened her mouth to speak but found that her tongue got stuck before it could make the words. It would be rude to talk about his crippled wing. Except that Leontine himself had said it was okay to talk about it, right? Except that people didn't always mean what they said, and he'd looked sort of angry when he said that, and now all the troubles of dealing with people were starting to clog up her thoughts. This was why she liked working with computers and with machines.

"Just get on with it," Leontine said. "I haven't got all day."

"Okay. Would you like a new wing?"

"Why would I want that?" He spread his wings wide behind him, or as wide as he could. One of them was strong and elegant, as powerful as any Arpak's wing. The other, short and twisted, didn't stretch out even half as far. "Oh, of course, to make me look like all the others."

"Why would you want that?" Ashley shook her head. "Who cares how you look?"

"Exactly."

"This is for flying."

"I can fly already."

His wings beat the air, and he lifted off his feet to hover above the chairs and benches. The pages of the textbook fluttered in the wind of his wings.

However, one of those wings flapped a lot faster than

the other to keep him in place, and he wobbled in the air as if he was about to fall sideways.

"It'll let you fly better. I'd make it out of plastics and aluminum, so it's super light but as strong as your good wing. It would strap along the other one so you can control it. See, I came up with some designs already..."

Ashley pulled a pile of papers from her pocket and carefully unfolded them. Leontine landed in front of her, and she held the pages out. He practically snatched them from her hand, then stood peering at the diagrams for a long time. She didn't understand his expression. He looked eager but sad too, and his finger tapped against the page as rapidly as his crippled wing had beaten at the air.

"No." He thrust the pages back at her. "I don't want this."

"Why not?"

"Because these wings are me, and I don't want to hide who I am from the world."

"It wouldn't be hidden. People could see you have a special wing. Plus you could fly better."

"I get along fine flying like I do now." He strode out of the school chamber.

Ashley peered after him. "I'd want a better wing. Wouldn't you, Octo?"

The robot nodded.

Ashley walked out into the main tunnel. The class on casting chains had descended into a free-for-all, kids chasing each other, shaking chains and ropes and strings, throwing around whatever spells came to mind. She saw wild bursts of sparks, sprays of water, flowers growing from the concrete, bright lights, and imaginary animals dancing in the air. It wasn't like any school she'd ever been to.

Twylan stood off to one side, shaking her head and laughing.

"Do you want to join?" she asked. "I don't know what the point is anymore, but it's a lot of fun."

Ashley shook her head. "I can't do magic, but if you ever have a science class, count me in."

"Science, math, English, we should be learning it all, like kids up there do." Twylan pointed at the ceiling and through it to the streets of LA. "As well as learning to use our powers better. But who are we going to learn from if reading from books doesn't help?"

"Maybe learn from each other?" Ashley suggested. "You're all good at something, right? Like, you're great with spells, and Kix knows about sewing, and Leontine knows how to fight and how to boss people around."

"He certainly tries." Twylan laughed. "Maybe you have a point. Starting tomorrow, we'll be learning a different way."

CHAPTER THIRTEEN

"This can't be right," Hank said.

He stood staring at a hillside in Elysian Park. The hill was scattered with hardy bushes and low trees but was otherwise unremarkable. Less than twenty yards away, cars rumbled past. This didn't make any sense as a place to run a business, and it made even less sense as a place for magic.

"I'm telling you, it's here." Lotty walked up the hill, peering at the bushes and trees as she went. "You can't always put a magical warehouse in a normal building, so sometimes they get hidden in other places instead."

"This is some kind of joke. I don't know why or what the point is, but you're trying to make me look like a dumbass, and I'm gonna kick your ass for it."

"Couldn't you try trusting me, just this once? Those of us who have a harder time passing for human, we look for different solutions. Not everything is about dressing up and blending in. Sometimes it's about getting out of sight."

"Like those kids down the tunnels." Hank said those

words with a snarl. It had taken him a while to find out who had lured him into that alley and handed him a beating, taking a few of his teeth out along the way. Real effort had gone into wringing that information from the local gossips, but now that he knew, he was going to have his revenge. He just needed to finish his homework assignment first.

Lotty stopped at the stump of a wide tree.

"Here," she said.

"This is what you call a warehouse?" Hank stared at it, incredulous.

"No, this is how we're getting in."

"So it's a secret door?"

"Better: a secret ventilation shaft."

Lotty pressed a nodule on the edge of the stump. The whole of its top swung back, revealing the end of a tube with a thick wire mesh about six inches down. Peering through it, Hank saw a cavernous room below, rows of shelves filled with boxes and jars. His eyes lit up with greed, and he let out a long, low whistle of appreciation.

"We're gonna get more than our homework out of this."

"I knew you'd like it." Lotty smiled. "Going around the magic stores like the other students, that's too obvious. This is the real source. They supply most of the magic stores in LA."

"Which means that they handle enough magical goods and ingredients to sell to the whole city and beyond."

"Exactly."

Hank extended a finger, and a narrow jet of white-hot flame leapt from the tip. He ran it around the edge of the wire mesh that blocked off the tube, cutting it loose, then lifted it out. Then his face fell.

"Wait, how we gonna fit down there?" he asked. "I can fit my arm down, but that's no good, and even you're not small enough to wriggle through."

Lotty raised her hands.

"Slither and shake, flow down like a snake," she chanted.

Both of their bodies wobbled, stretched, and shifted. Hank yelped in shock, then grinned in anticipation as he realized what was going on. He still had his arms and legs, but his body had narrowed down to the width of a fat snake, and all his bones felt as though they had turned to putty. Lotty tipped over headfirst into the hole, then slithered out of sight. Hank leaned in, laughing at the way his new body worked and followed her.

The two of them wriggled down the ventilation shaft, then dropped from the warehouse ceiling, landing between the shelves. Lotty waved her hand, dismissing her spell, and they returned to their normal shapes, standing amid a bounty of magical goods.

"Hell yes." Hank rubbed his hands together. "Now let's get looting."

Back up on the hillside, a tree shifted, moving in the opposite direction from the blowing wind. The bark rippled, and Heather Fields appeared. She had been there for hours, standing amid the trees, watching nature flow by, invisible to the world as long as she chose to be part of the forest. Now, she emerged from it, letting go of the magic of the Tolderai. She walked over to the tree stump and peered down into the warehouse below.

From the pocket of her flannel shirt, she pulled out her phone. If this had been her forest, she would have dealt with the criminals directly and brutally, but she was new to LA, and it was important to respect other people's territory.

She dialed a number, and it was quickly picked up.

"Lucy?" she said. "It's Heather. I've found something you ought to see."

The warehouse manager was a dwarf named Sgarny Olafs-dotir, and she didn't appreciate having her lunch interrupted. She appreciated the possibility of thieves even less.

"What was your friend doing up on my warehouse? That's what I want to know?" She glared at Heather.

"She wasn't there for your warehouse, Sgarny," Lucy said. "You know full well that people walk in the park all the time."

"Well, they shouldn't. If I had my way, I'd ward the whole place to prevent days like today."

"Then everybody would know that there was a warehouse here."

"Yes, but they would know to stay away."

The three of them stood at the door of the warehouse. It was a door of ancient dwarf-hewn oak, hidden from humans by a wrinkle in the landscape and some subtly placed illusions. Only people who knew about the warehouse would ever find it, in theory at least.

Sgarny turned the last of three heavy iron keys in the warehouse's ancient and magically enforced locks, then slid back a heavy bolt. The door swung open on well-oiled hinges.

"One moment," Sgarny said as something started beeping. "We have some high-tech security too." She went to a keypad mounted on the wall and typed in a code. The beeping stopped. "Come on in."

Lucy and Heather followed her into the warehouse. It was a large space carved out of rock and dirt using dwarven magic and ancient tools. Rows of shelving, most of them more modern than the walls and door, stretched back along a room lit by glowing crystals. The shelves were stacked with boxes, bags, and crates, all filled with magical artifacts and ingredients.

Near the back of the warehouse, the crystals cast an unusual shadow across the wall: the shapes of two people, one large and the other small, both trying to climb up the shelves.

Lucy strode down the warehouse, her footsteps echoing back from the bare walls. Sgarny and Heather followed, the dwarf snarling with rage.

"How did you get in here?" she demanded. "If you've touched my gold, I'll throttle the pair of you."

"What a pair of dumbasses." Heather looked up at the criminals as they clung to the shelves. "You know you won't be able to reach that vent from there, right?"

Hank cursed. "You idiot, Lotty. How were we supposed to get out?"

"I was going to use another spell," she said.

"Then do it!"

Lotty took one hand off the shelves and hung precariously. She waved her fingers in the air, trying to weave magic while clinging on to her raised perch.

"Levi—"

"Oh no, you don't." Lucy, her wand already in her hand, shot off a counterspell. As the levitation magic was flying from Lotty's fingers, Lucy's power hit it, and the gnome's spell evaporated.

"Do it again!" Hank shouted as he climbed the last few shelves.

"Levitare!" Lotty called.

As she waved one hand for the magic, her other hand lost its grip on the shelf. She fell with a *crash* and Heather leapt on her, pinning her to the ground.

Hank had reached the top of the shelves. He stood, stretching out on tiptoes, straining with his fingers to reach the bottom of the tube they had slithered down. He didn't know how he would fit back into it or how he'd climb up once he was in there, but he could only tackle one problem at a time.

"You won't get away this time." Lucy pointed her wand at him. "Come down quietly, and we can end this."

"No way, pig!" Hank pointed the palm of one hand at her, and a fireball formed. "You can't stop me."

He flung the fireball straight at Lucy. She dodged, and it hit the ground where she had been, scorching the packed-earth floor.

She stepped behind one of the other sets of shelves, using its edge for cover as she tried to aim her wand. Hank kept flinging fireballs, forcing her to duck back out of sight.

"Argh!" Sgarny screamed in fury as she ran across the

warehouse and slammed into the shelves Hank balanced on. The whole stack shook, then started to lean as the dwarf threw her considerable strength into it.

"Whoa!" Hank wobbled, flung out his arms for balance, and for a moment seemed to right himself. Then the shelf tipped further. His foot slid out from under him, and he fell.

Hank hit the ground with a *thud*. The impact set his head spinning, and the whole front of his body felt like a giant bruise. He'd dropped the backpack he'd been filling with stolen goods.

"We meet again." Lucy stood over him, her wand pointing at his face and a wry smile on her lips. "Do you do dumb crimes for your entertainment, or is it to amuse the rest of us? Because there's no way you could be this bad by accident."

Hank muttered something under his breath. Lucy wasn't sure what it had been, and she was pretty sure she didn't need to know. She pulled a pair of magically reinforced handcuffs from her back pocket.

"All right, sunshine, you're nicked."

Suddenly, there was a bright flash. Flames like the blaze of rocket engines burst from Hank's palms. The force of them launched him across the room. He scraped the floor as he went, but it was worth it for the yells of shock coming from the Silver Griffin and her friends. His fire carried him the length of the warehouse in seconds, then shot him out the door and into daylight. His power almost exhausted, he stumbled to his feet and ran.

Lucy ran down the warehouse after him, but by the time she reached the doorway, it was too late. Hank was out of sight, leaving only a smell of smoke and two scorched trails across the floor.

"Looks like your mate has left you in the lurch," she announced while walking back to where Lotty lay, still pinned to the ground by Heather. "I guess you'll be taking the fall for all of this. Would you like to tell me what you were up to, see if it gets you a lighter sentence?"

"We fell into a hole in the hill," Lotty said. "Then you came in, and we got scared, so we decided to run away."

"I saw you opening that hole," Heather countered. "You got a better story for us?"

"I should give you a good kicking," Sgarny said. "Coming down here, trying to steal from my hoard."

She raised one of her feet, and Lotty stared in fear at the steel toecap of the sturdy dwarven footwear.

"It wasn't my idea!" she wailed. "We were doing our homework. If it was up to me, I would have robbed somebody else, somebody with less-sturdy shoes. Please don't kick me!"

"Homework?" Lucy asked. "Who sets something like this for homework?"

"Ms. Womack. She's..." A sudden thought occurred to Lotty. Sure, it was bad to be arrested by the Silver Griffins and at least as bad to be beaten by an angry dwarf. However, the consequences of giving away Womack's secrets might be worse. It was time to shut up before she made her situation worse.

"She's what?" Lucy asked. "Some sort of magic tutor? Or a crime one?"

Lotty closed her eyes tight so she couldn't see that steel toecap. "I'm not saying any more."

"Homework means education. Are you going to some sort of crime school?"

"Not telling," Lotty mumbled without conviction.

"You are, aren't you? You and mullet boy are learning magical crime. That's why I keep catching you in these rubbish robberies." Lucy laughed. "Well, it's detention time for you, and this time you won't be going to the principal's office. Not unless the principal's taken up residence in Trevilsom."

CHAPTER FOURTEEN

"Ready, Buddy?" Dylan held out his wand. "I want you to stop me when I try to cast a spell, okay?"

Buddy looked up at Dylan with the mixture of hope and wariness he always displayed when the boy's wand came out. Buddy remembered what it had been like to be a bloodhound, and while he was a perfectly happy dachshund, part of him missed the longer legs and more powerful body he once had. Dylan's magic had transformed him, and when he saw that wand, part of him hoped he might get turned back, while another part of him worried about how else he might get changed.

Mostly, though, he was just happy to play. Charlie had been playing with him a lot recently, all these strange games where he tried to get Buddy to do the same things over and over again. The treats and attention when he obeyed were good, but the repetition itself got a little bit boring. Playing with Dylan and with guests who Buddy didn't see in the back yard very often made it seem like there was more fun to be had.

"You're serious?" Sofia raised an eyebrow as she watched her friend wave his magic wand. "You're going to get your dog to catch spells?"

"Sure. He's a smart dog, and it'll help me fight off bad guys, so why not?"

Technically, he shouldn't be doing magic in front of Sofia and Lance, but that ship had sailed a long time ago, and he trusted his two best friends to keep the secret that he was a wizard.

Lance made a face and scratched his head through curly, close-cropped hair. "I don't know, man, this seems like something that could get us into trouble."

"I'm teaching him tricks. That's what you're supposed to do with dogs, right? It's not like we're doing this in the park, where we might interrupt other people and whatever they're doing."

"Like that time with the water balloons and the picnic?"

"Exactly like that! If we'd had Buddy trained up, maybe he could have warned us that we were about to soak Mrs. Romano."

"A water-tight argument." Sofia smiled proudly at her pun.

"Okay, let's do this." Dylan waved his wand. "Pila accersi!"

A ball flew from the end of the wand and hit the lemon tree at the far side of the yard. Buddy watched it land, then raised one paw and scratched his ear.

"You were supposed to catch it, Buddy." Dylan pointed at the ball. "Then we can build up to you catching me before I cast."

"Maybe you need to act more like a regular game of catch," Lance suggested. "Swing your arm back like you're gonna make a throw, yeah?"

He swung his own arm back and coiled his body like a pitcher at the plate, then swung around, propelling an imaginary ball toward the tree.

Buddy barked and jumped up and down, his head twisting back and forth as he looked for the ball.

"Okay," Dylan said. "I've got this."

He pulled his wand arm back, then swung it forward as he chanted the spell. A ball sprang from the tip of the wand, shiny and blue, and flew through the air. Buddy ran after it, launched himself into a jump, and missed the ball by three feet. In this way at least, he hadn't gotten used to being a dachshund.

Still, he wasn't going to be defeated. He rummaged around in the grass at the roots of the tree, found the ball, and carried it back. When he dropped it at Dylan's feet, there was hope in his eyes. Was the ball going to be thrown again?

"Good boy." Dylan patted Buddy's head and handed him a small, bone-shaped treat. "Now, I need you to act quicker, to stop me before I even start." He frowned. "How can I explain this to him?"

"Show him," Sofia said.

"Cool idea! Lance, can you pretend to be a dog?"

"Sure." Lance crouched next to Buddy and bared his teeth. "So I'm gonna leap on you when you start casting, right?"

"Right."

"What's my motivation?"

"Huh?"

"Like, why am I attacking you? Have you hurt me, or are you a burglar I'm trying to stop, or—"

"Madre de…" Sofia shook her head and shoved Lance out of the way. "This is not drama club, dummy. He only needs someone to jump on him. All right, I'm ready."

Dylan swung his arm back, magic trailing from the tip of his wand. "Pila ac—"

Sofia slammed into him with the full force of one of her comic book heroes, flinging Dylan to the ground. Crouching over him, she turned to Buddy and smiled.

"You got that, boy?"

Buddy waddled over on his little legs, looked down at the gasping Dylan, and licked his face.

"Aw, he's trying to kiss it better." Sofia helped Dylan get back to his feet. "Not much of a guard dog though, if he let me do that."

"Well, hopefully he's learned. Ready, boy?"

Dylan pulled his arm back, then flung it forward, casting the spell. A ball hurtled from the tip of his wand. Excited to see this game return, Buddy rushed after it.

"I don't think he got the point," Lance said. "Maybe if we dressed Sofia up to look more like a dog?"

"Yeah, no." Sofia shook her head. "I draw the line at my band uniform, and I wouldn't even put up with that if I had somewhere else to play the flute. Anyway, you can't expect this to work the first time. We have to keep practicing, show Buddy how it's done."

"So you're going to keep knocking me over all afternoon?" Dylan felt for bruises along his ribs.

"Hey, it was your plan."

"It was?"

"Sure, now get ready to take your knocks, wizard boy."

Dylan was on his back for the fifth time, and Buddy was standing over a pile of slobbery rubber balls when Ashley emerged from her treehouse and came to see what the fuss was about. With her clothes neatly arranged and with her hair tied tightly back, the younger Heron was a striking contrast to her brother, who was now dirt-smeared from the yard, his shirt untucked and askew, his dark hair flopping in every direction.

"You need to use scents," Ashley recommended once they'd explained their scheme to her.

"How would that work?" Sofia asked.

"Magic often creates a distinct scent, like anything else in the world. If you want Buddy to respond differently to magic, you need to start from that idea."

"All right, kid genius," Dylan said. "How do we do that?"

"Do you have a normal ball, one that isn't coated in magical residue?"

"Um..." Dylan looked around the yard. By the kitchen door, Eddie was playing with his toy trucks. One of them was loaded up with other toys, including a bright green ball. "Hey Eddie, can we play with your ball?"

Eddie looked from his brother to the loaded truck and frowned. He'd kind of forgotten that the ball was there, but now he was reminded, it seemed like an important part of the game.

"You can play with these." Ashley held up the magnetic, programmable marbles she used to model construction projects.

"Marbles!" Eddie grabbed the ball off the back of the truck and hurried over to make the exchange. Ashley's marbles were like the ornaments on the house's higher shelves or the keyboard of their dad's computer, something that he wasn't normally allowed to touch. The idea of playing with them was irresistible, even at the price of his green ball.

"Here." Ashley placed the green ball on the ground and one of the magical blue balls a couple of feet from it. "Buddy, I want you to pick up the ball that Dylan made with his magic. Can you do that?"

She pointed at her brother, then at the balls, watching Buddy the whole time.

Buddy, sensing that they expected something from him but not understanding what scampered over to Ashley. Faced with two balls, he had no idea which one to pick, the one that smelled of Eddie or the strange-smelling one. It was too exciting, being the center of attention, with all these balls to play with, and being given treats! His tail frantically waved back and forth as he tried to work out what Ashley wanted.

"This one." She pointed at the blue ball. "Can you get that and take it to Dylan?"

At last, Buddy understood. He picked up the funny-smelling ball and carried it to Dylan, who gave him a treat. He was getting good at this game, whatever it was.

Ashley set up the balls again. "Buddy, which one?"

Buddy picked up the funny-smelling ball and carried it to Dylan, who fed him again. This was the easiest treat he'd ever earned.

"Here." Sofia retrieved another ball from Eddie's truck. "Try different balls, see if he understands what it's about."

Ashley set the new ball down, alongside a different one of the balls Dylan had summoned.

"Okay Buddy, show us how smart you are."

Buddy sniffed at the balls. These weren't the same ones that had earned him his treats, but the expectant look of his owners told him that something was going on. Of course, these balls smelled different from the others, but one smelled of Eddie and the other smelled strange. He picked up the strange ball, walked to Dylan, and looked up at him uncertainly.

"Good boy!" Dylan said.

Buddy dropped the ball to gobble down another treat. He really must be a good boy since the snacks kept flowing.

"So now what?" Lance asked. "We dress him up in a cape and call him Superdog?"

"Superdog!" Eddie, hearing an idea even more exciting than the marbles, turned himself into a greyhound and started running around the yard, yapping at imaginary bad guys. Buddy, seeing another happy dog to play with, ran after him. Lance and Sofia stared, open-mouthed.

"Did your brother just…" Sofia pointed at the dog that was Eddie.

"Oh, yeah, you haven't seen that before, huh?" Dylan was awkwardly aware of how many family secrets he was giving away.

"Nuh-uh. That's so cool." Lance grinned. "I wish my little brother would turn into a dog. He'd be way more fun."

"Hey, Buddy!" Sofia picked up two of the balls. "You know which one to catch?"

She threw them both and Buddy ran after them, Eddie alongside him, chasing the magical ball.

"It worked!" Dylan, beaming, dropped his wand and picked up two more balls. "Buddy, how about these?"

Sure enough, Buddy chased after the right ball, with Eddie yapping and jumping around him. The kids kept throwing the balls, and he ran back and forth, receiving a treat whenever he brought back something funny-smelling.

After a while, he started to get tired, as well as full. Treats were good, but the novelty of having them all at once wore off. He nosed one of the balls into the long grass when no one was looking, so he could trade it in for a snack later. Then, as he brought a ball to Dylan, he noticed a stick by the boy's feet, one that smelled as strange as twenty balls put together. That had to be worth a whole day of treats.

He grabbed the stick and ran off down the yard to hide it.

"My wand!" Dylan shouted. "What if he casts a spell by accident? Buddy, come back!"

The kids ran after Buddy. Now it was an even more exciting game for him. He ran back and forth, dodging between their feet, panting and drooling over the stick. The Eddie dog ran with him, barking encouragement, getting in the way, and tripping people. The yard became a mess of fallen children, brightly colored balls, and frantic barking.

Charlie, who had been working in the house, emerged to see the scene of chaos. "What's all the noise about?"

Buddy ran up to him and proudly dropped the stick at Charlie's feet. It was dripping with dog slobber, and the handle was chewed up.

"We're teaching Buddy tricks." Ashley sighed. "Maybe we should have tried teaching Eddie instead."

CHAPTER FIFTEEN

"Elf Café?" Charlie asked as they walked into the restaurant. "Isn't that a bit on the nose for dinner with other magicals?"

"Kelly picked it," Lucy said. "It does seem nice."

The place was dimly lit but in a warm, welcoming way, not like some of the darkened dive bars Lucy had chased fugitives through. Kelly Petrie waved at them from a table over to one side.

"Last chance to get out of this," Charlie said. "I can fake a stomach bug or a call from the babysitter saying there's been a crisis."

"That's sweet of you." Lucy kissed him on the cheek. "If I can't say no to Kelly when we're working so closely together, I certainly can't lie to her to get out of dinner. Besides, aren't you curious to see what her husband's like?"

"Curious would be one word."

With fixed smiles, they walked over to the table and took their seats. They had both dressed up for the occasion. Lucy put on heels and a dress that didn't feature any superhero symbols, and Charlie tucked his shirt into his jeans. Of course, the Petries had outdone them. Kelly's red dress matched her lipstick and nail polish, and she'd accessorized with intricate earrings of delicate, dangling gold, while her husband wore a three-piece suit.

"Lucy, Charlie, this is Max." Kelly beamed at them.

"Pleased to meet you." Max shook both their hands. "Sorry if I've come out dressed too formally. I came straight from the office."

"What do you do?" Charlie asked.

"Investment banker, but don't hold it against me. Most of my work is for charities and pension funds, I swear."

"So you're a white hat in the murky world of finance?"

"An off-white hat, perhaps." Max chuckled, and the sound was genuinely warm and relaxed, unlike Kelly's stiff laughter. "It's hard to keep your hands entirely clean, but I'm trying to move what investments I can away from fossil fuels to green energy, among other things."

Lucy picked up a menu, using it to cover her surprise. She'd expected Kelly's husband to turn up fully suited, but other than that Max was nothing like she'd expected, far less stiff and full of himself than the man she'd imagined.

"Um, where are the meat options?" Lucy looked down at the menu.

"In another restaurant," Kelly said. "I thought I told you this place was vegetarian?"

"Oh, yeah, of course." Lucy half-remembered a brief phone call during which she'd been trying to talk a chimpanzee-shaped Eddie down off the ceiling.

"Max is going through a meat-free phase," Kelly added.

"By phase, she means the last ten years." Max winked. "I think she's still hoping to turn me back to the steak side. Don't worry though. The food here is fantastic, and I've ordered us some drinks to get past that awkward first few minutes."

As if on queue, a waiter appeared and set down two bottles of wine, one white and one red.

"Wasn't sure which you'd prefer," Max added. "These are on me. I'm celebrating a big win at work."

The menu was a broad and exciting range of flavors, including some dishes Lucy hadn't seen anywhere else. On Max's advice, they ordered various things to share so the Herons could try as many as possible, including crispy oyster mushrooms, long beans with rice, and mushroom risotto. Soon, they all had plates scattered with pieces of different dishes, and the wine bottles were heading toward empty.

"This is so good." Lucy scooped up another forkful of beans.

"Isn't it?" Kelly leaned forward. "Don't tell Max, but some of the best meals I've ever had come from eating at these vegetarian places. The chefs are so imaginative."

"You're not veggie yourself, right? I'm sure I've seen you scarf a hamburger at lunch."

"Max's good influence hasn't rubbed off on me quite that much yet. While I'd like to pretend it's something civilized holding me back from going vegetarian, it's really all about the burgers."

"Me, I couldn't give up a proper cooked breakfast. Bacon, sausages, eggs, a bit of black pudding, some toast on the side...I mean, a proper fry-up is a nightmare to get living here in the States, but I'm not giving up on the dream. Even just a bacon sarnie..."

Lucy's mind briefly drifted off to thoughts of sandwiches she'd once had, only to return to the tasty food in front of them.

"So what do you two do outside of work and the kids?" she asked. "What holds you together?"

Kelly smiled as she looked at her husband from the corner of her eye. "Music's the main thing. I met him at a jazz club."

"Sounds romantic."

"You'd think, but—"

A crash from the back of the room made all the diners look around.

"None of you are real elves!" a voice bellowed. "This is appropriation!"

Lucy and Kelly exchanged a look.

"Sounds like one for us," Lucy said.

"Uh-huh." Kelly drew a wand from her handbag, then stood, the wand concealed from other diners against the side of her arm.

"Charlie, could you and Max keep an eye on things out here?" Lucy rose with her wand pressed against her forearm. "We're going to pop back there and say thank you to the chef."

The two witches walked toward the kitchen, where the shouting of a moment before had subsided to a rumble of loud, erratic grumbling. The occasional crash told Lucy that although some of the waiters were still hurrying in and out with food, there was more than a brief interruption going on.

They peered through the door into the kitchen. At the back stood an elf, tall even for his kind, the points of his ears showing through the silver curtains of his hair. He wore skin-tight leather jeans and a laced shirt that hung open halfway down his chest. His eyes were wide, and he wobbled as he faced two aproned chefs.

"No, see, you can't do this." The elf waved a hand, and even across the room Lucy could smell the alcohol on his breath. He had a cut-glass English accent as if he'd stepped straight out of a drama about a Victorian country house, its elegant effect spoiled by the way he slurred his words. "Trading on our, on our, on our heritage. Making out like it's yours. It's not right. 'S'not!"

"Look, pal, I don't know what you've got going on with this Witcher cosplay gig," one of the chefs said. "But you're not at Comic-Con, see, so take your game elsewhere."

"We should grab him," Kelly whispered as they crept into the room.

"Maybe we can talk him down," Lucy replied. "Get him out quietly."

"Cosplay?" The elf straightened his spine as he glared at the chef. "Witch? I will have you know that I come from a fine lineage of, of, of... Of people who can do this!"

The elf waved his hands. Around him, pots and pans lifted off worktops and ovens, some of them steaming as they floated through the air.

"Behold, real elf cooking!" The elf drunkenly laughed as he banged the pans together. The kitchen staff stared at him with wide eyes.

"Still want to get him out quietly?" Kelly glared.

Lucy shrugged. "Let's just do this."

"Never was, never will be!" Lucy chanted, waving her wand.

The kitchen staff froze, and their expressions went blank as the spell took hold.

"Oh." The elf narrowed his eyes. Pans hit the floor with a *clang*. "Silver Griffins. Have you come to oppress me as well, to stifle my right to wield my God-given gifts?"

"Actually, mate, we're here to listen to your side of the story," Lucy said. "It's out of order, them naming this place after your people and not employing any of them. Am I right?"

"Exactly!" The elf waved his hands around. "This one understands. Of course, you would. You're English. Proper country. Sense of respect. Rule Britannia and all that."

"Aye, lad, that's right." Lucy thickened her Yorkshire accent, leaning into the clipped vowels and earthy consonants. "Now come out back, and we can talk proper about this, maybe have a nice cuppa."

She took the elf by the elbow and steered him out of the kitchen, into the alley behind the restaurant.

"You're from Yorkshire!" the elf exclaimed. "I fought for Yorkshire once, back in, back in... What was it? Big war, lots of swords, angry man with a crown... Something about flowers..."

"The Wars of the Roses?" Lucy was surprised. Either this guy had been living on Earth for six hundred years, or he was on something more than booze. Judging by the subtle, small wrinkles around the edges of his face and the widely staring pupils, it could be both.

"You know what I miss?" The elf leaned against the wall of the alley and gazed into the distance. "Cricket. No one in this place gets cricket. All their sports are over in a day. What's the point in that?"

Kelly emerged from the kitchen, carrying a pair of magically reinforced handcuffs.

"Let's get this guy cuffed and off to HQ," she said. "Someone else can process him for Trevilsom."

"There's no need for that," Lucy said. "He's just sad and wasted. All we need to do is get him home so he's off the streets and not flashing his magic around."

"He used magic in public, on Earth. You know the rules."

"The rules are there so we can deal with the real criminals, not so that we have to treat everyone like they're a menace to society."

"He is a menace!"

"He's a sloppy drunk."

"A sloppy drunk who—"

"Wait, did you say Trevilsom?" The elf pushed away from the wall he'd been leaning on. "I'm not going to Trevilsom. You can't make me."

He raised his hands and magic glowed around them.

"See what you did?" Lucy and Kelly said to each other in unison.

The elf mumbled a spell and a wave of force shot from his hands. Lucy dove aside, but Kelly was a fraction too slow. The attack caught her in the shoulder and flipped her head over heels into an open dumpster.

Lucy cast a spell of her own, lifting the elf off his feet so he couldn't run away. He still had his magic, and with a gesture and a few words he made creepers spring up from the ground, thorned greenery scratching Lucy as it entangled her legs.

"Gotcha!" the elf called, laughing.

Lucy summoned a magical blade from the tip of her wand and hacked away the creepers as the elf waved his hands around, trying to dispel the magic holding him aloft.

"Down!" he said. "I said down, but in magic, so that should work. Why am I still flying?"

Lucy cut herself free and strode toward him. He launched another wave of magical force, but this time she flung up a shield. The wave of power broke around her as she reached out, grabbed the elf by the ankle, and hauled him down. Then she seized his arm and twisted it up behind his back. "I wanted to let you off lightly."

"You still could," the elf said, a pleading tone in his voice. "No one needs to know. Ssssshhhhh!"

Lucy shook her head. "We can't let this go anymore. You attacked two Silver Griffins."

"*And* ruined one of my favorite dresses." Kelly, dripping with stinking garbage, slapped the cuffs onto the elf. "I hope they lock you up for life."

"It's only a dress," Lucy said.

"You would say that. You dress like you'd be happier wrapped in bin bags. Some of us put effort into our appearance."

Lucy bit back an angry response. Just because she didn't dress like someone from forty years ago didn't mean she didn't take pride in her appearance. As far as she was concerned, the right t-shirt could look as good as any suit.

"I'll take him to HQ," Kelly said. "Make sure he doesn't

get walked home. You sort things out in the restaurant. Tell Max I'll be home late."

Lucy drew a deep breath, trying to summon some of the warm feelings that had briefly sprung up between them over dinner.

"Sorry this evening got ruined," she said.

Kelly snorted and led the squirming elf away.

CHAPTER SIXTEEN

"You know I'm after a con woman, not an oil change, right?" Ellis looked around the auto repair shop with one eyebrow raised quizzically. The place seemed as far from magical as it was possible to get. Cars were on lifts in the maintenance bays, half-assembled engines spread out across worktops, heavy tools hung from the walls, and heaps of tires occupied every spare corner. The whole place stank of fuel and engine oil, with a hint of rusted metal and sweat for good measure.

"I'm sorry, which of us is from LA, and which of us is the ignorant out-of-town visitor hoping someone will help him?" Jackie rolled her eyes so far the pupils almost disappeared from view.

"I'm mighty grateful for the favor you're doing me by doing your job. Still, I don't remember anything in the file saying Womack works with engines."

"We're here to talk to someone else, someone who could lead us to her. Someone with contacts all across the magical underworld."

"You couldn't have simply told me that?"

"You couldn't have trusted me to know what I'm doing?"

Mechanics watched them as they walked, still bickering, to the back of the shop. There, a vast man in grease-stained overalls loomed over a desk, looking down at a scattering of crumpled receipts.

"Tax time, Gunther?" Jackie asked.

The man stiffened, then turned to scowl at them. He had one of the ugliest faces Ellis had ever seen on a human being, with a huge, craggy brow, a nose like a squashed tomato, and deep-set eyes above rows of wonky, poorly cleaned teeth.

"For all the good the government does me." Gunther glared at Jackie as if she was a wrecked car blazing away in the middle of his business. "Damn waste of paper."

The deep, gravelly sound of Gunther's voice finally made Ellis realize what was going on. The man was part ogre, that part buried deep enough in his ancestry that he could pass for human, but not so deep that it wouldn't be obvious to other magicals. He might look like a road drill had rearranged his face, but that appearance let him have a foot in both worlds, like a witch or wizard could, or a well-disguised elf.

"I know a good accountant who could help you out," Jackie said.

"You saying I'm too stupid to do this myself?"

Ellis peered at the form lying next to the receipts. To his surprise, it was already half-filled out in meticulous handwriting, the letters neat and square.

"I think you've had some help already." Jackie glanced down at the same form.

"My lawyer helped me. You remember lawyers, right? Guys with pencils and big books, can make your life lousy if you arrest an innocent man."

"Lawyer, you say?" Jackie's smile crept up her face, as predatory as a lion on the hunt. "So you've seen Gruffbar then?"

"Didn't say I was using Gruffbar."

"True, but there aren't many magical lawyers in LA, and certainly not many with a gift for tax evasion. So, where can I find him?"

"Don't know no Gruffbar."

"Okay, how about I drag you down to HQ, let you make one call, and we can see who turns up?"

Gunther's face seemed to shrink somehow, the features squeezing in together as they struggled to express his frustration.

"I been lending the dwarf an office out back," he said. "For services rendered. Last time I looked, he wasn't in there, so you might want to come back another day."

His attention shifted for a moment, gaze flitting across the noisy, grease-stained space around them. Following that glance, Jackie saw a midnight black Harley Davidson Deluxe, its paintwork shiny as new, with tools and engine parts neatly laid out around it.

"I guess you give him access to the workshop as well as the office?" she said. "I hear he likes to tinker."

"Dwarves." Gunther shrugged. "They love that crap."

"'Course they do."

Ellis followed Jackie to the bike. Nearby, a short figure

in scuffed leather pants was leaning into a crate of parts, rummaging around noisily.

"Nice boots," Jackie said to the figure's back. "Very practical."

"Thanks." A muffled voice emerged from the crate. "You want me to stick them up your ass, or you want to leave me in peace?"

"Oh, Gruffbar, is that any way to talk to an agent?"

The figure straightened and turned slowly to face them, revealing a broad-shouldered dwarf, his beard cut unusually short. "If this is an official conversation, I want to see your badge."

"Come on, Gruffbar, you know me."

"Badge."

Jackie sighed dramatically and pulled out the protective medallion bearing her field agent number 782. Gruffbar pulled out his phone and took a photo of the badge.

"For my records," he said.

"You want to see mine too?" Ellis smiled and took out his medallion, the number 399 shining across it.

"Sure, why not." Gruffbar took another photo. "Can't do any harm if I have to make a brutality case later."

"I'm not here to do anything brutal, only to ask a few questions. I'm sure a gentleman of the law like yourself can appreciate that."

"Gentleman?" Gruffbar looked at Jackie. "This guy for real?"

"I'm afraid so."

"Okay, what do you want to know, Mr. Gentleman Griffin?"

"Do you know anything about a witch named Meredith Womack?"

"I know a lot of witches. You'll have to be more specific."

"She came to town a couple of months back, on the run from the Griffins. Likes to run big schemes with bigger lies at their heart."

"So she's a con woman?"

"A magical one, yes, although she doesn't limit herself to that."

"You're looking for a magic criminal who does all sorts of magical crime?"

"That's right."

"Nice and specific. Real helpful."

"Here's the thing," Jackie said. "A witch like that might need a lawyer for her schemes or as a backup in case something goes wrong. When magicals need a lawyer, lots of them come to you."

"At which point, it's covered by attorney-client privilege."

"That's not about magical laws."

"Are you saying we're immune to the law of the land? Because I think some people in DC might disagree."

Jackie ran a hand over the black Harley. Gruffbar's eyes went wide.

"Get away from her," he snapped.

"Her?" Jackie smiled. "Seems you're very attached to this bike. If I look her over, might I have to impound her for illegal magical mods?"

"You got a search warrant?"

"I don't need one, for so many reasons."

"You touch my bike, and this conversation is over." Gruffbar folded his arms across his chest and glared at Jackie.

"You want to play tough?" Jackie stepped away from the bike, and her voice gained an extra edge. "Everyone knows you were working for Zero on his big scheme. It was only luck that you got away when we raided his place. You understand what that means, right?"

Gruffbar's scowl deepened. He'd gotten out of that situation by the skin of his teeth and spent the next week looking over his shoulder in case the Griffins turned up for him. Since then, things had quieted down. He'd gotten his legal business going again, picked up bit work for old clients, started reassembling something approaching a life. The whole time, he'd been waiting for this moment, the thought of it making his guts tense up at any hour of day or night.

"That's got nothing to do with this Womack you're after," he said.

"Wait, Zero?" Ellis laughed. "This guy was part of that whole crime ring from the tar pits?"

"Allegedly," Jackie said, the word thick with scorn.

"Then there's no reason to be yapping out here. Let's haul him in, see what he has to say in an interrogation room."

"That's not—" Jackie began.

"Sure," Gruffbar said, moving toward his bike. "Just let me tidy up a few things here, then we can head up to the Observatory for a nice chat."

He clicked his fingers, and the Harley roared to life. Before either of the Griffins could grab him, he'd leapt into the seat and was away, swerving and twisting through the bustling auto shop, mechanics cursing him as he hurtled past.

"You idiot!" Jackie yelled as she ran after him.

"What?" Ellis ran too, but he was no match for her, never mind the bike, which had reached the entrance already. He flicked his wrist, and his wand sprang from the quick release holster on his arm, straight into his hand. "Punctum!"

A short, sharp stab of magic leapt from the wand and hit the Harley's back tire, which burst with a *bang*. The bike wobbled, but Gruffbar kept his seat and kept riding out into the street, the burst tire flapping. He tried to turn, but the rear wheel scraped along the sidewalk, and the bike fell.

Gruffbar scrambled out from under his beloved machine. He was loathe to leave her behind, but what choice did he have? Heavy boots pounding the dirt, he ran.

Within seconds, Jackie was on him. She grabbed him from behind and slammed him against the wall. Ellis ran up behind them, puffing and panting.

"Got him," he gasped.

"You got him?" Jackie snapped. "Which of us is holding him right now?"

"I disabled the bike."

"Which was only necessary because you panicked him into running."

"He was gonna run anyway!"

"No, he wasn't."

"Sure he was. They always run."

"Not if you handle them right."

"Now that there is an—"

"By my beard," Gruffbar exclaimed. "Could you two stop bickering already and take me in? This wall is scraping the skin off my face."

Jackie eased her grip on Gruffbar.

"We're not taking you to HQ," she said.

"Oh, so it's straight to Trevilsom without due process?"

"We're not arresting you at all."

"What?" Ellis and Gruffbar said in unison.

Jackie let go of the dwarf, who turned to face her, his eyes narrowed in suspicion.

"Why not?" he asked.

"Because right now, you're not doing any real harm. A couple of cantrips on your bike, which I expect you to remove before I come by here again, and that's it. Sure, you were involved in something bigger before, but I can't prove that, and you don't seem to be doing more now. Whereas this Womack, well, I've read the file, I've listened to my partner here's stories, and I know she needs to be stopped.

"So, here's the deal. You help me, and I help you. Tell me something about Womack, and I leave you to get back to your totally legitimate activities, knowing that I'll be by to keep them that way."

Gruffbar stroked his beard and watched her thoughtfully. "How do I know I can trust you?"

"What better option do you have?"

He contemplated that one a moment longer, then nodded.

"All right, but I don't have much. I'm a lawyer, not a spymaster. There's an elf I know, Vessfall, used to be in the Ultimate Magical Fighting League. He's better acquainted than I am with people who like their long cons. He contacted me a few months ago, while I was still working for Zero. A friend of his had come in from out of town, and she wanted help setting something up. Financial arrangements, contracts, building hire, all that legal jazz. Some on the magic side, some on the mundane. If your target likes big cons, this could be her."

"So what was in these contracts?"

"I don't know. I was too busy running errands for Zero to take the job. But you find Vessfall, and you might find Womack."

"You're right. You don't have much. Not sure I should let you off for that little."

Gruffbar shrugged, looking a lot more confident now that they were negotiating.

"Take it or leave it. It's all I've got."

Jackie looked at Ellis and raised an eyebrow. "Well?"

"It's all we've got too," he said reluctantly. "Least it gets us started."

Jackie nodded. "All right, Gruffbar, you can go piece your bike back together. Remember, I'll be watching you."

The dwarf hurried off to retrieve his battered Harley, leaving the two Silver Griffins alone in the street.

"Next time, learn to use a little damn subtlety," Jackie said. "You're not chasing fugitives over state lines anymore. This is actual detective work."

Ellis frowned but bit back his response. He needed Jackie's help for now, but once this was over, he could wave LA and all its inhabitants good riddance. Right now, that felt like a mighty appealing idea.

"Yes, ma'am," was all he said.

CHAPTER SEVENTEEN

Lucy sat in her parked car, a cup of tea in one hand and a bunch of printed pages in the other. Fitting in the Silver Griffins' management training around the rest of life was proving a little tricky, so she took any opportunities she could find. Instead of hopping onto her phone when she had ten minutes to spare, she would pull out her revision notes or try to make progress on an assignment.

Right now, having arrived at school ten minutes before she was needed, that meant reading a handout on project management. It was full of acronyms and jargon—PESTLE analysis, Gantt charts, critical paths, SWOT tables, a whole list of things that had meant nothing to her a week ago and didn't mean all that much to her now.

She'd thought that promotion in the Silver Griffins would be all about improving her magical skills, but instead, it was all this sort of stuff, about logistics and personnel and how to create more efficient processes. She felt as if she was sinking into a mire of bureaucracy.

"At least you're on my side." She smiled at her Wonder

Woman cup. "Do Amazons have to understand questions about employee engagement?"

The cup remained silent, but at least a sip of tea provided some comfort.

She flicked through the page of the handout. It had started as a mundane management course, with a few extra details flung in by someone who knew about magicals. So there were exercises and instructions for how to evaluate the strengths and weaknesses of a project, which mostly talked about social and financial factors, but with an extra question at the end about what to do if there were dwarves involved. Reading through the handout was dull enough in itself, but she felt patronized by the way magicals were flung in as an afterthought. How was she supposed to take this stuff seriously when it wasn't written for someone like her?

There had to be a better way of learning.

Her phone *beeped*, telling her that study time was up. She shoved the handout into her bag, gulped down the last of her tea, picked up a bag of homemade cookies from the passenger seat, and headed into school.

Music Club was clearly in session. The sound of amateurish instrumentation, all played to different time signatures, drifted through the halls. There was probably a tune somewhere beneath that chaos, and Lucy strained without success to identify it. Not that the song mattered all that much. It was great that the kids got a chance to express themselves, however that expression came out.

"Hi, Lucy." Annie the admin waved from behind her desk. "Are you here to pick up Ashley?"

"No, she's playing with a friend. I'm here to meet with

the hiring committee." Lucy opened the bag and held it out. "Here, have a biscuit. They're full of oats and raisins."

"Ooh, that's practically healthy." Annie took a cookie and nibbled at the edge. "So tasty, as well! I don't know how you manage it, with the kids and the job and all."

Lucy shrugged. "Just practice, I guess. I've been juggling those balls nearly my whole adult life, so it's second nature by now."

"Do you know who the committee's going to hire yet?" Annie leaned forward, eager to get in on the gossip first. Her duties took her all over the school, which made her the nexus for rumors and news, and she liked to maintain that position.

"We're meeting today to decide. I have a favorite, but..."

Kelly had a different opinion, and she could be very persuasive. This was going to be a tough fight. That wasn't why Lucy had made cookies, but she wasn't ashamed to wield them as a social weapon if that helped.

"Well, good luck." Annie smiled. "Principal Reyes isn't in his office yet, but you can wait for him there."

The office had been set up for the meeting, with three chairs arranged in a small semi-circle facing the principal's desk. Coffee, water, and snacks were waiting for the committee. Also waiting was Kelly, taking up the furthest of the three seats.

"Hi, Kelly." Lucy tried to make her smile seem friendly.

"Lucy." Kelly looked up from her notebook. "I see you've taken time out from your busy schedule of walking criminals home."

Lucy sighed and sat down in the seat farthest from Kelly. There was no point going over the restaurant incident again. The result hadn't been great, and nothing could change it now. The poor drunk elf was off to Trevilsom for a short stretch while he learned the error of his ways. Lucy hoped there would be someone there who could talk to him about the issues driving his behavior and maybe turn him away from alcohol. Ordinary prisons had councilors, so magical ones must too, right?

"Oat and raisin biscuit?" Lucy said, holding out the bag.

"No. Thanks."

"I don't suppose you've changed your mind about who we should hire?"

"Certainly not. And you?"

"No, I still think that Heather Fields is the best candidate."

Kelly tapped a pen against her notebook, pulling a thoughtful face. When she looked up at Lucy, there was something penetrating in her gaze. "Fields reeks of magic. She's clearly a witch. Is that why you want to hire her so badly, to help out one of our own?"

"It can't do any harm, having someone here who understands magic. After all, we both have kids here who inherited magic from us. It would be useful to have a teacher around who understands the implications, and who can cover things up when they go wrong."

"Hm." Kelly looked unconvinced.

"It might even lead other witches and wizards to send their kids here, make it an asset for the magical community."

"Having magicals around means more reason why we need a disciplined teacher like Banks, someone who can assert order. That way the children will be less tempted to act up."

"They'll be less tempted if the lessons are engaging and fun, and that's something Heather brings."

"Heather... You know her, don't you?"

Lucy froze. She hadn't meant to refer to the Tolderai chief in that familiar way, the name had slipped out, and now it was a problem. Not only a problem because of how it might affect the hiring process, but a problem for keeping the Tolderai safe. Lucy hadn't told the Silver Griffins about the existence of the tribe of woodland witches and wizards, and though she hadn't told any outright lies, she had gone out of her way to avoid telling the truth. The Tolderai valued their secrecy, which had kept them alive down the years. The wrong words from her now could ruin that.

"She's an acquaintance, someone I've run into a couple of times," Lucy admitted, deliberately keeping the story vague. "You know how it is. You tend to meet the same magicals around the place. She's always seemed like a good person to me."

"Oh, Lucy." Kelly shook her head. "We can't pick a teacher this way. It's nepotism."

"It's not like she's a friend of mine, only someone I know."

"The principle stands."

"Look, I didn't even know that she was going for this job until she turned up for the interview, and I wouldn't be arguing for her if she wasn't also the best candidate. It's my children's education at stake here too, not just yours."

"And you're going to ruin that for the sake of some

'acquaintance.'" Kelly made air quotes to go with the last word. "Real classy, Lucy. Proper Mother of the Year Award stuff."

"Hey, you leave my parenting out of this! I'm doing a perfectly good—"

Lucy shut up as she heard voices approaching. Mary Holmes and Principal Reyes walked in, caught up in their conversation and apparently oblivious to the tension in the room.

"Thank you for coming in again, ladies." Reyes settled down behind his desk. "Coffee?"

While he poured, Mary took the remaining seat between Kelly and Lucy.

"Here." Lucy set the bag of cookies down on the principal's desk where they could all reach them. "Have a biscuit with your cuppa."

"Don't mind if I do." Reyes bit into a cookie and smiled. "Delicious as always, Lucy. Kelly, thanks for sending 'round the minutes from the initial panel meeting. That was really useful."

Lucy silently cursed herself for forgetting to read that email. She hadn't seen the details of what Kelly had written about the interviews, but she was sure that the results would show Kelly's preferred candidate in a better light than hers.

"So, we're down to two." Mary also reached for the cookies. "Banks or Fields. I don't suppose either of you two has changed your minds?"

Kelly and Lucy shook their heads.

"As I said at the time, Banks has the experience, the qualifications, and the air of authority." Kelly enunciated every word for effect. "He's clearly the better choice."

"Heather Fields is creative and hands-on." Lucy looked at Reyes. Those were qualities he liked to live up to, and hopefully ones that would win him around. "That sort of thing is priceless."

Reyes sat back, cup in hand, and raised an eyebrow. "Mary, you've had time to reflect. Who do you prefer?"

"It's tough, but on balance, I think I'd pick Fields. Yes, she's new to classroom teaching, but with support, she could grow into the role. You can teach an adult to do discipline or plan a lesson, but teaching them creativity is far harder, and that's the part she has."

"Hm." Reyes leaned further back in his seat and stared up at the ceiling. "My instinct is to agree with you, but I think this time, my instinct might be a problem. You know I love a creative, hands-on approach, and I think that might blind me to Fields' weaknesses, as well as Banks' strengths. He doesn't teach as I would, but I need some balance on my staff." He rubbed his eyes and gave a tired laugh. "Second-guessing yourself is no fun at all, huh?"

Lucy looked around the room. Two all again. They were still tied, no closer to deciding before, and they couldn't put it off again.

"If I may..." Kelly reached into her bag and pulled out four sets of identical papers. She handed one set to each of them while keeping one for herself.

Lucy's heart sank as she read. These were printouts of emails from parents, mostly on the PTA, raising concerns about school discipline. It was ridiculous. Everyone knew that they didn't have a problem. Kelly had clearly gone around all the most uptight parents and got them to write in so she could use it to win this argument.

How could Lucy counter that? These were genuine messages from genuine parents, and judging by Reyes' expression, they had hit a raw nerve.

"A number of parents have approached me recently, in my capacity as a PTA member." Kelly barely stifled a smug smile. "They have concerns about the balance of influences in the school, and whether enough is being done to get the children ready for a world in which they won't always get to be creative, where following the rules is simply part of life. It seems that this hiring has provided a catalyst to bring out their concerns."

Lucy glared. That "catalyst" had been a bunch of calls from Kelly, but she couldn't prove that, and even if she did, what difference would it make?

"We have to set aside our personal biases." Kelly looked pointedly at Lucy. "Whether that's in favor of a particular teaching style or someone we know. This is about what's best for the children."

Reyes sighed and set the papers down. He looked across the desk at Mary, two professional educators balancing the comments of parents against their training and experience.

Mary sighed too.

"I suppose they have a point," she said. "Leaning into creativity and expression is part of what we do here, but it can go too far." She laughed. "Try leading our orchestra at the start of the year, and you'll soon hear what I mean. Creativity and expression are great for young minds, but so are clear boundaries and adults who know what they're doing. Banks has that." She looked at Lucy. "Sorry, but if this many parents are concerned, I have to change my view."

Three to one. Kelly was getting her way, Heather wouldn't get the job, and Lucy couldn't see any way to change that. It was maddening. She needed time to rally other parents, ones who would take her side, but there was no more time. Today was decision day.

Kelly had outmaneuvered her, while she hadn't even realized there were maneuvers to make.

"Mr. Banks it is." She forced a smile. "I'm sure he'll be an asset to the school. Now, who wants another biscuit before we go?"

CHAPTER EIGHTEEN

The deep bass beat of house music throbbed through the IT support team's room. Charlie had brought in a new system to avoid arguments over what they listened to, and under that system, today was Steve's day. He could pick whatever music he wanted, as long as it wasn't so intrusive that other people couldn't work. Since the others didn't want the music switched off on their days, they mostly tolerated what the others picked, not using the intrusive clause to silence music they didn't like.

Charlie was starting to regret coming up with the system. Sure, it had ended some of the petty squabbles between his colleagues, who were all younger than him, but there was a limit to what his eardrums could tolerate.

Maybe he should find a way to make the speakers stop working for an hour or two...

"Are you proud of yourself, office dad?"

The sound of Gail's voice made Charlie jump. He hadn't noticed her leave her seat since he'd been deep into his work, and the music had drowned out the sound of her coming around to stand by him.

"You mean the music?" he asked.

Gail nodded. "If you can call it that."

"You won't be complaining when it's your choice tomorrow."

"Oh, no I won't, and I'm picking out some really choice tracks to get my revenge on Steve."

"Um, I'm not sure that's the right way to approach music."

"It's the right way to approach everything." She peered over his shoulder at the screen. "What are you working on?"

Charlie quickly toggled windows to hide the program he had been running, one of his creations.

"Wait, did someone ask us to do some coding?" Gail leaned in close, her voice an angry hiss. "Are you holding onto the real work for yourself?"

Charlie laughed nervously. "No, this is something of my own. Remember, you were talking about side hustles? Well, this is mine."

"I'm bored. Show me."

Charlie thought about the hidden window, with its sprawling diagram of interconnected lines and colored disks at the nexuses of those threads. A map of the magical internet, working off a separate drive from their normal work, one bound up in security runes and concealment spells. That was where Charlie monitored the magical side of the internet, partly from idle curiosity and partly in case there was anything Lucy needed to know about. It was work he was proud of and that he absolutely could not let his colleagues see. That was the challenge of being employed out here among non-magicals.

He needed an excuse to explain away what the program was, or better yet an excuse for not showing Gail what he was doing. As he scrabbled around in his brain for an idea, a handy distraction presented itself.

"Uh, boss?" Kieran, the youngest member of the team, swept aside his floppy hair to look straight at Charlie. "I think we have a problem."

"What sort of problem?"

A phone rang, which was weird, because people usually emailed IT support, knowing that was the best way to get a coherent answer.

"The email server's doing something weird," Kieran said. "Like, it's not responding to—"

"Call from the deputy head of finance," Steve called across the room, clutching the phone. "He says he can't access his emails."

A phone rang again. This time Gail took the call.

"Yep?" she barked into the receiver. "Uh-huh. Uh-huh. Okay, we'll look into it." She put the phone down. "That was the senior sales manager. Says none of his team can access their emails, and apparently, that means they can't do their jobs, as if they were any good at them anyway…"

Charlie refreshed the workflow system and saw a stack of tickets that had come in over the past few minutes, all about the email system.

"All hands on deck. Whatever you were doing, it can wait. We need to get this up and running before a mob of angry executives lynches us."

He hastily divided the tasks between them, and they

rushed to get into the system, to work out what was going wrong and how to fix it. If there was one thing the team feared, it was receiving more tickets for work.

The frantic clatter of keyboards accompanied the music still blaring from the speakers. Now, its thudding bass and frantic tempo seemed appropriate, a musical mirror to the intensity of their efforts.

While a diagnostic ran, Charlie took a moment to glance at his magical internet surveillance tool. Something was flashing amber near the center of the diagram, a handful of lines with an on-and-off glow, but he didn't have time to dig deeper now.

"Backup's running," Gail announced. "I've got sales and customer service on there first. Should I tell them?"

"Go for it," Charlie said. "Let them know we're still looking for the root cause, but at least they can keep working for now."

An empty cola can sailed across the room and bounced off Steve's head.

"Ten points!" Kieran shouted and flung his hands up.

"Oh, it's on!" Steve downed the last of his Mountain Dew and pulled his arm back, ready for a throw.

"No!" Charlie snapped. "We need to stay focused, or we're all getting fired."

"Come on, boss, we're just—"

"No, you were goofing off, and now is not the time. Get. To. Work."

Heads went down, and the frantic typing returned.

"Idiots," Gail muttered, just loud enough for them all to hear.

"Found it." Steve looked up from his screen. "We have a

worm. Charlie's security system stopped it from doing what it was supposed to, copying all the contents of our email accounts and sending that info out. It's still doing half a job though, and that's causing the crash."

"Isolate that part of the system," Charlie ordered. "Come up with a couple of best options to fix it. I'll go upstairs. They need to know about this one."

He got out of his seat, straightened his tie, and unfastened the assorted locks and bolts that secured their special den. Blinking, he emerged from the dimly lit and safely locked world of the IT support team into the glowing corridors of the cloud computing company. He wasn't often called to deal with anything away from his desk, but this was big news, and better to get ahead of it.

He strode down the corridors, past executives in sharp suits and administrators in cheap ones, a janitorial staff member cleaning up a spill, and another one watering the plants. There was a whole world beyond the doors of IT, and normally he was happy enough to ignore it until he could go home. Today, he felt like they were all watching him in expectation.

Outside the managing director's office on the top floor, a PA was glaring at her screen.

"You're an IT guy, right?" she asked. "I was expecting a message about a meeting this afternoon, and I've got nothing."

"Email system's down," Charlie explained. "Took the calendar with it. We're working on fixing the problem."

"I can still get on the Internet, right? I mean, this won't lock me out of social?"

Charlie hesitated. If he had his way, social media would

be blocked on all the computers forever, for security's sake. However, that was a conversation for another day.

"Best not to for now," he said. "In case it makes the problem worse."

In case that was how the worm got there in the first place, and it was still trying to wriggle through their defenses.

Charlie walked into the MD's office. It was like every other senior executive's office he had ever seen, with an uncluttered desk, a great view out the window, the comfiest chair in the whole office, and some minimalist abstract art on the wall to create an air of culture. A dozen impressive-looking leadership books sat lined up on a shelf, two of them battered, probably bought early in the director's career, the others clean enough that they were probably for show.

"This about the emails?" the director asked.

Charlie nodded. "That's a symptom of something bigger. Someone put spyware into our system. We might never know where from: could be competitors, could be a ransom thing."

"Damn," the director said. "What did they get?"

"Nothing, I think. We caught it in time. But next time... Well, we should look at tightening up security. I've made a few suggestions before..."

The director gave a mirthless laugh. "All right, you win. Send me a list of recommendations by the end of the week, and I'll read them this time. Meanwhile, how long until we have email?"

"My team is shifting people to the backups already.

Beyond that?" Charlie shrugged. "I'll tell you when it's finished."

"Well done to your team for dealing with it so quickly. Let them know the pizza's on me if they need to stay late tonight or any night until this is fixed. Congratulations on containing it."

"I'll pass that along."

Charlie headed back to the confines of the IT support room. As he walked through the door, the kind of guilty silence that only came when people had been talking a moment before hit him. "Go on. Out with it."

"Doofus and doofus here were saying that our lives would be easier if the emails stayed off," Gail said. "Wondering how long we could keep it that way."

"It was a joke!" Steve exclaimed. "No need to get your panties in a twist."

"I'm certainly not letting you get them in a twist," Gail snapped.

"Oh, like I'd—"

"The MD sends his congratulations," Charlie interjected. "Job well done, and he's buying dinner for us if we need to stay late to fix it."

"Staying late?" Kieran looked around in alarm. "I have a raid tonight!"

"Dude, this is real life," Steve said. "It takes priority over Warcraft."

"Yeah, but..." Kieran sighed. "Fine, I guess, if there's pizza."

"Why always pizza?" Gail asked. "I say we get sushi this time."

"Raw fish? Urgh! I don't want to eat anything that wriggles…"

As his team settled into their usual combination of bickering and work, Charlie returned to his station. When he unlocked his monitor, the map of the magical internet flashed back up. The amber warning from earlier had turned to red.

He zoomed in on it, threads of connections splitting out to show him details, names, and codes appearing next to virtual objects. There had been a black hat attack inside the magical internet too, an attempt to infiltrate one of the discussion sites he provided security for. The worm he saw there looked awfully familiar.

He pulled up screen grabs of the code for the worm in their system and compared it with his alert. He'd need a much closer examination to be sure, but these two looked like they were related. His security code had already traced a likely source for this second attack, an open Wi-Fi hot spot here in LA.

Someone had walked into a cafe in Los Angeles and used their laptop to launch a preprogrammed attack. It looked like the targets were unrelated, which probably meant that it was gathering data for sale or ransom. That was good to know. What would have been better to know was who was behind it. Someone within the magical community or they wouldn't have been able to attack the net's secret side. Someone local, today at least. And obviously, a criminal.

A magical LA criminal. He knew someone who could deal with that.

Watching carefully in case Gail came over again,

Charlie bundled the evidence together in a secure shared drive, stuck a link in an email, and sent it to Lucy. Maybe she could help track down whoever had done this.

He wasn't sure how he would explain that to the director though. "Sure boss, the company's safe. My wife the witch caught a lizard man trying to get into our servers. She's sent him to prison in another dimension."

Good thing there was no rush to come up with a cover story. Charlie closed his magic monitoring window and got back to fixing the emails.

Around him, the great takeout debate continued to rage.

CHAPTER NINETEEN

Her wand illuminating the way ahead of her, Lucy descended into the tunnels under LA. It was a route she was growing increasingly familiar with, a series of rusted ladders and long-abandoned tunnels, some of them deliberately built to connect and others knocked together by time and enterprising hands. It all created a warren of passages that eventually led to the home of the Underfoot Brigade. The last stage was a ramp, running from narrower tunnels into a wide one, cavernous enough to hold a whole community.

Underfoot Hall, as she'd started calling the place in her head, was illuminated by its usual mix of fires and mismatched electric bulbs. A few of the teenagers who lived there were wandering around, but most had gathered toward the far end of the hall, where a buzz of chatter emerged. Lucy hefted the bags she'd brought with her and headed in that direction.

Twylan emerged from one of the improvised shacks, her magical eyes glowing in the dim and inconsistent light.

"Mrs. Heron!" she said in a softly musical voice. "It's so good to see you."

"Please, call me Lucy. Mrs. Heron is my mother-in-law, and Agent Heron is the one who hunts down rogue magicals. I'm here as a friend."

"Okay, Lucy." Twylan smiled warmly and pointed at the bags. "Can I help you with those?"

"It's more the other way around. I brought you some supplies."

"You don't have to keep doing that."

"I want to. I don't like thinking about you kids living down here in the dark, without proper houses or parents looking after you."

"You know that we chose this life, though?" Twylan took one of the bags and led the way to the community's storeroom shack.

"If your magic worked normally, you would've had some very different choices."

Twylan shrugged. "I'm happy with how it turned out. All my friends are here, like one big happy family."

"Don't you want anything more?"

Twylan stopped stacking cans onto a shelf and stood for a long moment, considering the dreams that she had long kept quietly curled away inside her, like delicate birds that she was afraid to let out into a storm-tossed world.

"I would like a chance to be part of magical society," she said. "To talk with other witches and wizards without them staring at me like a freak because of this." She gestured at her eyes. "To have a real job and a house and all those things. It's not going to happen, so I have this instead."

A cheer from down the hall made her smile. She set the remaining food down and took Lucy by the arm.

"Now we have something else down here that you should come and see."

Most of the Underfoot Brigade had gathered facing one side of the tunnel, where an elf stood, magic flying between his fingers. On the opposite side, a smaller crowd sat quietly, scraps of cloth in their laps, watching as a gnome in a sequined t-shirt talked.

"This is Kix's class," Twylan whispered. "She's teaching magical sewing."

As Lucy watched, the gnome held up two squares of cloth, pinned together along three of their edges.

"Have you finished pinning?" Kix waved her example. "Let me see."

Her handful of students held up their pieces of cloth, which they'd fastened together with collections of mismatched pins. One of the pieces fell apart in its owner's hands, and Kix darted forward to help him fix it. Distracted, the kids started chatting to each other, and one drifted off toward the other class.

"When we tried for one class, no one could agree on what it should be," Twylan said. "So now we have two to choose from, and next time we'll run something different against the popular one. It's like *American Idol* for teaching."

Lucy couldn't help wondering if that was any way to run a school. Then again, she wasn't these kids' age, and she wasn't the one stuck down here, looking for ways to learn.

"How can the teachers plan ahead if they don't know whether they'll keep teaching?" she asked quietly.

"Oh." Twylan bit her lip. "I hadn't thought of that. I should talk about it with Leontine."

Kix was back at the front of her diminished class.

"Now, put your hand inside," she said, demonstrating on her material, "and cast the first spell." There was a glow from between her pieces of fabric. "Then use the stitching spell to join it all together."

She waved her fingers, and a needle hovered in the air, then took a series of swift, stabbing dives through the cloth. A few seconds later, the pieces were stitched together. She turned the results inside out to hide the seams, then stuck her hand through the gap between the materials, and the hand disappeared.

"Invisible pocket!" she explained. "Now I'll come around and help while you finish yours."

A few of the kids focused on their work, needles flying erratically about, making something approximating Kix's work. Others, bored with the lesson or frustrated when the spells didn't work as they wanted, dropped their materials and wandered off. Poor Kix watched them go sadly, then turned to help her few remaining students.

"What's the other lesson?" Lucy asked.

"Come see." Twylan led Lucy across the tunnel to the boisterous crowd watching Siltor the elf.

Siltor held himself more like a stage magician than a teacher. He was posing for the crowd with a wide grin and his arms outstretched, fingers wiggling.

"Stop," he called, and his audience went quiet. "Hammer time!"

A pair of hammers appeared in each of his hands. He flung them into the air one by one and started juggling.

The hammers spun and twirled, bounced off each other, stopped to hover for a moment at the top of their arcs. The things they did seemed nearly impossible.

Then Lucy noticed that, every so often, one of them didn't quite touch the hand it was supposed to be in. "It's an illusion."

"That's his specialty," Twylan agreed. "He can put on quite a show."

Siltor ended by flinging his hammers, one by one, at members of the class. Each one vanished right before it hit, but the targets still all flinched. The students cheered and clapped, his targets as loudly as the rest.

"Before we go any further, I'm going to need a blank space." Siltor spread his arms wide and an arc of midnight black filled the air in front of him. "Of course, I'll write your name."

As Lucy watched, her name appeared from the darkness in glowing stars. There were whispers in the crowd, then more gasps and cheers.

"Why did he pick me?" Lucy asked quietly.

"He didn't," Twylan replied. "Each one of us sees our name."

"Neat trick. The lad's got some skills. What's he supposed to be teaching?"

"Illusions."

"I don't see him explaining it or anyone else practicing."

"Let's talk about the elephant in the room," Siltor exclaimed.

He waved his hands and a gap opened in the wall. An elephant stepped through, waved its trunk, and bellowed at the class.

"Or maybe the room in the elephant?"

The elephant turned, the ground shaking at its footsteps, to reveal a handle on its side. Siltor turned the handle, and the elephant's flank opened like a door. Inside was a sunken bedroom, with silk sheets on the bed and a chandelier hanging from the ceiling, like something from a celebrity's home in a magazine profile. Again, the students cheered and applauded.

Lucy stepped away from the entertainment that passed as a class, and Twylan followed her, lips pursed.

"You're right," the younger witch said. "They're not learning. He's just showing off." She sighed. "I thought we were getting there."

"Sorry to burst your bubble, but it's important to understand what's happening."

Twylan nodded. "We had such high hopes, but it's hard. Most of us haven't been to school in years, so we don't remember exactly how it works."

"Trust me," Lucy said, "as someone who sees this from the other side, the students never quite understand what a teacher is really up to."

"We tried to write a curriculum, a list of all the important things to learn, but no one could agree on what should be in it. Then we tried getting Leontine to teach, but, um…"

Twylan shifted uncomfortably from foot to foot, not quite wanting to say what she was thinking.

"Maybe he's not the teaching type?" Lucy offered.

"Yes, that's it." Twylan smiled sadly. "Maybe none of us are."

"You could be, Twylan. You're smart, considerate, good with people…"

"What would I even teach?"

"Magic, of course."

Twylan shook her head again. "No, I couldn't. You need to make people listen all the time, and they're always watching you, and…no."

"Well, let's both think about it." Lucy put a hand on the girl's shoulder. "Between us, I'm sure we can find a solution."

Leontine emerged from one of the shacks and walked over to them, flexing his wings.

"How's class going?" he asked.

"Same as before." Twylan sighed. "Going nowhere."

Leontine scowled. "They should all shut up and listen. This could be good for them."

"Do you like to shut up and listen?" Lucy asked.

"Sometimes," he said without conviction. Then another thought crossed his mind. "Why are you here?"

"Because there are some things you kids are definitely good at. You see people moving about in the streets, notice which magicals are about, and if they're hiding underground. I hope you can help me find a criminal gang."

Leontine grinned and cracked his knuckles.

"We're all on board for that. We've even started cleaning up the neighborhood ourselves."

"A little," Twylan said. "Although we've probably done better at that than at teaching."

"Well, what I'm looking for might be a school. Someone is secretly teaching magical crime, and I'm trying to track them down."

"You think they're in the tunnels?"

Lucy looked around her. The Underfoot Brigade had shown that places like this could become a schoolroom of sorts and how good they were for keeping secret lives hidden. Still, they weren't the only option, and right now, she simply had no idea where to look.

"That's one possibility although my gut's telling me to look elsewhere."

"My gut's telling me it's time for a snack," Leontine said. "You coming?"

They walked over to the canteen shack, where he started assembling a sandwich, only to abandon it when Lucy pulled out a bag of cookies.

"These are the best." Twylan licked her lips after a mouthful of cookie. "You're the best."

"Hell yes." Leontine had wolfed down two cookies in the time it took Twylan to eat a half. "Now we're distracted. You said you're looking for a crime school?"

"I think so." Lucy sighed. "The only solid lead I have is a gnome I arrested, who now won't talk, and the guy she was committing burglaries with, a wizard with fire powers and a bad mullet."

Twylan and Leontine looked at each other.

"This guy, does he wear sleeveless t-shirts?" Leontine asked.

"Yes, I think so."

"Is he missing his front teeth?"

"You know him?"

Leontine laughed. "We're the ones who knocked those teeth out."

Twylan frowned. "It's not funny, hurting someone like that."

"Come on, Twy, the guy deserved it. He was menacing homeless people for small change."

"Now he's escalated to burglary." Lucy thought about what she'd seen: the failed attempts at robbery, the half-baked plans, the poorly applied magic coupled with excessive self-confidence. This was exactly the kind of third-rate criminal who could be convinced that he would benefit from a crime school, that he was going to become the next big thing. He was being encouraged to commit more serious crimes and ones that directly hit the magical community.

"Do you know where I can find him?" she asked.

"Not sure," Leontine said. "We kept a lookout around a regular spot until he turned up."

"I've put together some notes," Twylan offered. "Based on the places we've seen him, which way he came from, and what else is nearby. I thought it might be useful in case we had to deal with him again."

"Maybe you should be a detective instead of a teacher," Lucy said. "Show me what you have."

CHAPTER TWENTY

"Gather around, class." Womack did her best impression of a proper teacher. Part of her wondered if it was even an impression anymore. After all, if she was educating these people, did that mean that she'd crossed the line and become the thing she was imitating? Where did fraud end and real teaching begin?

Probably somewhere past her plan, in which half of these fools would pay her for the right to go set up their schools on her "model," unaware that it was all sham and improvisation, while the prime meat became recruits to work with her on other schemes. Every student here was a profit point for Womack, with a future as either a mark or a colleague, and all those colleagues were likely to become marks too. Even that part would only kick in after she'd milked them all for merchandise and information through their "homework exercises." She should've done something like this years ago.

"I set you all hacking targets and the challenge of using

your magic to carry out the hacks," Womack said. "So, who wants to impress me with what they came up with?"

She looked around the class. Even after a few had dropped out or just disappeared, like Lotty and Hank, her numbers were steadily growing. Word was seeping out in the right circles to keep the recruits discreetly drifting in. It would have been even better without those losses, especially Hank, who had the potential to be talked into something dumb and useful further down the line. Like most of her work, this was a numbers game, and the aim was to come out ahead, not win every single time.

"I can already program malware," said a shifter with a twitch in her eye. "I used performance-enhancing magic to speed me up, get the program written quicker and better. It let me hit my targets before all the other attacks made system admins jumpy."

"Well done. It's not the most original approach, but it's one you can apply to other crimes. Transferable skills are always worth developing."

She made a note on the whiteboard, a record of what the shifter had done. Things felt more official when she did that. Something about the smell of dry wipe ink and the squeak of the pen across the board made everything more convincing.

"Who took a different approach?" she asked.

"I created some adaptive magical code," another student said. "The magical component let it get around the first few mundane countermeasures it encountered."

"Very smart," Womack said. "Remember, most mundane systems are vulnerable to magical code if you have the skills to write it." She added that one to the board. "What did you get from the target systems?"

"Found some Bitcoin, so I stole that."

"Bitcoin, huh?" There was a con Womack could respect, convincing everyone to buy into a currency you'd invented. She wished she'd come up with that one herself. It was so big that it was practically Wall Street work. "Is that worth anything today?"

The whole class laughed, including the bitcoin thief. The yoyo movement of virtual currencies might make for a good punchline, but that string of ones and zeros was well worth stealing.

"Let's get another perspective." Womack looked around. "Someone who thinks outside the box." Her gaze settled on Snivvery. "Come on then, what did you do?"

Everyone turned to listen. Despite her indifference to all of them, Snivvery had become something of a hero to her classmates. She was usually the first to finish any task and the one who got the best marks. If she'd bragged about it, they would have hated her, but the distance she held between herself and her classmates left space for admiration to grow.

"I cheated," the Willen said.

That drew another laugh. Wasn't cheating the whole point of what they did?

"Go on," Womack encouraged.

"I used magic to trick some nerds into hacking for me," Snivvery said. "I don't know computers, but I know people, so that's what I worked with."

"I can't fault that logic." Womack scribbled on the

board. "Outsourcing is almost always an option, but it has some serious risks. Who can tell me what they are?"

A door at the back of the room opened. To Womack's surprise, Hank walked in, looking even more shifty than usual. Unusually, he didn't glare back at the people looking at him but instead took a seat at the back of the class.

"Good of you to join us at last," Womack said. "I don't suppose you know whether Lotty will be along as well?"

"Don't know." Hank stared firmly at the floor.

That didn't seem right. He hadn't even looked around for his friend, which meant that he knew she wasn't here, and he probably knew why. Foreboding crept up Womack's spine.

"Pair up." She fell back on another of those teaching tricks that saved her from doing any work. "Take it in turns to practice your distraction spells."

As the air filled with hypnotic beams and showers of glittering sparks, Womack walked to the back of the room and leaned in to speak to Hank.

"Can we have a word outside?"

He grudgingly got to his feet and followed her into the corridor, out of everybody else's earshot.

"Where have you been the last few days?" Womack asked.

"Nowhere."

"Don't lie to me, Hank. I'm an expert. You're nowhere near good enough for me not to notice."

"All right, I'm not telling you." He crossed his arms and glared at her, sullenness turning to defiance. "That honest enough?"

"If you want to stay in this school, you'll tell me right now," Womack snapped. The more he resisted, the more certain she became that she needed to know what was going on.

"Maybe I don't want to be in this school."

"Bullshit. You came back today, even in this mood. You want to be here. Now tell me what's going on."

Hank's shoulders sagged. He looked down at the floor, and his cheeks flushed with embarrassment.

"We got busted by the Griffins again," he said. "Me and Lotty, while we were doing that theft assignment."

"You got away again?"

"I did, but they caught Lotty. Far as I can tell, they've got her locked up."

Womack kept her face blank, masking her sudden rush of fear. If the Griffins had Lotty, she might tell them about this place, and they might charge in to bust it up. Except that they'd had Lotty for days, and there hadn't been a raid, so maybe the gnome had kept her mouth shut. That showed more character than Womack had credited her with.

"The Griffins you escaped from," she said, mentioning Hank's limited achievements to restore some of his confidence and encourage him to talk. "Was one of them a blond guy, short hair and a goatee, wearing a dark suit with red sneakers?"

Hank shook his head.

"There was the Griffin who nearly busted us before, the witch with an English accent, wearing some sort of dumbass superhero t-shirt. The other one, she had short hair and one of those shirts like lumberjacks and old rock guys wear. There was a dwarf too, but I think she owned the place."

Not Ellis, then. That came as a relief to Womack. If the guy who had been hunting her made a connection to the other robberies, he could put the whole puzzle together. Then she was in serious danger.

Still, this woman had caught Hank and Lotty twice, and while it could be a coincidence, Womack couldn't take a chance on that. She had to assume that someone was closing in. That wasn't a reason to shut up shop. She'd put too much effort into this scheme to abandon it. However, it did mean that she needed to take action.

"You idiot." Snivvery's low and disdainful voice made Hank's head shoot up, and his face instantly twisted into an angry scowl. "You ran robberies so stupid you got caught twice, and now the Griffins are coming for us."

"I didn't get caught," Hank retorted. "Lotty got caught. I got away."

"I'm sorry, you're right, you didn't get caught yet. You're saving that until you can get the rest of us arrested too."

"No one's getting arrested," Womack said.

"Lotty did," Snivvery pointed out.

"You think you're so much better." Hank stalked across the corridor, then leaned in to shove his face right into Snivvery's. "You don't even do the work yourself."

"That's what makes me better. That and having some actual skills." Snivvery held up her hand, holding Hank's wallet.

"Hey!"

Hank grabbed for the billfold, which disappeared from view, deftly slipped away by Snivvery's sleight of hand. His temper rising, Hank swung a punch at the Willen, who dodged out of the way, leaving his fist to collide with the wall.

"You rat-faced little—"

Hank took another swing at Snivvery and missed again as she dove out of the way, laughing darkly. Other students were emerging from the classroom to see what the commotion was about, and they started cheering on Hank or Snivvery, depending on who they wanted to see hurt more. Womack watched in frustration as the situation collapsed into chaos, with the wizard and the Willen running back and forth, kicking and punching each other.

How did real teachers put up with this nonsense?

"Enough!" she snapped and pulled out her wand. She flung a spell, lifting the bickering pair of students off their feet and away from each other, to ineffectively flail a foot above the floor. "Your enthusiasm is admirable, but save it for out there in the world."

She set them down, and they stood glaring at each other, seconds away from fighting again. She needed something to distract everyone right now.

"As our friends are demonstrating so well here, knowing your opponent is key to success." She stepped between Snivvery and Hank and gestured at each of them in turn. "Snivvery is too fast and agile for Hank to beat senseless. Hank is too strong for Snivvery to fight back effectively. If either of them wanted to win this confrontation, they needed to know the other one's weakness, a way around these strengths."

Hank snorted and scowled, unhappy at becoming the subject of more criticism. Snivvery, ever the admirer of a weaselly way, laughed and shook her head at the way their teacher had turned things around.

"We're criminals, and that means we're going to get into conflicts," Womack said. "Although preferably not fistfights in the halls. Before getting into a conflict, you should learn about your opponent. Their strengths. Their weaknesses. Their allies. How they handle a problem. This applies to the targets of crimes as well. How does a shopkeeper defend his store? What sort of person is the mark of your con?

"So, the big question for today's class, how can you find out about your opponents?"

"Hacking," someone called.

"An obvious answer, given our last assignment, but a valid one. How else?"

"Watch them."

"Stalk them!"

"Read their Facebook."

"And Twitter."

"And Insta."

"And—"

"Enough social media," Womack cut in as answers threatened to turn into general chatter. "It's an important source, but not the only one. Today's assignment, to test how you handle all your sources, is to gather information on a specific Silver Griffin. All I'm going to tell you is that she's a witch, based here in LA but with an English accent. You need to find out who I'm talking about and as much about her as you possibly can, all without drawing her attention."

A hand went up at the back of the crowd.

"What is it?" Womack asked.

"On the other assignments, we all had different targets. Why are we all going after this one lady?"

It was exactly the sort of question Womack would have asked, and she silently cursed herself for finding students with brains. She didn't want to tell them the truth. They might panic and leave the class if they thought the Griffins were closing in.

"It's for comparison," she said. "I will be ranking your assignments based on who brings me the most thorough and valuable information, with a prize for the best one." That got their attention. The gleam of competition shone in their eyes. "Well, what are you waiting for? Get out there and find her."

Womack watched her class hurry off, some of them speculating about what the prize would be. That part she could decide later. For now, she needed to start planning. Whoever this Silver Griffin turned out to be, Womack had to throw her off the trail.

Last to leave was Hank, still standing where she had set him down, his fists clenched at his sides.

"I could have kicked her ass," he muttered while watching Snivvery walk away.

"Of course you could." Womack smiled at him. "Save that energy. I might need you to kick a Silver Griffin's ass instead."

CHAPTER TWENTY-ONE

Lucy and Jackie strolled through the darkness, wands in their hands. LA was quiet in the way that it only got around three in the morning, and even then, some parts of the city would be bustling with night workers, determined drinkers, and the sorts of people who hovered around the fringes of society. That last group was what the pair of Silver Griffins were looking for tonight, and one individual in particular.

"Why are you so keen to catch this Hank guy?" Jackie asked. "He sounds like he's a petty thug with a taste for fire."

"It's not only about him. It's about who he's connected to," Lucy said. "I think someone's running a magical crime school here in LA. The person in charge isn't going to show themselves, so I have to chase down whatever reprobates I find linked to it."

"This Hank is one of them?"

"The only one so far, apart from a gnome we already caught, and she's not talking. According to Twylan and the

Underfoot Brigade, this is one of the places they've seen Hank skulking, so it seemed worth checking out."

They ambled down the street, surveying the buildings to either side. They were mostly warehouses, with varying levels of magical and mundane security. They'd already had one guard come out to flash a torch at them and ask wary questions, and their evasive answers, meant to avoid mentioning magic, had only made him more suspicious. At least he hadn't called the cops. Those sorts of encounters were awkward, trying to explain things away without admitting their business to the mundane authorities or wiping the potentially valuable memories of cops.

"Thanks for coming with me," Lucy said. "This lad already got away from me twice. I don't want it to happen a third time."

"No problem. I didn't have anything going on tonight anyway."

"No hot date or extra yoga class?"

"I wish. Applegate saddled me with some dude from out of town, and now I'm too busy helping him hunt a fugitive to make plans of my own."

"This doesn't count as plans?"

"I figure that Silver Griffin work is a good enough excuse to shake off other Silver Griffin work. If it means I get some time off from babysitting the bozo, I'm all for it."

"Is he that bad?"

Jackie rolled her eyes. "Don't even get me started."

A movement caught Lucy's eye. Was it her imagination, or had she seen a dark figure slipping across the open ground next to one of the warehouses?

"Over there," she whispered. "I think I saw someone."

Wands at the ready, they crept toward the chain-link fence surrounding the warehouse and its loading zone.

"I know this place." Jackie squinted to read a sign in the darkness. "They mostly deal with food and toiletries, but the owner's a wizard, and he uses it as a cover to store and distribute magical ingredients. Puts it on the books as organic produce so he can explain small sales to specialist stores."

"Sounds like exactly the sort of place that a trainee magical thief might target."

They reached the fence. Everything looked normal, no movement, nothing out of place. Sill, Lucy's wand tingled in the palm of her hand as if it sensed that something was amiss.

She crouched and ran her fingers along the lower part of the barrier, feeling the links of heavy wire. Then suddenly, that feeling wasn't there. Her hand went straight through.

"Ostende mihi re vera." She waved her wand.

The section of fence her hand had gone through vanished. In its place was a gap cut through the wire, the severed ends pulled back to make a hole a large man could fit through.

"Looks like my mate Hank brought his wire cutters," Lucy observed.

"Or a blowtorch spell." Jackie fingered the ends of the wire. "Look at that, melted through. Fits what you told me about his powers."

Lucy took a moment to examine the warehouse, checking for any signs of a security guard or that someone had triggered a silent alarm. There was nothing. "Let's follow him in. Catch him in the act."

They crawled through the gap. Beyond was an empty staff car parking lot, then parking space for trucks. Past that were the rollup doors that led into the warehouse's parking bay.

"Is it me, or is one of the doors up?" Jackie asked.

"It's not you." Lucy watched the deeper darkness that was the gap at the bottom of that door. "Let's go check it out."

"Wait!" Jackie grabbed Lucy's arm to hold her back. "Magical warehouse, remember, and that means…" She waved her wand. "Revelare!"

The parking lot lit up, revealing the lines and sigils of a network of spells. They looked like alarms rather than traps although Lucy wouldn't have wanted to bet her life on it.

"How did he get through that lot without setting them off?" Lucy asked.

"Same way we will. Careful footwork."

They walked across the parking lot, picking their way between wards, stepping over spells. Every time the symbols started to dim, Jackie cast her spell again to see where they were going. Slowed by caution, a thirty-second journey took them several minutes, and Lucy kept glancing back in case someone came along the road, or a security guard appeared around the corner and demanded to know what they were up to. Fortunately, the night remained as still and silent as it had been.

"In we go." Jackie ducked to get under the partially open bay door and into the warehouse. Lucy followed.

The space immediately behind the doors was dark, but a doorway at the far side led to the warehouse proper, where a flashlight beam swung back and forth.

"That him?" Jackie whispered.

"How can I tell?" Lucy whispered back. "That could be anyone holding that light. Our perp, Mickey Mouse, the Prince of Wales…"

"I hear Mickey's scared of the dark, so it's probably not him."

Still moving slowly and quietly, they made their way across the loading bay and into the warehouse proper. The only light was the flashlight shifting in the darkness and some dim patches of moonlight that crept in through the skylights. The two Silver Griffins walked even more cautiously for fear of bumping into something in the dark and making a noise their target might hear.

Whoever it was, they were looking for something. They worked their way slowly down the aisle, surveying stacks of goods, occasionally stopping to look more closely. That slow progress gave Lucy and Jackie time to catch up until they were only a dozen feet away and could make out the shape of a human man, relatively tall and well-muscled.

"Put the torch down, Hank." Lucy raised her wand. "And put your hands in the air."

For a moment, the figure hesitated. Then the light dropped, hitting the floor with a *crack*. The impact must have broken the bulb because it immediately threw them into darkness.

The sound of footsteps told Lucy that their target was getting away.

"Omnis lux!" She waved her wand, casting a thin sheet

of magic across the entire warehouse. Slowly, a light swelled from the darkness.

A silhouetted figure sprinted away from them through the shelves and stacks of crates. Lucy and Jackie gave chase, far faster than on their regular weekend runs.

The guy swerved left, dodging off through the stacks.

"I'll follow." Lucy gestured down another gap between the shelves. "You try to cut him off."

Jackie was faster than her, so she had a better chance to get ahead. She nodded and sprinted away while Lucy kept up her pursuit.

She rounded the corner in time to see the guy turn again. He was trying to lose them in the maze of boxes and crates. However, they were Silver Griffins, not lab rats, and they weren't going to get thrown off that easily.

Lucy rounded the corner again, panting from the run. She couldn't hear the target's footsteps anymore although she could still hear Jackie dashing around the edge of the warehouse, trying to cut him off. Where had the guy got to?

Movement made her look up. The dim glow of her spell, still slowly rising in brightness, silhouetted a figure moving up one of the stacks, climbing toward the top.

"Nice try, mate!" Lucy called. "I see you."

He climbed faster, hurrying toward the top, and Lucy went after him. It was years since she'd last been bouldering, but old instincts kicked in. She hauled herself up the pile, sticking fingers and toes into the gaps between pallets of tinned food, using her hands to keep her in place while her legs drove her ascent. It was strangely satisfying, but there was no time to enjoy the moment as the suspect disappeared over the top.

Lucy clambered faster, swaying from side to side as she shifted her weight to keep her balance. At last, her hands reached the top, and she hauled herself up.

From here, she could see across the warehouse. It was like being a giant perched on the top of a city, except that the skyscrapers were made of cardboard and packed full of baked beans. Running away from her across the tops of those stacks, head down and arms pumping was a man in a black t-shirt.

The guy reached a gap between stacks of boxes. Head still down, he leapt across, landing with a *thud* that made the next pile wobble. While he was catching his balance, Lucy ran after him.

The guy was two openings ahead of her, but that last landing had thrown him off. Lucy reached an edge and leapt, landing in a superhero pose on a stack of crates labeled as rice. One gap between them now.

Without looking back, the guy staggered across his stack and made another leap. Lucy jumped at the same time, not letting him open space. This time, the stack wobbled as she landed on it. Rather than pause to catch her balance, she flung herself forward, keeping up her momentum. She jumped across one more gap and landed on the same pile as her target.

They were at the edge of the warehouse, with nowhere left to go. A shout told Lucy that Jackie was on the ground in front of them, ready to catch the guy if he climbed down.

"Got you, sunshine." She pointed her wand at him. "Hands in the air."

"Agent 485?" The guy in the black t-shirt turned. At last, the rising light let Lucy see his face. Not Hank the street thug, but Ringo Fuller, bounty hunter.

"Level Three?" Lucy arched an eyebrow. "What are you doing here?"

"Don't suppose you'd believe I'm chasing a fugitive?" he asked. For once, he wasn't wearing his shades, and there was a nervous twitch around his eyes.

"Not bloody likely. Looks like we've got you bang to rights, a law officer robbing a warehouse. Not that I was a huge fan, but it's still sad to see that you've come to this. I mean, what's the point?"

"I'm not saying anything until I've talked to my lawyer," Fuller said.

"Of course not." Lucy sighed, then gestured off the side of the stack with her wand. "Go on. I'll leave your hands free for now, so you can climb down. If Jackie sees you doing anything suspicious, she'll tangle you in chains and let you face a rough landing."

"Agent 782's here too, huh?" Fuller crouched on the edge of the boxes, then swung his legs over. "Guess I'm honored."

"No, lad," Lucy corrected. "You're nicked."

CHAPTER TWENTY-TWO

The practice room was a new addition to the tunnel base under the Herons' house. Dylan had built it using his magic and some help from Ashley's machines to give himself a place where he could safely practice his magic. This way, there was no risk of revealing himself to the world or of more magical accidents like transforming Buddy the dog, or summoning a rain forest in the school playground. It was a space hidden from view and safe from serious consequences, somewhere he could work on becoming a better wizard.

His mom had wanted to call it the Danger Room, and she'd had that big grin when she said it, like it was the cleverest thing ever. To Dylan, that just sounded silly. He wasn't going to be in any danger. If anything, he would be safer while he was down here, and so would the people he would otherwise have been around.

The Safety Room. Could he call it that, or was that even more dumb?

"Wanna cookie," Eddie announced from where he was playing with his trucks at the side of the room.

"Sorry, I don't have any cookies." Dylan pressed a hand to his rumbling stomach. "I wish I did."

"But I wanna cookie!"

Dylan sighed. His parents were both busy with work, so they'd made him responsible for looking after Eddie for the next two hours. He loved his little brother, but Eddie wasn't always helpful when he was trying to concentrate. Arguably, he was always unhelpful, even if it was sometimes in an entertaining way.

Buddy walked in with a patter of paws from the next room, where he'd been chasing a ball, and came to sit next to Eddie.

"Good dog." Eddie wrapped his arms around the dachshund's neck. "Good Buddy."

Dylan sighed again, this time in relief. Buddy should be able to keep Eddie distracted for a while.

Dylan raised his wand, aimed down the long, empty room, and gathered his magic.

The small metal badge on his shirt buzzed, and a voice emerged from it.

"Hi, Dylan, are you there? It's Twylan."

"Hiya." Dylan smiled. He liked the tunnel girl. She listened to him in a way most older kids didn't, and she knew a bunch of neat magic tricks. "Can I help with something?"

"I'm at the entrance to your tunnels. Is it all right if I come in?"

"Of course! I'm in the practice room."

A few minutes later, Twylan walked in, her long brown

coat sweeping out behind her and magic flickering from her eyes. She had a bulging bag hanging over her shoulder.

"You know you can just come in, right?" Dylan asked. "That's why we built the connection to your tunnels."

"I know, but this is your space. It doesn't feel right to walk in without asking."

"I asked you to come and help me!"

"Wylan!" Eddie walked across the room and wrapped his arms around the girl's legs. "Come play trucks?"

"Later, I promise." She tousled the little boy's hair. "I brought you a treat."

She took a cheese slice from her pocket and handed it to him.

"Cheese!" Eddie grabbed the slice and headed back to his corner, peeling back the wrapper as he went. "Buddy, we got cheese!"

"You know his favorites already," Dylan commented.

"It's nice when people remember these things." Twylan put her bag down and rummaged inside. "So, are you ready for a lesson?"

"Yes, please! The rest of the Brigade must be really lucky, having you to teach them magic all the time."

"That's not quite how it works." Twylan frowned, an unusual expression for her. She enjoyed working with Dylan or with anyone else when it was only the two of them, but her efforts to teach classes in the tunnels had descended into rowdy chaos, like almost every effort to educate the Brigade. She didn't know what she was doing wrong, and it bothered her. At least here with Dylan was one place where she could feel like a success.

She took a watermelon from the bag and set it on the floor a dozen paces from Dylan.

"Is that our snack?" Dylan asked.

"No, this is for learning. You can do all sorts of practice with a melon."

"Monkeys like melons," Eddie declared.

The air around him shimmered and the small boy turned into a capuchin monkey, with golden fur framing his mischievous face and his dark tail swishing back and forth. He scurried over to the melon and grabbed it with both hands.

"Oh no, you don't, Curious George." Twylan shooed him away with a laugh. "You have your toys. This one's for Dylan."

Eddie took a few steps back, then sat watching Twylan and the melon. His tail kept swaying from side to side behind him, drawing Buddy's attention, who wandered over to watch.

"All right," Twylan said. "Today, we're going to start with the spell that got you in so much trouble."

Dylan blushed. "Do we have to?"

"If you can face this, you can face anything. Besides, you magically grew a tree to stop Zero's dwarf friend, right? You've already faced this fear and won."

Dylan nodded reluctantly. It had been one thing to grow that tree in the heat of the moment, when there were villains to stop and his family was in danger. Now, casually picking up his wand to do something that had gone horribly wrong—and with Twylan and Eddie watching him—that was uncomfortable.

"You've got this, I promise," Twylan said.

Eddie looked and clapped.

Dylan drew a deep breath, nodded, and pointed his wand at the melon. "Crescent plantae."

Magic welled up from inside him. In a sense, it was always doing that. The world was full of magic, constantly churning away, begging to be released. That was why he had so much power. Not because it came from inside him, but because it came from all around. He was vaguely aware that it didn't work like that for everyone, that most people had to work hard to find their power. For him, once he started, the challenge was holding it back.

The wand made magic easier to control. He kept a tight grip on it as the magic ran from his head, through his heart, down his arm, and out. It was like a stream of energy that surged through him, bright and refreshing.

The magic reached the melon and found a seed there, a small dark spot within the moist red flesh and tough green shell, a point of untapped potential. As the magic flowed into it, the seed sprouted. A shoot rose through the melon while a root went down until both pressed against the outer husk. Months of growth went by in moments. Then the top of the melon trembled, and the tip of the shoot burst through.

"Well done," Twylan praised. "Now keep it going. See how far you can grow it while still controlling the magic."

Dylan grinned and let the power flow. The shoot grew and twisted, turning into a long tendril from which leaves spouted. The root emerged from the bottom of the melon and crept out across the concrete floor, looking for earth where it could dig in and feed.

The power grew stronger in Dylan. He was still

directing it, but there was more than he had intended. It turned from a trickle into a rush. The melon shook. Its husk cracked, then burst apart, showering them in red fruit and seedlings, all of which were still growing with the last surge of the interrupted spell.

"Sorry," Dylan mumbled, wiping melon from his face.

"Don't be sorry." Twylan laid a hand on his shoulder. "You did great. Look how far you grew that first melon before you lost control!"

The plant still sat amid the ruined fruit and the hundred other seedlings that had started to grow. Its tendrils ran for three feet across the floor, with lush green leaves hanging from them, and there was a long, sturdy root.

"Thanks." Dylan smiled. "Now what?"

"Now we try again." Twylan took another melon from her bag.

Eddie turned from a monkey into a bear cub, then used his paws to scoop away the shattered gourd, eating pieces as he went. Buddy helped, nudging pieces of shell across the floor with his nose. Then the two of them sat to watch as Dylan pointed his wand at the new melon.

"Crescent plantae."

They went through the same process with that watermelon, then three more. Each time, Dylan's plant grew a little larger before his power overwhelmed the spell's structure and dozens of seedlings burst the melon apart. The last one he grew had melons of its own, round fruits bulging with life and flavor before the original exploded.

Eddie, who was now a lizard, made a rasping sound that could have been a laugh as he swept fruit from his face with his forepaws. Buddy was running around excitedly, gobbling up pieces of melon. Even Dylan was laughing now although he was trembling too, the strain of controlling the spell's power having shaken him to his core.

"I don't know how my mom does this," he said. "Or how you do it. You have so much power, and you keep it under control like that's the most natural thing in the world."

"Not all of it." Twylan pointed at the magic that constantly flickered from her eyes, bright tendrils dancing across her cheeks, leaving behind dark and sooty streaks. "If I could, my life would be very different."

"Do you wish you could?" Dylan asked.

"Some days, yes. I imagine what it would be like to live in a normal human house, go to human places, have a job like other witches do." She smiled sadly. "But if I had that life, I wouldn't have met Leontine and Kix and all the others. I wouldn't be part of the Underfoot Brigade. I might never have met your mom and you guys through her. Those are things I wouldn't give up for the world."

She drew a deep breath, then continued, "As for keeping power under control, that comes with time. You keep practicing, and at first it's difficult all the time. Then it starts to get easier. Then it gets to a point where you don't even think about it most of the time. You just do it."

"So you never lose control?"

"Occasionally. When things are really difficult, or I'm tired or hurt. It's okay for that to happen sometimes. You're never going to have perfect control, but as long as you do your best, everyone who matters will be proud of you."

"Mom seems to have it under control all the time."

"That's part of the magic of being a mom. I bet your clothes seem to get clean with no effort too, and she naturally knows where she needs to drive you every day."

Dylan laughed. "Maybe I've underestimated how much work mom-ing is."

"We all do."

Twylan took the last three melons from her bag and set them down on the far side of the room.

"Last bit of practice today," she said. "This time something more fun. A competition to see who can make the biggest mess with one spell. You can use whatever spell you want."

Dylan thought about it for a moment. He knew that there were spells out there to blow things up or to rip them apart. Those weren't the sort that anyone taught a twelve-year-old, and he was okay with that. After today's practice, he should play to his strengths.

"Crescent plantae," he shouted, putting all the force he could into it, unleashing a torrent of magic.

Inside one of the melons, a hundred seeds burst with life. The melon shattered, and juice flew, leaving behind a tangle of roots and shoots.

"Eddie, do you want a go?" Twylan asked.

The air around Eddie flickered, and he turned into a miniature rhinoceros. With a bellow, he charged across the room and slammed into the next melon, crushing it between his hardened head and the wall. When he turned back to them, a chunk of green shell hung from his horn.

"My turn." Twylan lowered her voice to a whisper. "Displodo."

The last melon flew trembling into the air. It hung for a

moment in the center of the room, then burst apart so hard that it painted every wall with its insides.

"Wow," Dylan said, as he and Eddie stared wide-eyed at her handiwork.

"Thank you," Twylan said. "Although I'm afraid we'll have a long job cleaning it up."

Dylan grinned. "Don't worry, Ashley built a robot for that. Mom-ing is hard work, remember, and none of us want to have to do it."

CHAPTER TWENTY-THREE

Lucy sat with her feet up on the couch, a pen in her hand, textbooks, handouts, and pages of scribbled notes scattered around her. She stared again at the assignment she was supposed to complete, a complex, multi-part case study about managing an office move. There were questions on finance, on handling people, on planning the move itself. It was so detailed that she was surprised they didn't ask her to pick what color the walls should be and what sort of carpet to install. Yes, there were magical components to do with spell-proofing and providing for the needs of different races on the company's staff. For the most part, it was the sort of mind-numbing, spirit-crushing office grind that she'd thought she was avoiding by working for the Silver Griffins.

She got up, stretched, and went through to the kitchen so she could make a cup of tea. Tea was her friend. Tea wouldn't let her down in this moment of crisis. Tea understood.

While the kettle boiled, she contemplated what she was

learning from the training course. Not the stuff the materials set out to teach her, like strategies for managing awkward staff or how to plan a company retreat. No, the thing she was learning was what being a manager meant, what Applegate had to deal with daily. She wasn't the bright-eyed young Griffin she'd once been, so she was under no illusion that it was all fighting magical beasts and saving the world from rogue wizards. However, she'd never appreciated what a vast heap of admin it was or how much of that might fall on her if she got a promotion. It would be great to have more power over her work, but was this really what she wanted?

Tea in hand, she returned to the couch. Maybe if she looked at the assignment from a different angle, that would help. What sort of person would be running the imagined office? She could pretend to be them, add some fun to proceedings.

"I'm the supervising troll," she announced to the empty living room. "No, wait, I'm a dwarf with an MBA. My interests include golf, skiing, and hoarding gold for the glory of my ancestors." She sipped her tea and sighed. "I am a very bored witch and wish I'd never gotten into this business."

She picked up some notes, but as she ran her gaze across the words, her brain skipped across them, taking nothing in. That was no good at all.

Perhaps if she did something else for a while, she would be able to face the assignment. She needed to relax, reset her brain, shake off the stress and the jumble of acronyms that seemed to spring up whenever she was working on the course. She needed some time to be herself, not the troll or dwarf or even witch who could successfully move a whole Silver Griffins base from one location to another.

Setting the notes aside for a second time, she headed into the dining room. Eddie had set up a den under the table, building a nest around himself from blankets and cushions, and there he sat, acting out epic conflicts between his superhero action figures.

"Want to do some baking?" Lucy asked.

Eddie scratched his head with Batman and made a thoughtful face.

"Yes," he said at last.

He crawled out from under the table and followed her into the kitchen, where he set Batman up to watch out for the Joker while they cooked.

"How do muffins sound?" Lucy turned on the oven.

"Chocolate?" Eddie asked.

"If you want."

"Yes."

"Chocolate muffins it is."

She got out the low, battered folding table on which the kids had done their cooking since Dylan was small. There she set down a plastic bowl and a sieve.

"I need you to sift out any lumps, okay?"

Eddie nodded earnestly. Baking was serious business.

She weighed out flour and cocoa, measured a spoonful of baking powder, and turned to hand the results to Eddie. To her complete lack of surprise, he had turned into a capuchin monkey, one of his favorites at the moment. Slender fingers reached for the ingredients.

"Wash those hands first, please," she instructed.

Washing inevitably involved a lot of splashing and some

blowing on soap bubbles, while Eddie waved his tail around in excitement. Then came the challenge of drying off an energized monkey with sodden fur. That was enough of a routine now that she could get him back at his table in a few minutes, as long as she made encouraging noises and didn't let him get too comfortable at the sink.

"All right, sweetheart, it's time to set you to work." She draped an apron around his neck and bent to tie it behind him. "I'm like some sort of Victorian gentlewoman indulging in child labor, sending kids up the chimney to clear out soot. Would you make a good chimney sweep, do you think?"

"Ook!" Eddie mimed sticking a brush up a chimney, as he'd seen in Mary Poppins.

"I don't know. That was a bit half-hearted. You'll never get old London town clean like that. Give it another go."

"Oooook!" This time his arms flew wildly up and down as if he'd grabbed that chimney brush and was giving it his all.

"Okay, I guess that'll do, lad." Lucy handed him the bowl containing the flour, cocoa, and baking powder. "Time to get sifting."

Eddie held the bowl carefully in both hands and started pouring the dried ingredients through the sieve, which he shook back and forth using his tail. It made Lucy wish that she had more arms, so she could get all the things done she needed to.

While Eddie was busy, she grabbed a bowl of her own, measured in sugar, oil, and milk, then added an egg. She mixed them with one eye on her bowl and the other on Eddie, making sure that he didn't scatter too much flour around the kitchen. She'd added extra in the certainty that some would get spilled, but past a certain point, a three-year-old assistant could lose so much in ingredients that the recipe didn't work.

"Are you ready to mix it all?" she asked once he'd finished sifting the dry ingredients.

"Ook!"

"Brilliant. Can you fetch a wooden spoon?"

Eddie took hold of the step he used to reach the sink and pushed it down the line of kitchen cupboards. Then he hopped up onto it, bouncing on his springy monkey legs, opened a drawer, and pulled out a spoon. He gripped it in his tail and waved it with a flourish.

Lucy laughed. "I get it. You have a tail. Now come help me bake, or we'll never get muffins."

That was more than enough to motivate Eddie. He leapt down off the step and hurried over to his table. There, he did the stirring while Lucy slowly poured her mixture into the dry ingredients.

"That's it." She scraped the last of the sugary gunk into the bowl. "Keep going, make sure it's combined."

Eddy gripped the spoon with both hands and stirred harder, his face wrinkling in concentration.

"Do you want to make them double chocolate muffins?" Lucy held up a bag of chocolate chips.

If there had ever been any doubt about the answer, a stream of "ooks" eradicated it. She tipped a handful of the chocolate chips into the recipe and set Eddie to stir again while she put paper liners in the muffin tray.

Eddie's attempts to spoon the mixture into them got a little messy, with strands of muffin mix getting draped across the table, the floor, and, of course, his fur. Enough went into the muffins to make it all worthwhile, and if there was lots of cleaning up to do after, it would be worth it for how proud Eddie looked as she slid the tray into the oven.

He stood, watching the oven expectantly, one chocolaty paw stuck in his mouth.

"You know that's going to take at least twenty minutes, right?" Lucy asked.

The little monkey looked from her to the clock and back as if begging her to speed up time.

"Let's get you cleaned up. That should kill five minutes, at least."

Cleaning Eddie turned out to be as much about him licking the uncooked batter from his fur as it was about soap and water, but Lucy managed to steer him to cleanliness in the end. They were nearly done with the whole soggy business when Lucy's phone buzzed with a call from work.

"Back in a moment, sweetheart." She left Eddie to finish drying his hands and walked out of the room, answering the call as she went. "Agent Heron here. How can I help?"

"It's Applegate," her manager declared in a booming voice. "Want to talk to you about this guy you brought in last night."

"Ringo Fuller? Jackie and I caught him breaking into a warehouse down by the river, probably to steal magical supplies. I haven't linked him to the crime ring you set me on yet, but I think it's only a matter of time. He's always been a bit of a shifty bugger."

"We're letting him go."

"What? Why?" Lucy's hand tightened around the phone. "I worked hard to be there and stop another theft, risked my neck chasing him across the goods in that warehouse. Why on earth would you let the bloke get away now when I caught him red-handed?"

"Those hands of his aren't as scarlet as you think."

"He'd broken in. We found the hole in the fence, the spell he used to hide it, saw him rummaging around the warehouse…"

"Apparently he's taking an official bounty hunter training course to try to get from level three to four. As part of his assessment, he has to carry out a series of tasks set for him around the city, including surveillance work and covert infiltration. The people running the course arranged with the warehouse owner to use the place for one of these assignments. Fuller was supposed to cut through that fence, get around the magic, and find an artifact hidden inside."

"Pardon my French, sir, but that's the biggest pile of wank I've ever heard. How long did it take him to spin you that line?"

"Actually, it was the course administrator who told me, after we contacted the warehouse owner. One of the rules of the course is that Fuller isn't allowed to tell people what he's doing."

"All that was pretend?" Lucy stared at the wall as she tried to take it in. It did explain her recent encounters with Fuller, the way he'd been lurking idly around places rather than chasing down targets, failing to catch them before she did. Still, she would have called it nonsense if the story had come straight from him. "I suppose it's only fair to let him go then."

So much for a lead on the thieves. She would have to go back to stalking Hank's haunts, hoping to catch him doing whatever he did that wasn't committing rubbish robberies.

"Mr. Fuller isn't asking for an apology—"

"I'd bloody well hope not!"

"—but technically you arrested an innocent man, so tread lightly next time you run into him."

"There's nothing innocent about Ringo Fuller."

"That there? That's what you absolutely cannot say, at least for a while. We don't want to look like we're picking on a legally licensed agent."

"Right you are, sir. Was there anything else?"

"That's all. Good effort catching him, Agent Heron. It's a shame it didn't work out."

She hung up and stood in the middle of the living room, staring at the papers she'd scattered around. She wished her assignments were a little more like Fuller's, something hands-on. She would take in much more of the information that way and have a lot more fun with it. Then again, practical activities probably weren't suited to a management course, whereas they were virtually a necessity for a bounty hunter.

She'd been so sure this was her next lead on the crime school.

Maybe it was. After all, there was a lesson to be learned here by her as much as Fuller. The tasks they'd been set weren't only about the specific details, like whether she could process invoices. They were about what made the learning sink in, for the sort of people who needed that learning. Trainee managers needed to get used to paper-work, and someone who couldn't cope with that shouldn't manage. Trainee bounty hunters needed to be willing to risk capture and its consequences, and someone who couldn't face that should fail, whatever the exercise was. What was the equivalent for a gang of magical thieves?

A hoot snapped her out of her thoughts. She walked back into the kitchen, where Eddie had taken the form of an owl and perched on the counter opposite the oven, watching the timer tick down. A delicious smell of chocolate already filled the air.

"I'm not sure how wise it is to sit here watching those unless you want to keep feeling hungry."

Eddie half-raised his wings and turned his attention back to the oven, where the muffins were rising. His mom was here for company while she washed up and cleaned off the surfaces where they'd worked. The room smelled of baking. Those were two good things to keep him going. He could happily wait.

CHAPTER TWENTY-FOUR

Womack sat back in her swivel chair and looked around her office. Three hours ago, she hadn't had an office. Even as the principal of her self-made crime school, it hadn't felt like a necessity. Her approach to discipline was less "see me in my office" and more "go do this shitty task," with a side order of public mockery to enforce the point. Still, appearances mattered, and setting the right tone was critical to how people saw you. The school experience's improvised style was supposed to draw her students in, to make them feel like they were building the place up almost as much as she was. It was a way to get them invested. This meeting called for an entirely different approach.

Was the plant by the window too much? Womack had seen that some leaders put plants in their offices, whether to humanize themselves or to foster the illusion that they weren't stuck within those four walls all day long. It wasn't as much of a constant feature as the desk toys and the management books, but it helped set the scene. The risk was that she might have overdone it.

There was a knock at the door. Too late to rethink the plant now.

"Yes?" Womack called as if she didn't already know who it was.

Snivvery, dressed in a suit to play the role of a personal assistant—for a suitable fee, of course—opened the door far enough to poke her head around.

"Your two o'clock is here, ma'am," she said. "Mr. Gruffbar."

Credit where it was due, Snivvery kept a straight face throughout although Womack could see the glimmer of amusement in her eyes. Sure, they were all about the lies, but this one had a touch of the ridiculous to it.

"Show him in, please," Womack said.

As the dwarf walked in, Womack pushed aside a carefully prepared pile of papers and locked her computer screen as if she had been looking at sensitive documents and not playing Candy Crush. She stood and extended a hand.

"Good of you to meet with me, Mr. Gruffbar," she said.

"Just Gruffbar is fine, Ms. Womack."

"You can call me Meredith." She deliberately added the tone of forced familiarity that made corporate executives sound on edge. "Please, take a seat."

She pulled out a notepad and sank into her chair. Across the desk from her, Gruffbar leaned back and looked around with the careful, evaluating eye of a dwarf. Instead of a suit, he wore bikers' leathers and a pair of old army boots, and he carried with him the smells of leather and motor oil. He wasn't what she had expected from one of the best lawyers on the magical side of LA, or at least one of the best ones willing to work with the openly criminal class. In her experience, those were the best lawyers anyway since they had the most challenging job, although high finance lawyers came a close second for similar reasons.

"Second time you've reached out to me through Vessfall," Gruffbar said. "You must really need legal representation. Who are you planning to murder?"

He said it casually, but Womack was smart enough to catch the layers hidden in that question. On one level, there was the serious though exaggerated query about what sort of work lay ahead. On another was the joke, the idea that only murderers needed lawyers, that there was something desperate here, a strand of dark humor to see what would make her laugh. Then there was the test: was she stupid enough to give away something big? A lawyer like Gruffbar needed to know how dumb a potential client was as much as she needed to know that about a mark. For her, stupid was appealing. For him, it was a warning of trouble ahead.

"Actually, I don't want to hire you as a lawyer," she said. "At least not this time. I'm after a consultant."

Gruffbar looked around the office again as though he was reevaluating everything he had seen, including her. Yet again, there were layers to that because Womack could see that he was buying time to think through a response as he fitted the pieces he saw into a new framework.

"Consultant on what?" he said at last.

"Local law enforcement. I hear that you know as much as anyone about the workings of the Silver Griffins in LA. Given your experience, you probably understand what you've seen better than most. I want you to tell me about them."

Gruffbar nodded and looked at her, weighing her in the balance of his mind. He held out a hand. "Attorney-client privilege is invaluable even if I'm not writing up your contracts."

"Of course." Womack pulled a wad of used bills from her desk and handed them to him. "The fee we discussed, plus a little extra to thank you for your help."

She could afford that extra. The students were tackling their assignments with more enthusiasm than she could ever have imagined and bringing her most of their proceeds without questioning it. If she'd taken this sort of cut as a gang boss, she would have faced a revolt by now. Instead, they smiled and handed her everything she wanted.

For a long moment, Gruffbar held the cash in the palm of his hand. Was he really counting twenties by weight? Womack had met dwarves who could do that with gold coins, so it wasn't inconceivable, but the delicacy of judgment involved for paper money would be staggering.

He nodded, pocketed the cash, and leaned back in his chair again.

"You have me for two hours. What do you want to know?"

"How effective are the Silver Griffins around here?"

"On the whole, too damn effective, though there are weaknesses. They've had a lot of good recruits over the past decade, solid wands on the ground. With better coordination, they'd be one of the top offices in North America. Word is that the regional manager is heading for early retirement, so there's a make or break moment coming up."

Womack scribbled notes as Gruffbar talked. This wasn't the part she needed to know, but she didn't want to give away too much about her priorities. Attorney-client privilege was fine when dealing with the Griffins or the police, but it made no difference among the criminal fraternity, and she had no idea who else was paying this guy.

"There's a Griffin after me," she said. "I want to know more about her, whether she's one of those solid wands you talked about."

"I know the one you mean, Jackie Kowal. She's good. Old magical stock. Her ancestors worked for the Griffins back when this town was nothing but a village around an elm tree and some lost-looking Conquistadors. She's a decent witch and smart enough to do the job, but her real specialty is the physical stuff. Fast, aggressive, mean right hook."

He rubbed his chin as though he could still feel a bruise there.

"How do you know who it is? I only now told you I had this problem."

"She came to me a few days ago, asking questions that could lead to you. Had an out-of-towner with her. Guy with flashy shoes, still trying to shake off his hick accent."

"Ellis." Womack said the name like a curse. "So he's the one who set this English witch on me."

"English?"

"Apparently she has an accent, English or Scottish or something like that."

"Wait, what does she look like?"

"I thought you were the expert?"

"By my beard, do you want my help or not?"

"I do for now, yes, but that could change."

Gruffbar shrugged. "Your money, your choice."

Womack drew a calming breath, then continued, "I haven't seen the witch myself, but apparently she's in her early thirties, casually dressed, brown ponytail, average height…"

"Superhero t-shirts?"

"Yes."

"Then you have more problems than you thought because that's not Kowal. That's Lucy Heron."

"She's a bigger problem?"

Gruffbar hesitated. He was a professional, so he was supposed to be objective. However, he wouldn't be doing his job if he ignored valuable personal experience.

"My opinion might be biased since it's based on my problems with her. That said, if there's one Griffin you don't want after you, it's Heron. She's smart enough, tenacious, and oozing with magical power. Far as I can tell, her whole family is, and sometimes she brings them along for the ride."

"Shit." Womack had given up any pretense of making notes. She pressed her thumbs against her temples, trying to massage away tension that threatened to escalate into a headache. "I'm going to have to do something to get rid of her."

"As your lawyer, I recommend that you back the pits off from that," Gruffbar said. "I wouldn't touch a fight with Heron using an ogre's war ax."

"How bad can she be?"

"She brought down Zero."

"Well, now she's after me, and that means I need to take her down first."

Gruffbar snorted and got out of his seat. "Take my advice. Whatever you're doing, put it on hold until she stops paying attention. It's the only way you get through this a free woman."

"Where are you going?"

"As far away from this as possible. If you need a lawyer once the dust settles, which you will, you know where to find me."

He walked out, leaving open the very real door of her very fake office.

Womack gritted her teeth. No point getting mad at the messenger. At least now she knew who was after her, and she could start planning to deal with her.

Snivvery appeared around the doorway, unfastening her tie. "Tell me I didn't just hear that. That the Griffin who brought down Zero is after us now."

Womack glared at her. "What, you were sitting there with your ear pressed to the door?"

"Thin partitions." Snivvery tapped the wall to emphasize her point. "This is what happens when you rent cheap office space."

Womack sank back in her seat, trying to let go of a sense of anger that was shifting toward Snivvery as the only target left in the building. Let emotions control you, and they would ruin everything. "Think of it as an extra challenge. I wouldn't be providing you with much of an education if it was easy."

"There's challenging, and there's madness." Snivvery

planted her hands on Womack's desk and stared across it, straight into her teacher's eyes. "We can't take on the woman who took down Zero."

"We can and we will."

"You're supposed to be the smart one, so how come I have to teach you how the world works? We are not up to that, especially not with idiots like Hank on our team. I get that this isn't really a school and that you'll be out of here once you have what you came for. But I'm not going to cover your back if you bring the worst of the Griffins down on us."

Womack drew a deep breath and kept her face still. She needed Snivvery. More importantly, she needed not to face the questions the others would ask if Snivvery upped and left.

"I get that it's scary," she said. "Willens aren't made to face tough things like this. You're better than that, Snivvery. You use the best of your people's instincts, and you overcome the worst. This is a time to overcome. Because yes, we have Griffins after us. That's how it works when you're a magical criminal. We also have all the resources we've gathered, all the people lining up to learn from me, and we know who we're looking out for.

"When smart people see a threat coming, they avoid it, as you want to do. The smartest people, they turn the tables. They cut the threat off before it even gets close. We're the smartest people here, no matter what some Silver Griffin thinks."

Snivvery watched her through narrowed eyes. Womack could practically hear the gears turning in her head.

"You're so full of shit," the Willen said with a small laugh and stepped back from the desk.

"That's why you're learning from me." Womack grinned. "Now go put the practice dummies out. I have this evening's lesson to plan."

CHAPTER TWENTY-FIVE

"Will you put that damn thing away?" Jackie snapped. "An app is not going to lead you to a suspect."

"It ain't the app that does the leading," Ellis corrected, still gazing at his phone. "I'm pretty sure I told you that already."

"Then why are you looking at it?"

"Because the app reflects the spell, and the spell's starting to close in. Least I reckon it might be. Hard to tell some days."

Ellis tapped the top of his phone as if he was trying to shake something loose. Lines danced across the black background of the screen, then settled into the same tangled mess that had been there a moment before. If the spell was achieving something, Jackie couldn't see it.

"I'm hungry." She weighed up the options ahead of her as they walked down Sunset Boulevard. "Let's eat."

"What if I'm not hungry yet?" Ellis was surprised to hear those words spring from his mouth, an instinctive response to Jackie's terse tone. Normally, he was an easy-going guy, but the past few days had worn on his nerves.

"Aren't you?" Jackie raised an eyebrow.

Ellis drew a breath. Some instinct told him to fight back, not to let her assumptions be right. However, he didn't want to do that to his stomach.

"Guess I could eat," he said. "Anywhere good around here?"

"All sorts of places." Jackie gestured at the nearest doorway. "You tried Masa yet?"

Ellis shook his head. "My hotel's nearer the airport. I haven't tried too many places around here."

"Then you're in for a treat, especially if you like pizza."

"Who doesn't?"

"True."

As they walked into the restaurant, a woman waved at them from one of the nearby tables. Ellis recognized her, though it took him a moment to work out why.

"Jackie!" Lucy called as she waved. "Want to join us for lunch?"

"Sure." Jackie settled into one of the mismatched wooden chairs at the table where Lucy and their friend Sarah were already sitting. "Ellis, this is Lucy, another Silver Griffin, and Sarah, a witch and a doctor."

"Not a witch doctor though." Sarah smiled as she pushed back a few strands of her long red hair. "I practically never put a curse on anyone."

"Best I'm careful just in case." Ellis smiled as he took a seat across from her. "Jackie can tell you that I'm the kinda guy you're gonna wanna curse."

"At least he has the decency to admit it." Jackie rolled her eyes.

"Well, he seems very nice to me," Sarah said.

"You've only now met him."

"I have good instincts."

"You have terrible instincts. Remember that guy from the yoga retreat?"

Ellis turned to Lucy.

"We met on the train, didn't we?" he said. "On the way to your headquarters. You're the Scottish lady."

"English," Lucy said. "You Yanks all sound the same to me, so I guess we're even. What brings you to town this time?"

"Same as last time, chasing down a fugitive."

A smiling waiter appeared, interrupting the conversation long enough for them to order drinks and scan down the menus.

"You should try the deep dish," Sarah said. "It's really good here."

"I dunno. I get to visit Chicago pretty often," Ellis said. "LA deep dish isn't likely to compete."

"Trust me. It's really good."

"Well, how could I say no to a smile like yours?"

While the others were placing their orders, Ellis took a moment to look around the restaurant. It had a homey vibe with its warmly painted walls, a few pictures, mismatched wooden furniture, and friendly waitstaff. Its smells were enough to convince him that they'd made the right choice, as his stomach rumbled in response to all the delicious aromas wafting around.

"You're not a local Griffin, are you?" Sarah asked Ellis once the waiter was gone. "Do you travel around a lot?"

"That's right. I track down magical fugitives who cross over jurisdictions and accompany the ones that need to be taken elsewhere."

"Like the U.S. Marshals?"

"Kinda like that, yes, only with more wands and none of those flashy star badges."

"Let me guess. You have a different sort of flashy badge?"

"Only the same amulet a lot of other Griffins carry, but sure, you could consider that flashy."

"Can I see it?"

"Honestly, look at this!" Jackie laughed. "You've only met the guy, and you're asking him to get it out for you."

"Jackie!" Sarah blushed and slapped her friend on the arm. "You know what we're talking about."

"Hey, I'm not judging. I've invited plenty of dates back to my place to play hunt the amulet. Just not many guys I've newly met in a pizza shop."

"I'm sorry about Jackie." Sarah turned her attention back to Ellis. "She's very, um…"

"Oh, I know," Ellis said. "We've had a few long days together."

Feeling a little like a third wheel, Lucy took a moment to cast her gaze around the place. Magicals were as fond of pizza as any human being, some of them more so. Dwarves in particular enjoyed the way it reminded them of miners' flatbreads back in Oriceran. That meant that there were usually a few magicals in the place, suitably disguised. She spotted a couple of dwarves who had used platform shoes and long coats to cover how short they were, as well as someone with the bulky coat of an Arpak hiding their wings. It didn't matter where in LA she went, there was no getting away from the magical community, and honestly, she was happy with that. After all, these were her people.

Then she spotted one of her people doing something they shouldn't. An elf with her ears hidden under a striped beanie hat walked close behind a customer on the way to the door. There was a small flutter of magic, a bulge disappeared from the unwitting customer's pocket, and a wallet appeared in the elf's hand.

"Excuse me a minute." Lucy got out of her seat.

She followed the elf out the door and around the corner before catching up to her. When she tapped her on the shoulder, the elf turned with a forced smile.

"Can I help you with something?" the elf asked. She had a brightness that made her seem young, but it was hard to tell whether that youthfulness was real or an elven thing.

"You can hand over that wallet."

"I'm sorry, I don't know what you mean."

"Really?" Lucy flashed her Silver Griffin medallion. The elf stiffened but didn't say anything. "That's a heavy coat you're wearing for the time of year. Mind if I look in the pocket?"

"Actually, I do, and I'm pretty sure the Scottish cops don't have any jurisdiction around here."

"For your information, Griffins can act on magical crime wherever they go, and I'm English, not Scottish."

"I thought Scotland was, like, part of England?"

"Don't tell a Scot that. They'll kick you right in the

sporran. Now move your hands away and let me into that pocket."

"Okay, okay."

The elf made a big show of moving her hands away from her sides. Lucy was about to reach into a pocket when she realized what she had almost missed. She grabbed the elf's wrist, shook it, and caught the wallet as it fell from her sleeve.

"That's mine," the elf said.

"Really?" Lucy opened the wallet and pulled out a driver's license. "You're Godfrey Humboldt, aged forty-nine, from Washington DC?"

"I've had some work done since that photo, been through a lot of changes."

"You've grown a lot of hair back too. Those plugs must have worked really well."

The elf's eyes darted back and forth, evaluating her options for escape.

"No point in running," Lucy said. "I'm not taking you in for this. But now I know what you look like." She pulled out her phone and took a photo of the elf. "Soon my colleagues will too, and if any of us catches you using your magic to criminal ends, you'll be off to Trevilsom faster than I can say God save the Queen. Got it?"

"Uh-huh." The elf's shoulders slumped in relief.

"One other thing," Lucy said. "You've not had someone training you in magical pocket-picking, have you?"

The elf shook her head.

"Not heard anything about a school for that sort of stuff?"

Another shake of the head.

"Oh well, it was worth trying. If you do hear anything, call the Griffins and ask for Lucy Heron. Help me out, and I'll be more lenient next time I catch you carrying someone else's cash. Got it?"

"Uh-huh."

"Good. Now clear off. My lunch is getting cold."

Lucy walked back into the restaurant and up to the counter, where she handed the wallet to a confused-looking waitress.

"Found this outside the door," Lucy said. "Might belong to one of your customers. I'd check the driver's license if I were you."

"That's good of you." The waitress opened the wallet and whistled. "That's quite a tip someone almost left. Good thing there are honest folks around here."

"Yeah, good thing."

The food was waiting when Lucy got back to her seat. She took a big bite of her California pizza, enjoying the spinach, sundried tomatoes, cheese, and delicious sauce.

"What was that all about?" Jackie asked.

"Pickpocket," Lucy explained. "One with sparkly fingers."

"You look weirdly disappointed for someone who stopped a crime."

"I was hoping for a lead on my case. I know not every magical theft is going to be linked to this crime school business, but a lot of them have been recently, and I could really do with finding out who's behind it."

"Did you say crime school?" Ellis looked up from his conversation with Sarah.

"Yes, why?"

"The fugitive I'm after, she learned her craft from a wizard called Daltry. He ran a sort of a crime school in New York for a while, nothing too big, but it got itself a reputation."

"You think she might be following his lead?"

Ellis looked at Jackie.

"What do you think?"

Jackie, her mouth full of mushroom and sausage, took a moment to respond.

"Could fit what the dwarf told us," she said at last. "Financial arrangements, building hire, that says you're setting up something more than a quick casual con. Teachers need classrooms and equipment. If she's charging people for lessons, she'd need a way to collect and launder the money."

"If Womack was doing something like that, she'd be mighty careful about it. Take her time, recruit her students carefully, not show her hand to the world. Reckon she's been out here long enough to do that by now."

"How long?" Lucy asked.

"A few months. Three at least, maybe a little more."

"That fits. A few odd thefts led into this case, ones that could have been her acquiring materials for her school. Then the real crime wave started a few weeks ago. That could be when she started running classes and handing out homework assignments."

"You know anything else?" Ellis leaned forward eagerly, and his tie almost fell onto his pizza. Sarah caught it and tucked it aside, then sat back, happy to eat her lunch and listen to her friends at work.

"They've been robbing magic stores and warehouses,"

Lucy said. "Getting a lot of the same supplies, but in larger quantities. There have been some other things too, like one week there was a spate of coin-matching game scams, and a few days ago it was magical computer hacks."

"So a bunch of powered criminals are learning new tricks," Jackie said. "Then they're going out to practice them together."

"It's more than that." Ellis pushed his plate aside, pulled out a pen, and spread a napkin in front of him. He drew a circle, then a scattering of smaller dots around it. "When Womack goes big, this here is how she works. One central scam, a long-term plan that's supposed to keep running, then around it, a whole bunch of distractions. Usually, they're separate things, but what if she's linking it all up through this school?"

"So the thefts are the core crime, building up supplies, while the rest are distractions?"

"Exactly."

"Distractions from what?"

All three Silver Griffins stared at the napkin, their brows furrowing in concentration.

"Do criminals have franchises?" Sarah asked. "Sorry, that was a silly question, wasn't it?"

"No." Ellis gave her a big grin. "That might be the smartest thing I've heard all day." He tapped the center of the napkin. "Lucy said they're stealing the same supplies as before, but more of them, right? Well, that sure sounds like what Womack would need if she were supplying other folks, getting them ready to set up their schools."

"It's perfect," Jackie said, and for once she smiled at Ellis. "She teaches them her tricks, sells them the supplies, and sends them out to set up schools elsewhere. They probably keep paying her afterward as well, a fee for consulting services if they get stuck, and to keep playing off her reputation."

"Well, if that ain't the darnedest thing." Ellis shook his head. "Capitalism in action. You got any leads on where we can find this school?"

"Some, but nothing strong yet," Lucy said.

"Then let's go back to your office when we're done here, see what we can come up with together. First though, I'm gonna enjoy this fine pizza, fine company, and finally working out what we're dealing with."

CHAPTER TWENTY-SIX

Ashley crouched next to Buddy, fastening the straps on the harness she had built for him. It stretched along his body and down his legs, with components sticking out all over. There were wheels, lights, tubes, runes, and a little black box behind his head.

"It's only a prototype," she explained as she fastened the final buckle. "Especially the magical components. I don't understand those well enough to know the optimal placement, so these are best estimates based on limited data. We can reconfigure it once we've carried out some field trials."

Buddy looked back at the devices strapped to him, wriggled his spine, and gave a short, curious bark. This was all interesting, and it was nice that people were paying him attention, but he wasn't sure how he felt about being wrapped up. Then Dylan offered him a dog biscuit, and he decided that it was all fine.

"You're saying we should try it out?" Dylan asked. The way his younger sister talked sometimes left him a little bewildered, in awe of the family's technological genius.

However, he'd come up with the magical parts for the harness, so he at least understood some of what was going on.

"I don't think that we should use Buddy to track down real magical criminals yet," Ashley said. "I made some targets. Let's set them up and see what he'll do."

They left Buddy to play with Eddie on the patio and carried Ashley's targets to a spot near the side of the yard. Each target was a life-size cardboard cutout of one magical or another, including a gnome, a Willen, an Arpak, and a Kilomea. The kids stood the fake criminals up on folding bases, and Dylan sprinkled a little magic over half of them. He found it easier to do now that he got regular practice. As long as it wasn't a large amount of magic, he could perfectly control what came out, even without turning it into a spell. It was exciting to think about what he might manage soon.

They went back to the patio, where Buddy was licking a giggling Eddie.

"All right, Buddy," Dylan said. "It's time to see if your training has stuck." He pointed across the yard. "Go catch the magic!"

Caught up in his master's enthusiasm, Buddy bounded away, only to stop in the middle of the lawn, unsure what he was supposed to be doing. Tongue hanging from his mouth and tail twitching, he turned to look back at Dylan.

"The people." Dylan pointed. "Go catch the magic people!"

Buddy waddled over to the lemon tree, picked up a stick from the ground, and brought it back. Then he looked up optimistically at Dylan.

"Good Buddy." Eddie patted the dog on the head.

"Maybe this needs to be more like what we did before," Ashley said. "Try throwing the balls for him again, get him thinking about what's magic and what isn't."

Dylan picked up one of Eddie's rubber balls, to Buddy's great excitement, then pulled out his wand. Both arms went back and forward. Two balls flew off down the garden, one from his hand, the other from the tip of the wand.

Buddy ran after the balls, his little legs racing. The mundane ball bounced off the cardboard Willen, but he ignored it, running past the targets and after the magic ball as it disappeared into the bushes at the side of the yard. The children waited several minutes for him to return.

"Where Buddy go?" Eddie asked.

"After the ball," Ashley said. "I don't think he understands about targets yet."

"I'll go get him." Dylan walked over to the bushes and held out a dog biscuit. "Here, Buddy. Good boy. Come and get a treat."

There was no response from within the bushes.

"Buddy?" Dylan crouched to look around for the dog. Instead of Buddy, what he saw was a hole in the fence beyond the bushes, at the exact place the magic ball had flown toward.

"Oh no." His heart sank. "I think he's gotten into Al's garden."

"We have to get him back," Ashley said in a matter-of-fact tone. "Before someone sees him in that harness."

She got down on hands and knees and crawled under the bushes, then squeezed through the gap in the fence.

Dylan reluctantly followed her. The opening was even tighter on him, and he was glad that he was slim or he would have gotten stuck.

They emerged into a patch of bushes at the bottom of their next-door neighbor's yard. Al was weeding farther up. He knelt next to a flower bed, gray hair protruding from underneath his baseball cap, a trowel in his hand and a bucket next to him, tugging up weeds one at a time. He had his back to them and a pair of old headphones on, and he was whistling along tunelessly to the radio.

The magic ball had bounced off something and rolled out into the center of the garden. There it sat in the grass underneath a tree, bright red against the green. Buddy was waddling toward the ball.

Dylan got to his feet and was about to go after Buddy when Ashley grabbed his arm.

"Careful," she whispered.

"Why?" he hissed back.

"The harness must have knocked against something on the way through the fence. It's gone active."

Dylan looked again at Buddy. Sure enough, the devices spread across the harness had stirred into life. Flashlights were pivoting in their mounts although their light didn't stand out in the middle of the day. The wheels were turning, but they hadn't yet lowered into active positions. The box behind Buddy's head had risen slightly. Most worryingly, half a dozen tubes had risen along his back.

"Are those the dart guns you talked about?" Dylan asked.

"Of course," Ashley said. "What else would look like that?"

Dylan could think of a few things, but he was very aware that it didn't matter. What mattered right now was not getting their neighbor shot.

Ashley pulled a plastic box from her pocket. It had several buttons on it and an antenna protruding from the top. She took out a screwdriver and a fistful of tiny circuit boards then started opening the box.

"Stay here," Dylan whispered. "I'll go grab him."

He crept up behind Buddy, who was sniffing around the ball, trying to decide whether to pick it up or to grab a funny-shaped stick instead.

"Got you." Dylan grabbed the dog.

One of the runes on the harness flashed. A magical glow appeared like a bubble around Buddy. Dylan's hands slipped off the protective spell, and Buddy stumbled forward as if Dylan had pushed him. Sensing a game about to begin, the dog dashed off across the garden.

Dylan glanced over at Al, who seemed oblivious still, lost in the music and the slow pleasure of gardening.

Deciding that the coast was clear, Dylan ran after Buddy. His legs were ten times as long as the dog's, and it was easy to catch up. Or it would have been if not for the wheels. As he got close, they descended from their positions on the harness as the plastic legs swung down. The wheels spun faster, then hit the ground, and suddenly Buddy sped away, his legs flailing uselessly under him.

Dylan ran after the dog as he wheeled in circles around the garden, each loop carrying him closer and closer to Al. Ashley cast aside her electronics and joined in, the two children chasing the fugitive pet.

"He's going to hit Al!" Ashley said in alarm.

"No, he's not." Dylan pulled out his wand. "Rigescent indutae!"

A blast of icy magic shot across the yard. It almost hit Buddy, but another of the runes flashed and the magic dissipated around the dog. The rune went dull gray, its protective power spent, and Dylan raised his wand, ready to try again.

One of the tubes pointed at him. He barely had time to dive aside before there was a soft *phut* sound of compressed air releasing. A tranquilizer dart shot past Dylan and buried itself in a tree.

Buddy's wheels carried him in another rapid circle around the lawn. He was heading straight toward Al now, and the tranquilizer guns, once activated, were going wild, twitching this way and that as if sniffing out targets. One of them pointed straight at Al's unprotected back.

"Preatereo!" Dylan exclaimed.

This time the spell got through, turning the dart gun aside at the very last moment. There was a *phut* of air, and a dart soared over Al's head.

Dylan and Ashley froze as Al looked up.

"Pesky flies," Al muttered, then turned back to his weeding, whistling along with the music emerging from his headphones.

Dylan's spell hadn't only turned the dart gun. It had also turned Buddy and the harness from their path. The dog rushed down the yard, ears flapping in the wind, his remaining dart guns pointed at Dylan and Ashley.

"Oh no." Dylan tried to remember a defensive spell, but his mind went blank. He could feel the magic longing to be released all around him, but that only made it harder to concentrate since he was afraid the power might get out of control. He didn't want to be responsible for another rainforest.

Ashley snapped the parts of her remote control back together and pressed a button. The dart guns sank against the harness. Ashley turned a dial, and the wheels turned with it, directing Buddy straight at Dylan, who caught him with both hands.

Buddy licked Dylan's face and wagged his tail. This was one of the most fun games they had ever played.

"Time to head home." With a sigh of relief, Dylan shoved the dog through the hole in the fence, then followed him. Ashley gathered up her pieces of electronics and followed them through.

Eddie was waiting on the other side, kicking a ball around the lawn. On seeing him, Buddy leapt from Dylan's arms and ran off to play. The wheels on the harness folded up, and the whole thing went into standby mode.

"So much for training him to catch bad guys." Dylan gestured at the untouched cardboard targets.

"This was only the first trial," Ashley pointed out. "We were always going to have to complete a succession of iterations if we wanted to make a crime-fighting dog."

"I suppose. At least he didn't kill Al."

"He was never going to kill him." Ashley laughed. "The worst he could do was catch him in a magic net."

Dylan went pale, thinking about how close they had come to revealing the existence of magic to their mundane neighbor. He didn't know the "never was, never will be" spell yet. They would've had to call in the Silver Griffins instead. Then they would have had to explain everything to his mom, and… Well, it was good that it hadn't happened, that was for sure.

On the other side of the fence, Al got up from his weeding, shook his legs, and tried to roll out the ache from his shoulders. He enjoyed work like this, but he had to admit it got harder with the passing years.

He turned and saw something gleaming against the bark of a tree.

"Is that a dart?" he muttered as he pulled it out. He looked around in confusion. "Where on earth did that come from?"

When no gun-wielding gamekeepers appeared, he shrugged and went to drop the dart in the trash. Sometimes life threw little mysteries at you, things you'd never get answered. At least he knew what he was doing with the weeding.

CHAPTER TWENTY-SEVEN

Lucy stood in an alleyway, a backpack over her shoulders and a flashlight in her hand. She glanced at the time on her phone. If Heather didn't turn up soon, she would have to give up on this, which would be a shame. By her reckoning, she had found a way to kill two birds with one stone, and she didn't want to see that fall through if she could avoid it.

Heather Fields appeared at the end of the alley dressed in a flannel shirt, faded jeans, and sturdy boots. She looked far more comfortable than she had in the school gym, and not only because she wasn't facing an interview panel. Smart clothes weren't Heather's bag. Well-worn, casual clothes fit her whole demeanor.

"Sorry I'm late, Lu." She strode up to Lucy. Despite the better fitting clothes, an air of tension slipped out around her stern and sturdy facade. "It's harder to find my way around a city. There are no mosses or animal smells, none of the things you can navigate by, you know?"

"I navigate more by road signs and Google Maps," Lucy said. "I can see the appeal of asking the trees though.

They're better looking than a sign at an intersection and less likely to give you backchat than a phone."

"I don't know, I've met some pretty sassy trees."

Lucy narrowed her eyes. "Are you taking the piss, or can you really have a conversation with a tree?"

Heather almost smiled. "That would be telling."

Lucy pulled up a manhole cover, and the two of them descended into darkness, using flashlights to illuminate their way. The rusted rungs of a ladder ground against Lucy's palms, but she didn't mind much. She was getting used to this route by now.

"Urgh." Heather looked around as they walked along an abandoned tunnel. "This place is even worse than the streets. The concrete's all around, and the only living things I can sense are lichen and rats."

"Why have you moved to the city if you hate urban life so much?" Lucy asked.

"To hunt."

"Then you're definitely in the wrong place. The only wild animals you'll catch around here are foxes and raccoons, and shooting at them is likely to summon the police."

"It's not animals I'm after. There's a creature that the Tolderai have been battling for centuries, a thing that lives in smoke and ash. We think it might have come back here, so I've come to wait and watch until it reveals itself."

"Is there anything I can do to help find it?"

"Thank you. For now, we wait. I'll let you know if that changes."

They walked on for a while, Lucy contemplating what Heather had given up to get her target. Could she have taken a big step like that? She didn't have a forest to give up, but her neighborhood was the closest equivalent, and it would have been difficult to let it go.

"It must be tough living here when your heart is with the trees."

"I find places. Parks mostly, or abandoned ground where nature has started growing back. It's not the same as living in the forest, but it lets me recover a little, to restore my energy."

The tunnels wound around and down, deeper into the ground below LA. Lucy knew what some of them had been, including failed transport projects, Cold War hide-aways, and other fractured pieces of urban infrastructure. Others she hadn't worked out yet. Many of them had similar musty smells and a sense of still air and pressing gloom. It was easy to understand why Heather would dislike it so much, but to some other people, it was ideal—the perfect safe, hidden space.

They walked down a ramp and into the broad tunnel that was the home to some of those people. They'd installed more electric lights since Lucy was last down here, and she was relieved by that. The open fires the Underfoot Brigade also used for light and heat seemed like a dangerous thing to her, with those flames so close to their improvised homes of flammable materials. It couldn't be healthy for the kids to live in a space full of soot and smoke. It was their space, and she wouldn't have taken it from them for all the world, but she was happy that they'd made some changes.

Twylan was sitting underneath one of the new lights, along with Kix the gnome. A pile of cloth sat between them, most of it offcuts and pieces of old clothes. Both girls had some of that cloth in their laps, and a pair of some-things darted through the material, bright, silvery points shooting back and forth in front of each of them.

"Now turn it over," Kix said to Twylan as they approached. "Give it a good tug. See how much sturdier that seam is."

Twylan tried to pull apart two pieces of faded cotton and smiled in satisfaction as they held firmly together. "It's amazing how much difference the stitch makes."

"Hi guys, what are you up to?" Lucy asked.

"Learning to sew," Twylan said.

She held out her hand and whispered a spell. The shining point that Lucy had spotted before flew over to hover an inch above Twylan's fingers. It was a needle.

"Not conventional sewing then?" Lucy watched as another needle darted through the air in front of Kix, so fast that it became a blur, streaks of silver against the dark-ness of the tunnel wall.

"Kix knows all sorts of smart tricks," Twylan said. "Magic pockets, sewing by spell, binding in magic so ordi-nary clothes will keep you dry in the rain."

"You get more out of enchantments this way than if you cast them after a garment is finished," Kix explained. "I come from a long line of seamstresses and tailors, so I know how to combine spells with the craft."

"How are the other lessons going?" Lucy asked.

Twylan and Kix looked at each other, then let out a coordinated sigh.

"It turns out that teaching is harder than we thought," Twylan said. "Even when you know the subject you're teaching really well. Everyone wants to learn in theory, but they get bored or fidgety, and it all starts going wrong. Competing lessons seemed like a good idea until we realized that people weren't learning. It was entertaining, and that's fine, but..."

"But it's a distraction instead of an education?"

"Exactly! After a couple of days, Leontine stopped the whole thing. Except even that went wrong. He meant well, trying to remind people of how important education was and how we needed to cooperate for the good of the whole Brigade. But he was frustrated and disappointed by then, so it came out badly."

"What she means is that the fatheaded Arpak had a big angry shout at everyone," Kix added. "Then some people shouted back. Others took sides, and soon half the Brigade was caught up in a massive row."

"He did try," Twylan said. "That was pretty much the end of anybody's interest in trying to teach each other. If you talk about it now, they all start grumbling about Leontine."

"So no school?" Lucy asked.

"No school."

Lucy turned to Heather, who had hunched over to look more closely at Kix's sewing, admiring how the magic worked, deconstructing and evaluating it with the mind of an experienced witch and tribal chief. Now that she had something to consider other than the tunnels, she looked a lot more relaxed.

"What do you think?" Lucy asked. "Could you do it?"

"Do what?" Heather asked.

"Teach these kids. You're looking for pupils, they're

looking for a teacher, and you're all magicals. It seems like a great fit."

Heather frowned and rubbed the back of her neck.

"I dunno, Lu," she said. "You know why I didn't get that job. I don't have experience. I can talk about plants, but I'm not used to the classroom."

"You're used to teaching in unusual places, and it doesn't get more unusual than this. Sure, it's a tunnel instead of some forestry station or outdoor activity center, but the principle stands. You could teach them about plants and nature. In fact, that would be great for kids who are stuck down in these tunnels all day. You'd just have to work some other things in too, like maths and English and spells."

"You know there's only one math, right?"

"There are lots of them. I counted, using maths."

Heather laughed. "Okay, English. Still, I'm no expert on that."

"No teacher is an expert on everything, but you know spellcraft, and that's important here. I bet you've been teaching things to others for years, right?"

Heather nodded.

"Well then." Lucy smiled. "I admit, the conditions aren't great. There's no pay on offer, and you'll have to spend a lot of time down here in the dark. But these are great kids. They know LA in ways no one else does, and they can help you learn your way around while you're teaching them. You'll get experience at teaching, which will be helpful for future jobs, and you'll be doing something good for the community."

"You have it all worked out, haven't you?" Heather asked, raising an eyebrow.

"A master plan of my devising." Lucy grinned. "Well?"

"What do you think?" Heather asked Twylan.

"I think it's a lovely plan," Twylan said. "Let's give it a try. Do you have something you could teach us about right now?"

For a brief moment, Lucy thought she caught a flicker of panic behind Heather's calm expression. Then the Tolderai's gaze found something on the tunnel wall. She walked over, carefully eased a tiny green plant from a gap in the brickwork, and came back to them.

"I'm ready," she said.

Twylan whistled, a sharp blast that carried down the tunnel and brought the rest of the Underfoot Brigade running. The motley crew assembled, a mix of magicals, each with their disappointment or deformity from Leontine's crippled wing to a Willen with no whiskers. At a gesture from Twylan, they sat on the ground and watched their guests expectantly.

Twylan smiled and gestured at Heather. "This is Ms…"

"Fields."

"…and she's a teacher. Lucy brought her here to see if she might want to teach us."

There was a chorus of groans and discontented muttering.

"I get it." Heather raised her voice to cut through the noise. "School can be boring, and it can be annoying. Today, we're going to talk about something that's never dull: life."

She cast a spell, and the tiny plant in her hand grew, roots running out between her fingers, leaves unfurling in every direction. Smaller plants started to bud off from it. As each one took shape, she pinched it off the trailer it was growing on and handed it to one of the teenagers. Those without a plant yet cupped their hands and expectantly waited as she walked among them, handing out those tiny green pieces of life, something they seldom saw down in the tunnels.

"Each of you gets a plant of your own. I'll teach you how to look after it, both with magic and with simple care. Along the way, we're going to learn the names for parts of the plant, how it works, and maybe a little about how it evolved to be like this. Does that sound interesting?"

The Brigade nodded, even surly Leontine. It wasn't only her words that had caught them or the plants she was handing out. It was her tone, the way she talked with total confidence that they would and should listen. She commanded attention like the tribal chief she was.

While Heather started talking about plant parts, Lucy tapped Twylan on the arm and led her off to one side.

"I brought you these." She pulled a bag of home-baked muffins from her backpack. "And some other supplies I thought you might be low on."

"You really don't have to keep doing this," Twylan said.

"I want to, sweetheart. What's the point of having money if you can't use it to help others out once in a while? Besides, you've earned it this time."

"Earned it how?"

"The information you gave me about Hank. I haven't caught him yet, but it's been really useful in understanding the pattern of crimes we're looking at. I even caught another suspicious character thanks to you."

She didn't need to mention that they'd let Ringo Fuller go. He was one of the most suspicious characters she knew, and Twylan's information had given her a chance to make his life uncomfortable for a few hours. Heck, it had probably helped with his training. There was nothing like a real live chase to keep a bounty hunter in shape.

"Thank you." Twylan accepted the food and soap Lucy offered. "Maybe I could do more for you, help to earn what you're giving us?"

"Sure. If I think of anything you can help with, I'll let you know right away."

They looked over at the others. Siltor was standing next to Heather at the front of the class, proudly holding up a leaf he'd grown while she pointed out parts of the plant.

"I think this could work," Twylan said.

CHAPTER TWENTY-EIGHT

Womack stood on the roof of the building she'd been renting for the school. It was such an ordinary building in many ways, a small, disused office nestled in a development that hadn't quite taken off. A place that no one had been paying any attention to. The sort of location that wouldn't leave a jarring gap in anyone's memory if they stopped knowing it was there, stopped even seeing it as they walked past—the type of place that could slip quietly out of view.

She had been working on the runes and sigils since she first moved into the building. Her research had been meticulous, working out which symbols would best hold the complex network of spells she needed to cast and what forms would make them most powerful. Some she'd marked out in spray paint, others in blood, a few she'd carved into the roof's flat surface. One she had burned on using a welding torch. The lines running between them created a spiderweb pattern, but this time she'd reversed the web's purpose. It wasn't there to catch someone. It was there to keep her free.

She scrolled down the screen of her tablet, reviewing her list of supplies. Everything she needed for the subsidiary schools was ready, but getting that exactly right had never been as important as this. All that took was a bagful of ingredients to give her students confidence in their new endeavors, to make them feel prepared. The supplies for the spell were far more exacting, and some of those weren't ready yet. Students had dropped out or failed assignments, meaning that they hadn't delivered what she had asked of them. It would have been frustrating if she wasn't used to others' failures by now. You could never rely on anyone, and it was important to plan for when they let you down. She'd add the missing ingredients to upcoming assignments, and soon she would be ready.

Then, one glorious day, she would cast the spell. Wards would rise around this building. It would fade from memory and view, taking her with it. She would disappear as surely as an abandoned alias. Only the people she invited would remember that she was here, never mind be able to find the place. It would be the perfect headquarters to run her empire, an ingenious combination of criminal network and corporate franchise, constantly churning out new trainees to drive expansion. First across America, then across Earth, and finally into Oriceran. She would become the secret spider at the heart of an invisible web.

This time, she had exceeded even her expectations.

She checked the markings on the roof one last time, then headed down the stairs into the building. It wouldn't be good to keep her students waiting. They could be an impatient bunch.

They were all in the classroom when she arrived. Snivvery sat near the back and off to one side while Hank was front and center, waiting for his teacher's attention and a chance to prove himself. The way the others had spread out between them was like a map of the class's social dysfunction, with Hank's accomplices gathered around him, those who aspired to be Snivvery settled around her, and a few others scattered across the no man's land between. Womack smiled. These developing tribes were more tools she could work with. A little unhealthy competition would help to keep everyone motivated.

"Good morning, class," she said brightly. "I have a few announcements before we start today.

"First of all, we're getting near the end of the course you signed up for. Most of you have done very well. You'll be graduating soon with honors and, if you want it, one of these..."

She lifted a bag onto her desk and opened it for them all to see inside. A selection of magical ingredients was revealed, along with a bound instruction book.

"Think of it as a thank you gift to acknowledge all your hard work and an offering for the future. In here, you'll find everything you need to set up a course like this of your own, including my instruction manual and curriculum. It's felt good knowing that I'm helping spread knowledge to you all, and I'll feel even better knowing that you're passing that knowledge on, making the world a better-informed place. And of course, making a handy profit for yourselves in the process."

She winked, and most of them laughed. Snivvery gave a knowing smile that said she saw through the bullshit and that she approved. Sure, give them a gift made of things they'd stolen themselves. Set them up to be reliant on Womack for years to come and to keep feeding her a chunk of their profits in return for her help. Snivvery wasn't going to buy in, but she might adapt the scheme herself somewhere down the line.

"Obviously, I hope that some of you will stay on for the advanced course," Womack continued. The advanced course was a new idea she'd dreamed up the previous night, and she was enjoying considering what she could talk "advanced" students into doing. "However, I know many of you will be keen to get out there and start earning. After all, that's what this was about."

She closed the bag and put it back under her desk. She might leave it there later when she left the room as a way of seeing who had the initiative to steal from her.

"Second announcement, and tied to your upcoming graduation, there will be two homework assignments today.

"One is an open methods theft, your chance to go through all the things you've learned and apply the approaches that suit you. I'll be looking for innovative plans, so don't be obvious. Burglary, fraud, mugging, hacking, do whatever you think you can do in style.

"The second assignment is this."

She waved her wand, and an image of Lucy appeared in the air. Next to it was a list of all the things they had learned about her from a previous assignment. It wasn't as much as Womack had wanted, but it should be enough to get them started.

"As my A-grade students already discovered for themselves, this is Lucy Heron of the Silver Griffins. She's been a problem for us all term, and now it seems she's closing in. So, we need to resolve the Heron problem, both to keep you all safe and to stretch your skills that bit further. After all, we've not done much person-centered work so far."

Hank stared at the picture, his face filled with fury. Where his hands clutched the sides of his desk, smoke drifted from charring wood.

"You want us to kill her?" he asked.

"Not necessarily," Womack said although she wasn't going to dissuade him from that approach. "Your assignment is to come up with a plan to get her out of our way, however that works. Again, think about the skills you've learned so far and how you can apply them, as well as your unique abilities. If you want to work in groups, you can, but you'll need to prove to me that you've all contributed at both the planning and the execution stages. As always, if you want guidance, you can come and talk to me.

"Now, on to today's class, advanced variations on the grandfather con..."

Lucy and Sarah ran along the path next to Silver Lake Boulevard, enjoying the view of the lake. After Heather's comments about how she missed being near nature, Lucy had found herself hit by some of the same feelings, and it was refreshing to be somewhere a little less built up.

MARTHA CARR & MICHAEL ANDERLE

"Your out-of-town friend seems nice," Sarah said as they jogged easily along.

"My friend?"

"The one working with Jackie."

"Oh, Ellis! Yeah, he seems like a decent lad, despite what Jackie says on the subject."

Sarah laughed. "We can't all live up to her standards."

"Can anyone?"

As they approached Silver Lake Meadows, a woman emerged heading in the opposite direction, with a corgi on a leash.

"Isn't that Esther Romano?" Sarah asked.

"Oh, yes," Lucy said. "Guess we'd better stop for a minute and say hello. The fact that we're running won't be enough of an excuse for her."

They slowed as they approached Esther until they were jogging on the spot right in front of her.

"Hello, girls," Esther said. "What are you doing out here?"

"We're running, Esther," Lucy said. "You're taking Duke for a walk?"

The corgi yapped at the sound of his name.

"That's right." Esther patted her dyed blonde perm. "It does him good to go a little farther, see some dogs he wouldn't see near my place, you know?"

"Lucky Duke."

"It's great that you girls make all this effort, with the running and the yoga. Good to keep yourselves in shape for your young men."

"It's really for ourselves," Lucy pointed out. "It feels good to stay fit and healthy."

"Of course, of course, but it doesn't do any harm to look nice and slim." Esther looked at Sarah. "You got a man to look good for yet, honey?"

"Not at the moment, Esther."

"Well, I'm sure you will soon, honey. Catch like you, a doctor and all. You know, there's this guy I met in the grocery store last week. He'd be perfect for you. Nice smile, good arms, real friendly."

"I'm not sure Sarah's after a grocery store clerk," Lucy said.

"Why not? He's got real good eyes."

"We should get going," Sarah said before they could discuss her dating options any more. "See you soon, Esther."

Off they went, along the dirt path through the meadow.

"She means well," Sarah said. "It's a good thing Jackie wasn't here for that."

They laughed, imagining their friend's reaction if she'd been the one Esther wanted to set up.

Off to one side of the path, the low bushes rustled as if in the wind. For a moment, Lucy felt a tingle of magic in the air. Then her foot slid on something smooth and snatched her attention away from it. She wobbled, wind-milled her arms, and almost fell.

Sarah wasn't so lucky. Her legs shot out from under her, and she fell flat on her back with a *thud* and a gasp.

"Ow." She clutched her head.

"Are you all right?" Lucy offered her friend a hand back to her feet.

"I think so, but what was that?"

The two of them looked at the patch of the path they

had run over. Despite the heat of the summer sun, it appeared to be covered in ice. Sure enough, when Lucy reached down, she found that the surface was freezing with a thin mist evaporating from its surface.

"How did that get there?" Sarah asked.

Lucy peered into the bushes. Was it her imagination or was something moving there? "Magic," she said.

"Why?"

"If I didn't know better, I'd say it was someone trying to break my leg."

"Do you know better?"

"Not this time, no."

Lucy took off at a sprint, charging straight at the bushes. They rustled as someone or something made its getaway. By the time Lucy was close enough to peer in, the bushes were empty, and there was no sign of whoever had occupied them.

Sarah walked up behind her, still clutching the back of her head.

"The ice is melting," she said. "Can't have been there long."

"Then we were the targets. Do you know of anyone who's out to get you?"

"No, should I?"

"Probably not. This is the problem with being a Silver Griffin. You draw all the worst sorts of attention."

CHAPTER TWENTY-NINE

Dylan was in the magical practice room when Twylan and Leontine arrived. This time, he had got the melons himself or at least got his mom to buy them. They sat in a row at the end of the room, all ready for the next lesson.

Twylan smiled when she saw that. "We don't have to use melons every time."

"Oh." Dylan blushed. "I thought...I mean, the last lesson was really helpful, and..."

"You enjoyed blowing something up at the end?"

Dylan nodded and grinned.

"Well, then I'm sure we can do that," Twylan said. "First, we're going to do something with a bit more delicacy." She took square sheets of colored paper from her bag and laid them down next to each other in the middle of the floor. "I got this idea from Kix and her craft projects: magical origami."

Leontine stood in the doorway, watching them with crossed arms and a scowl. Dylan felt intimidated by the older boy at the best of times. He was tougher and more streetwise, seeming almost like a grownup but without the burdens that adulthood carried. His frown added to his intimidation value. Still, Dylan was determined not to let that feeling show.

"Are you going to practice with us?" he asked.

Leontine shook his head. "Twylan said I had to come along."

"I didn't say you had to come here," Twylan said. "Only that you had to get out of the tunnel. You've been in a bad mood all week, and it's affecting the rest of the Brigade."

"Where else did you expect me to go if not with you?"

Twylan hesitated. She hadn't thought that part through. She had assumed that Leontine would have something he would enjoy doing, like going for a walk or reading a book or...well, something. Now she considered it and realized how dependent everyone in the Brigade had become on each other for entertainment. Apart from those who were happy to sit making things on their own, they were pretty much each other's world. Where else was Leontine going to go except with her?

"Do you like machines?" Dylan asked.

"I guess."

"My sister's working on something in her workshop, if you'd rather do that than spells."

Leontine took a moment to weigh up his options. At least in a workshop, there might be something he could help with, a machine to repair or disassemble. He walked off down the tunnel Dylan had pointed out, leaving the others to their magic.

Sure enough, Leontine emerged in a room laid out with all sorts of mechanical equipment. There were work-

benches along two sides, shelves full of boxes of components, tools arranged on a shadow board on one wall, and
another large, well-lit workbench in the room's center.
That was where Ashley stood, gears and springs laid out in
front of her, a screwdriver in one hand and a soldering
iron in the other. Seeing her frown reassured Leontine that
he wasn't the only one who could get fed up with the
world.

"Hallo!" Eddie called from where he sat on the floor,
Buddy beside him. The little boy and the dog were pushing
wooden building blocks around, one of them using his
hands, the other his nose. "I'm buildin' a pimid."

"He means a pyramid," Ashley said. "I've been trying to
get him to work on more advanced shapes, but he won't
listen."

"I know that feeling."

Leontine thought back to the big argument in the
tunnels, the one that had almost ended their experiment in
schooling. All he had been doing was to remind the others
why this was important, why they ought to listen to him
and each other. Apparently, listening was too much effort
for his peers.

"Is that an old Silver Griffin carrier box?" He looked at
the scattered pieces.

"You've seen one before?" Ashley glanced up at him in
surprise. "I thought no one knew about these."

"I had an uncle who used to work with the Griffins
around the time they tried to introduce these as a replacement for carrier pigeons. He kept a few of them after. Used
to say it was important to remember that even smart
people could make stupid decisions."

Leontine picked up one of the gears and held it up to the light, enjoying the familiar shape and feel of it, those rows of neat little teeth. It was almost enough to make him nostalgic.

"I hope to borrow some ideas from it," Ashley said. "Old magical engineers talk about how well these things combined spells and technology, that they're a great example to learn from. Terrible idea beautifully executed, that's what one of my chat room friends said."

"What do you want the ideas for?"

"Buddy's harness." She pointed with her screwdriver at the harness, which lay neatly spread out on the end of the workbench. "I'm equipping him to fight crime. He'll be a wonder dog."

Leontine peered at the components attached to the harness.

"You gave your dog a gun?"

"Only a dart gun. And I think he would be far more responsible than some human gun owners."

"Is that a magic net?"

"How else is he going to catch anyone?"

"With his teeth, like a normal dog?"

"Buddy, smile!" Ashley called.

Buddy opened his mouth as wide as he could. It wasn't enough to wrap around any but the skinniest of legs.

"Point made." Leontine took another look at the pieces of the carrier box mechanism spread out on the workbench. "What have you learned so far?"

"That this is more complicated than it looks and very delicate. Also that nobody put the repair and maintenance manual online, so I can't consult that."

"Well, what are you trying to do?"

"To get it working. This is a broken-down old box mom found in a cupboard at her office. It needs some work before I can see it fly."

"Can I help?"

Ashley set her tools down and took a step back. "Yes, please, if you know something about them."

Leontine surveyed the pieces. It was years since he had seen Uncle Valnay, but he still remembered the smell of the man's house, a scent of mechanical grease and exotic spices. When he closed his eyes, he could picture Valnay's carrier boxes laid out on the table, one of them in pieces for maintenance, magical components lined up on one side, mechanical on the other, placed in order of what should go back in first.

One by one, he started lining up the pieces. The smooth, solid feel of them was as comforting as the sight.

"Have you got a soft cloth to clean them with?" he asked.

"Sure."

Ashley fetched a box of cloths from the shelves, and together they set about cleaning the pieces, working in companionable silence as they wiped away years of grease and grit. After a while, Eddie wanted to join, so Ashley gave him some other pieces to clean, ones that didn't come from the delicate machine they were trying to fix.

At last, all the pieces were gleaming and grit-free, laid out in their neat rows.

"This goes in first." Leontine pointed at a crystal that channeled magical power to give the box its motive force.

Ashley held the shell of the box under the light, and the two of them looked inside.

"There?" She pointed at a short pin projecting from the inside.

"No, that one." Leontine pointed at another near the bottom.

Piece by piece, they reassembled the machine, inserting cogs and spindles, crystals and springs. It was satisfying work, not only for its familiarity but for the sense of achievement that came with construction working well. Once everything was in place, Ashley took a pair of wings spun from toughened spider silk and attached them to the sides.

"How do we start it up?" she asked.

"Give it a message."

Ashley pulled a notepad and pen from her pocket and carefully wrote a short letter in glittery ink.

"Dear Dylan, this is a test message. I hope that it finds you well. Yours sincerely, Ashley."

She folded it neatly in half.

"Do I need to address it?" she asked.

"Does the note say who it's to?"

"Yes."

"Then the magic should pick up on your intentions. Put the note in."

Ashley dropped it into the box. There was a glow, and the wings began to flutter. The box, which a moment before had been completely inert, lifted off the workbench and slowly flew away, wings frantically flapping to keep it in the air.

"Why don't they use them anymore?" she asked as the box disappeared down a tunnel.

"Officially, it's because the pigeons already do the job better," Leontine said. "They're faster and more efficient than the early boxes, and they don't need a strict mainte-nance routine to keep them working. Unofficially, there were rumors that the pigeons started trashing the boxes in protest at having their jobs taken. After all, every message they carried turned into a meal of tasty worms. The people higher up were worried they might face an outright revolt, losing both message systems, so they shelved the boxes."

"Really?" Ashley's eyes went wide at the thought of pigeons, even magical ones, carrying out a sort of strike to avoid being replaced by machines.

"Maybe. I don't know how much of that's exaggeration, but I know they never tried to make better versions of the boxes, which would make sense if it was all about efficiency."

Ashley started packing away tools while Leontine wiped the dirt from the workbench. Eddie, having finished cleaning the pieces Ashley had given him, started a chasing game around the room with Buddy, then turned into a hare so he could get away faster.

"Thank you for your help," Ashley said.

"I enjoyed it. It's like fixing up the lights in the tunnel. Sometimes it's good to do something with my hands."

Leontine looked around the room. There was so much potential here, all the tools, all the components, and of course Ashley's incredible intelligence. She could make almost anything, but she had still been happy to lean on him for help. If she was willing to accept that support, couldn't he accept hers?

"That wing you talked about making for me," he said. "How long would it take?"

Ashley sucked on the end of her finger as she did some rough math. "Depends on how much homework I have and how much you're around for me to test parts on. I could probably get it made in a week or two."

"I'd like that, if you're still willing to make it."

"Sure. It'll be a fun challenge."

"Once I can fly properly, I can protect the others better and get to places I can't at the moment. It'll make me more valuable to the Brigade."

"I thought it would be worth having for the fun of flying, but those are good reasons too." Ashley took out a tape measure. "Can I start making measurements now?"

There was a *whir* as the box came back into the room, followed by Dylan and Twylan.

"This is so cool!" Dylan exclaimed.

The box landed on the workbench, and a scrap of paper fell out. Ashley unfolded it and read the message:

"Ashley, this box is super cool! Can we make it chase bad guys with Buddy? Dylan."

"Well done, kid." Leontine patted Ashley on the shoulder.

"Well done, you." She reached up and patted him in return. "Now let's take it apart. I have some great ideas for using components on the harness."

CHAPTER THIRTY

Lucy, Jackie, and Sarah sat around a table in Semi-Tropic, a bar with bare brickwork and a casual atmosphere. Lucy was vaguely aware that this was the sort of place where hip young people might hang out, but she had left any chance of hipness behind on becoming a mother, and she didn't mind. She was happily enjoying a rare drink with her friends on a warm, gentle evening.

Lucy hadn't been able to free up a weekend evening, but that had worked out nicely since the place was quieter than usual. They'd been able to get seats and get served without Jackie having to shove past anyone or battle for a bartender's attention.

"What is that thing?" Jackie stared at Sarah's orange cocktail.

"It's called a twenty-four carrot."

Jackie groaned. "Did you pick your drink because its name's a pun?"

"It made me smile."

"Urgh, it's like drinking with a toddler."

"A toddler would probably like a brightly colored drink."

"Although maybe not one with mezcal in it," Lucy pointed out. She sipped her lavender gimlet, which was wonderfully refreshing after another long, frustrating day of chasing down leads that went nowhere.

"I'm glad we finally got to do this," Sarah said. "It's been far too long."

"What are you talking about?" Jackie said. "We went to yoga last week."

"This is more relaxed."

"More relaxed than moving very slowly in a room filled with soothing music?"

"Some of those stretches really work your muscles."

"Ironic, given that you're the one of us who strains the least."

"Jackie's right," Lucy said. "You're so flexible that we could wind you up like a ball of string."

Sarah smiled and blushed. "Everyone has to be good at something."

"You mean apart from saving lives?"

They laughed, and all took a moment to drink.

"I thought you had to take that new guy everywhere with you." Sarah looked at Jackie.

"Ellis and I have come to an understanding. He works on my schedule, and I stop mocking him for his magic app. So yeah, no risk he'll be interrupting us this evening."

"I'm not sure Sarah sees that as a risk." Lucy shot her friend a sidelong grin. "In fact, I wonder if she had an ulterior motive in inviting us out."

"No!" Sarah blushed more deeply. "I wanted to see you

both. Sure, it wouldn't have been bad to see him again. He is quite funny…"

"Oh God, you think he's cute." Jackie put her head in her hands. "You know he has a goatee, right? I mean, it's right there on his chin. Someone save me from your terrible taste in men."

"I'm not sure she's the one with terrible taste," Lucy said. "Remember when—"

"All right, all right, let's not dredge up my past! If you want, I can arrange for you to meet up again one lunchtime. Then I can arrange to get an urgent call, and you can take him off my hands for an hour or two. Which, thinking about it, sounds like a win-win situation."

"I didn't mean to—"

"Don't play the innocent with me. I'm a detective, remember? I can sniff out dishonesty at a hundred yards." Jackie raised her nose and started sniffing comically at the air around them. "I smell lies, lust, and antiseptic, although that last one's probably from your work." She drew another deep breath, then frowned. "Is it me, or is something burning?"

"Very funny," Sarah said, "but my pants are not on fire."

"No, seriously." Jackie looked around, then down, and her eyes went wide. Lucy followed her gaze and saw smoke trickling from the legs of their table.

"Get back!" she shouted.

The three of them leapt to their feet as the table burst into flames. The glasses they had been drinking from shattered as their contents evaporated in the sudden, intense heat.

The bar erupted in screams and shouts of alarm. A

bartender rushed over with a fire extinguisher as people ran for the door. The chemical fog blasted from its nozzle, billowing around the burning table, but the flames kept coming.

"Everybody get out!" the bartender shouted.

At the back of the room, three people got up from a low sofa where they'd hunched over their drinks. One of them took off his hat, and the others pushed back their hoods. Lucy didn't recognize two of them, but the middle guy was all too familiar. This time, Hank had come looking for her.

"Sarah, help get people out." She drew her wand. "Jackie and I have something to deal with."

"You all have to get out, now," the bartender said. "These flames aren't going out. It has to be chemicals or something."

Sarah cast a spell, and the bartender's eyes went glassy. He walked with slow steps as she led him out of the building, following the other staff and customers.

On either side of the burning table, Lucy and Jackie raised their wands.

"Think you're so damn smart," Hank growled, holding out his hands. The muscles of his arms bulged, and fire flared from his fingertips. "Well, you ain't gonna look smart when I burn you to a cinder. You try and keep getting in our way then."

"You'd sound a lot tougher if it weren't for that lisp," Jackie said. "Maybe if you saw a speech therapist you wouldn't be so mad at the world."

"I don't have a lisp!"

"I think it's the missing teeth that do it," Lucy said. "Maybe those dentures you got fitted aren't sitting right?"

"Shut up!" Hank moved a hand self-consciously to cover his mouth, then jerked it away. "We're gonna make sure you never mess with us again."

A jet of flames shot from his hands and hit the burning table. What was left of it burst apart, and Lucy and Jackie had to dive clear of the blast.

When Lucy looked up, Hank was charging at her while Jackie was backing away from the other two, her wand twitching back and forth as she countered a string of spells. The flames were growing around Hank's hands, and a furious inferno blazed in his eyes.

Lucy rolled back across the floor, and a fireball hit where she'd been. She kept rolling as more came in, then ducked into cover behind the corner of the bar. She clutched her wand while fire lapped around the edges of the bar, its outer edges groping at her, the heat making her sweat.

"You think you're so damn clever," Hank yelled. "But I'm the smart one. I've got the learning now."

"Because you've been going to Womack's school?" Lucy called back to him.

"Damn right." Hank was coming slowly closer, and the flames crept farther around the bar, pushing Lucy back into a corner. "I'm gonna follow her plan and gonna have my gang. LA's gonna learn to fear the name Hank Zublensky."

"So it's not your plan?"

"It will be! I'm gonna make it mine. You'll see." Hank snorted in malicious laughter. "Except you won't be around to see nothing."

Hank pulled the flames back, gathering his power for

one last big blast to incinerate Lucy. At that moment, she rose from behind the bar and pointed her wand at him.

"Sonum aquarum!"

Water shot from Lucy's wand while fire burst from Hank's hands. The two met in the middle of the bar. With a *hiss* like a thousand snakes, the water became steam, a scalding cloud that filled nearly the whole room. "Looks like I quenched your little campfire."

"It'll take more than a trickle of water to stop me."

The steam glowed orange, and a torrent of flame shot through it, like the blaze from the back of a jet engine. Shooting blind through the concealing haze, Hank swept the fire across the space where Lucy had been. She leapt clear again while he reduced the end of the bar and the floor beside it to charcoal.

Water hadn't been enough, but Lucy had another idea.

"Vocare glacies," she chanted and pointed her wand again.

A blast of ice met that of fire. In the middle of the room, the two opposing forces obliterated each other, with more steam billowing out and water streaming onto the floor. No matter how deeply Lucy drew on her reserves of power, she couldn't push the flames back, couldn't wipe out what Hank was doing.

She swirled her wand in a circle, redirecting the ice magic. Instead of a jet of ice directly taking on the fire, it formed a wall between them. As the flames blazed away, the wall started to melt, but at least now she had a moment to think.

Water hadn't been enough. Ice was making a stalemate. The fire came from deep inside Hank, and merely facing it with its opposite wasn't enough to diminish that. She couldn't keep fighting raw strength with more of the same.

Her wand pulsed in her hand as a cloud of steam swept over her, caught by the air conditioning. She lost sight of everything: the bar, the ice, the flashes of magic where Jackie was battling the other wizards. There was only this empty, white space, and within it, she felt her mind go blank. It was like the moment after waking up, when she was sure there was something from her dream that she had meant to remember, but she couldn't quite latch onto it. Something about fire.

An image sprang to mind. The fire as a monster, a thing with a hungry mouth. It grabbed a balloon, opened wide, and swallowed it. The image was so strange in its dreamlike logic that Lucy laughed despite the danger she was in. As she laughed, she realized what the vision meant.

"Fire needs air," she said as the steam swirled away and the world returned. Directly in front of her, the ice wall glowed, the flames having almost melted a way through. She raised her voice. "Jackie, take a deep breath, quick!"

Lucy drew a big gulp into her lungs, then whispered a spell. "Caeli et abierunt."

There was a roar of wind as the air rushed out of the room. Hank's fire, starved of oxygen, went out.

Lucy knew she only had moments before she ran out of air or the spell ended and the room refilled. She flung herself at the diminished wall of ice, smashing through the thin layer that remained.

On the other side, Hank was leaning on a table, gasping for the air that wasn't there. His mouth was open, eyes wide with panic. Only soot stains remained of the fire around his fingers.

"Form to contain in bonds of chain," Lucy chanted with the last of her breath.

Steel chains shot from her wand and wrapped themselves around Hank, binding his arms and hands to his sides. Staggered by the impact, he fell against the table, then off it to the floor.

Lucy dismissed her other spell, and the air rushed back into the room. She turned to find Jackie standing over a prone wizard with a bruise on his cheek as she slapped him in handcuffs. The other guy was already on the floor, tangled in a mass of spiderwebs.

"Great work," Jackie said. "Now for the clearing up."

Lucy dismissed the ice wall shards and looked around the room. Flames had charred half of the place, and the rest was dripping with water.

She stepped into the street. Sarah had gathered the people from the bar in a single group on the sidewalk, and now a fire truck pulled up behind them. Fortunately, Applegate's car was approaching, meaning that there would be more Griffins to help with the cleanup.

"Hey, everyone!" Lucy held up her wand. "Never was, never will be."

Bar staff, customers, and firefighters stopped talking and went glassy-eyed. Their memories of the past half-hour would be gone, but now the Griffins only had fifteen minutes to clean up before they recovered.

"Do you have suspects to deal with?" Applegate asked as he got out of his car.

"Yes, sir," Lucy said.

"Then I'll sort out this lot while you get them away."

Lucy walked back into the bar. Jackie had their captives lined up and ready to be marched out. The contents of their pockets floated in a magical bubble: keys, wallets, phones, wands, even a pack of gum.

"I found these on all of them." Jackie held up three plastic cards with some worn orange symbols on them. "Do they mean anything to you?"

"Looks like key cards for an office." Lucy thought back over what she already knew and the insights she had gained. Students needed a classroom to learn in, and a deserted office would do the job. "If we can find the building these come from, I bet we find Womack."

"That's something, at least." Jackie smiled wryly. "So much for our evening out."

"Are you kidding? When was the last time we had a night this wild! Doesn't it make you feel young?"

Jackie shook her head. "We're still young. What I feel right now is too sober."

CHAPTER THIRTY-ONE

Lucy set her pencil down for a moment so she could consider what she'd drawn. In the middle of the classroom, a bowl of fruit sat on a table, where everyone in the art class could see it. She was glad they couldn't also see her attempt to draw the contents. By her standards, it wasn't bad, but the apples looked squashed, and the less said about the banana, the better. Still life might be a great way to practice drawing skills, but right now hers seemed more like messy scribbles.

"This is a lot calmer than last night," Lucy whispered, looking around at the focus on people's faces. Jazz played softly in the background, but the only other noises were the scratching of pencils on paper and the quiet, slow footsteps of the art tutor as she walked around the room.

"I could set the place on fire if you're missing that vibe," Charlie replied. "I thought you might not approve of that for date night."

"Calm isn't bad, especially if it means I'm not fighting for my life."

"That's good, but I think my fruit might be dead. I mean, it started all right, but the pear is getting darker and flatter every time I try to fix it."

"We don't have to do this again if you don't want to."

"No, I'm enjoying it. Makes a nice change of pace from coding. It wouldn't be a change if we were playing to my strengths."

Lucy smiled at her husband. She loved his easy-going manner, his willingness to try new things along with her. Art seemed a particularly fitting choice since they'd met in a gallery although they were both art appreciators rather than creators. Maybe with practice, she could paint a picture of him, capture that handsome face for future generations to enjoy. He deserved it more than a lot of the historical figures she'd seen hanging on gallery walls. Her installation wizard did more good for the world than some of history's aristocrats and dictators. Kindness should be immortalized every bit as much as power.

The tutor walked into the middle of the room and covered the fruit bowl with a cloth.

"Enough of that for today," she said. "You've all made great progress. Now we're going to do something fun for the end of the lesson."

She picked up a pile of printouts and stuck them to the wall as she talked. They were a selection of familiar faces: Mickey Mouse, Bugs Bunny, Garfield, and other famous cartoon animals.

"Cartooning is all about exaggeration," the tutor explained. "Mickey's ears, Bugs' teeth, the eyes of almost every character a cartoonist ever drew. We've spent the evening aiming for realism, so now it's time for something different. Get onto your phone and find a photo of an animal. It could be a pet, something you saw at the zoo, or someone else's image off the internet. Take a minute to look at that picture and think about what makes the animal distinctive. Do they have a small face, a fat body, a bushy tail? Try to draw a version of them that exaggerates that feature. Do it quick and messy. This is about impressions, not perfection. Then have another go, maybe with another feature. See how many cartoon animals you can make in ten minutes."

While the tutor brought around fresh paper, Lucy pulled out her phone and looked for pictures of Buddy.

"Snap." Charlie held up his phone with a picture of their beloved pet dog.

They both picked up their pencils and started to draw. Lucy drew Buddy extra-long first, with his body stretched out like a rubber band. She kept the head simple, so she wouldn't have to deal with too many details. Then she drew a different version exaggerating his ears, turning them into long rolls that flopped to the floor. Meanwhile, Charlie drew him with tiny legs and an enormous tongue hanging out of his mouth, capturing some of his irrepressible eagerness.

"I almost feel bad," Charlie said. "It's like we're making fun of him, and he's not here to defend himself."

"You know what Buddy's like. He'd be happy that we're thinking about him."

"We might have to take these home after class. Buddy cartoons are the sort of thing the kids would really enjoy."

"We could all have a go at drawing together!"

Lucy tapped her pencil against the page, considering what to add to her images. Would more detail help to make them more complete or distract from the features she had focused on?

"That's really good." The tutor appeared over her shoulder. "Now try exaggerating a less obvious feature to see how that changes the results. Pick something like…" She peered at the picture of Buddy. "…his shiny nose."

With quick strokes of the pencil, Lucy started sketching Buddy's face. She drew his eyes, the grinning mouth, tongue hanging out, and in the middle of it an enlarged nose, with a dark and shiny tip.

"It's as if you're revealing his inner character," Charlie said. "The way he's always chasing after interesting smells."

"I wish I could get him to do that for me," Lucy said. "A magical bloodhound in the body of a dachshund, sniffing out the criminals I'm trying to catch."

"The kids are already on it."

"Really?"

"Oh yeah. I found them with a bunch of battered cardboard cutouts in the back yard, teaching Buddy to go after the magical ones. It's the first time I've seen a Willen have their cardboard legs chewed off."

Lucy laughed. "Some days they amaze me."

"Only some days?"

"All right, every day." She leaned over to kiss Charlie on the cheek. "I still can't believe we made such a great family."

"I can." He smiled at her. "They had a great mom to get them started."

"Time's up," the tutor called. "Pencils away in the pot, take your work home with you if you want. I hope you had fun with this taster session, and if you'd like to sign up for a regular class, you have my email."

Lucy took her paper and pencils with her, headed out of the building hand-in-hand with Charlie, and down the street to where he'd parked his Prius. They got in and started the drive home.

"This training the kids have given Buddy." Lucy looked at her pictures while Charlie drove. "How far have they got?"

"Not as far as they'd like, but you know them, they're an ambitious bunch. He can tell a magical ball from a mundane one, and I think he was going after the right targets although it was hard to tell once he got excited and knocked them all down."

"So I might be able to use him to find a source of magic?"

"You want to recruit our dog to the Griffins now as well?" Charlie chuckled. "Because the family wasn't enough."

"Buddy is family."

"Fair point and I'm sure he'd be happy to join. It would give him something to use that harness on."

"Harness?"

"Oh, you've missed out on all the fun stuff. The kids have rigged up this crazy contraption covered in lights and magic and tranquilizer guns."

"Tranquilizer guns?"

"Don't worry. I've taken away the darts for now. I don't want them sedating us."

"I was more worried that they'd accidentally sedate each other."

"Might be worth it for an evening to ourselves."

They pulled into the driveway of their house and climbed out of the car. The only light on in the place was in the living room.

"We're home," Lucy quietly announced as they crept into the house.

Emily Sanders, Eddie's regular babysitter, appeared around the living room door.

"They're all in bed," she whispered. "Went down when I asked them to, good as gold. Even Eddie only insisted on showing me three different animal shapes first."

"Now there's someone we could draw cartoons of," Charlie said. "Eddie the endless string of animals."

They waved Emily off, then went to sit on the couch, Lucy curling up in the crook of Charlie's arm. She leaned against him, enjoying the warmth of his body against hers and the subtle, comforting smell of his skin.

"If the kids are in bed…" She ran a hand across his shirt.

"My dear, what are you suggesting?" Charlie grinned and trailed a finger down her spine, that gentle touch making her shudder.

Then Buddy waddled in, leapt up onto the couch, and rested his head in Charlie's lap.

"So much for that." Lucy laughed. "Even without the kids, we're never alone."

Buddy tipped his head on one side and looked at her with dark, curious eyes.

"Is it true what they say, Buddy?" she asked. "Can you find magic?"

Buddy panted and wagged his tail.

"I think he knows that word now," Charlie said. "The training's sinking in."

"Let's try something." Lucy curled her hands into loose fists and held both of them out in front of Buddy. Silently calling on her inner magic—that deep and powerful thing that had driven her ever since she was young, that had sometimes overwhelmed her as it threatened to do to Dylan—she pushed most of the power back and let a little flow into one of her hands. "Which one's magic, Buddy?"

Buddy looked at her, then sniffed each hand in turn. He raised a paw and planted it on her left fist. Lucy turned that hand over and unfurled it, revealing a spark of power on her palm.

"Well done, boy," she said.

Buddy sniffed her hand and licked it half-heartedly. He looked disappointed.

"If you want to train him to go after something, you have to give rewards when he gets it right," Charlie said. "I learned that from YouTube."

"Be careful what you learn on YouTube. Some of those makeup tutorials really won't suit your complexion."

Lucy focused on the magic in her hand, then set it to shape something from thin air. A moment later, a dog biscuit lay between her fingers.

Buddy panted excitedly at the sight of a snack appearing from nowhere. He snatched it up between his teeth, leapt off the couch, and waddled off to eat in a quiet corner.

"That's a bright lad we have there, protecting his prize

from the humans." Lucy smiled. "Looks like I have myself a right smart magic hound."

"What will you do with this modern marvel?"

"Same thing I do every night, fight crime."

"Even on date night?" Charlie ran a hand down her side.

"Maybe I can make an exception." She kissed him.

CHAPTER THIRTY-TWO

A wall of computer monitors stared down at Lucy like the faces of a bright and square-faced crowd, every one of them eager to please, practically yelling their brightly colored patterns of data. There were maps and diagrams, tables and charts, and somewhere near the middle, a screen full of incomprehensible letters and numbers where Ashley was editing her code. This was where Ashley was most at home, her computer lair beneath the house, and Lucy was happy for her to have all the technology she wanted if she used it like this.

Next to Ashley, Octo stood on what had once been a coffee table. The robot was up on all eight legs with a pile of papers sitting in the space underneath. A scanning beam ran across each page in turn before two of the legs twitched in to turn that page over or transfer it with precise movements to the out pile on the floor.

"Octo's nearly finished scanning Twylan's notes," Ashley said. "The software is picking out names, locations, and directions for that data set."

Lucy pointed at a map of LA on one of the screens. "This is the unoccupied office properties?"

"Everything I could find, based on government records, business data, and realtor listings."

Lucy marveled at the sight of it all. For her to do this, she would have had to read through those records one by one, if she even got the search terms right to find them. Ashley had automated the process, turning her computer system into a digital detective.

"You're brilliant." Lucy kissed her daughter on the top of her head.

"Can I make a video about this for my YouTube channel? My subscribers would think it was cool."

"Sorry, sweetheart, but I don't think we should turn a Silver Griffins investigation into a piece of entertainment."

"It's an educational channel."

"Still no."

Ashley sighed. "I suppose I can duplicate the process with some other data once we're finished. Use it to find historical landmarks visited by celebrities or something like that."

"That sounds much better for YouTube, and more people will want to see it if you mention celebrities."

Ashley made a face. "Urgh, clickbait."

Octo set aside the last of the pages, and Ashley hit a key. Her new code started running, and things shifted on the screens. Lists scrolled by, maps merged, figures danced as if by magic, and a new image coalesced at the center of it all, right in front of them.

"These are the most likely places." Ashley pointed at the new map. "That's taking into account relevant crimes, sightings of Hank, and office spaces that are either empty or were hired out three to four months ago by someone we can't discount as your suspect."

"What are the different colors?"

"A traffic light system. The deeper reds are the most likely locations, fading to yellow for less likely ones."

Lucy examined the map. Hank hadn't admitted anything about Womack and her school under questioning, but he'd still ended up being a huge help, even if he didn't want to. The information Twylan had gathered on his comings and goings significantly narrowed down the search. Most of the school's likely locations were concentrated in a few specific areas, meaning that Lucy could visit ninety percent of them without going more than a few miles from Echo Park. If she started in areas with big piles of red on the map, maybe she would get lucky and keep her search short.

"Did I mention how brilliant you are?" she asked.

"Once or twice." Ashley smiled. "I like hearing it though."

"I like saying it. You might be the smartest girl in the whole world. Now I need to get to work."

Lucy made her way through the tunnels, up a ladder, and out the hatch hidden by bushes on the side of their house. As she dusted herself off, she wondered if they should add an entry from inside the house, now that the kids weren't hiding their base from her and Charlie. It would make it easier to come and go unseen.

She pushed her way out past the bushes into the front yard.

"Hey there!" Al called from his yard. He was standing by

a flower bed, a pair of pruning shears in his hand and a bucket by his feet. "You trimming back those bushes at last?"

Lucy looked at the plants behind her. They were getting overgrown, but she wasn't sure she wanted to change that, given what they were hiding.

"Thought I might grow them out," she said. "See how they look with more leaves."

"Careful they don't take over. You have to keep an eye on that."

"I will."

Lucy headed into the house and picked up a dog lead off a table by the door. Drawn by the sound, Buddy rushed to meet her.

"You want to go walkies, lad?" Lucy snapped the lead onto his collar. "'Course you do."

Buddy looked a little disappointed when she put him in the car instead of heading straight off down the street, but he was smart enough to know that cars sometimes drove to parks or woodland, or even to the beach, where he could dig in the sand and splash in the surf. It helped that someone had left a chew toy on the back seat following a previous expedition so he had something to keep him entertained.

A drive through LA's sunny streets carried them to the first of the areas Lucy wanted to check. Ashley had sent the data to her mom's phone, and now it flashed up on the map app, making navigation easy.

The good thing about empty office buildings was that the parking didn't get crowded. Sure, there were people from other nearby developments using some of the parking spaces, but Lucy still found a slot where her Rivian could fit.

"Out you get, boy." She opened the back of the SUV.

Buddy looked around, mildly disappointed. This place seemed to be a lot of concrete paths and tall buildings. Pretty much any building was tall to him. He couldn't smell squirrels or deer or anything the countryside might have offered. There were the scents of a few feral cats, as well as raccoons, who had marked their territory in the moments between raiding local dumpsters.

"What can you smell?" Lucy asked. "Anything interesting?"

Of course, there were interesting things. The world always had interesting smells for a dog who took the time to appreciate them. Dropped takeaway cartons. Melted ice cream. Rats. The question was, which one should he go after?

Today felt like an ice cream day. Tugging on his lead, Buddy dragged Lucy down a street and around a corner to a creamy pink puddle with a half-crushed cone sitting next to it. He lapped at the ice cream, enjoying the sickly sweet taste.

"That's not quite what I had in mind," Lucy said. She crouched facing Buddy and held out two hands, one with magic and one without. As on the previous evening, he quickly identified the magical hand and was rewarded for it. "Good boy. Now, can you find any other magic around here?"

The next hour was as exciting for Buddy as it was disappointing for Lucy. LA was full of magic if you knew where to sniff for it, and all his practice with balls in the garden had made Buddy good at that sniffing. He might not have a bloodhound's body anymore, but he still had its mind and a good nose to go with it. He took Lucy to a nest of imps living on a fire escape, a broken wand in a trash can, a witch trying to eat a sandwich during a brief break from her office job, and five places where traces of magic lingered from castings within the past few days. Nothing about any of it said "secret magic school" to Lucy. She cleared out the imps, took the wand for safe disposal, and asked the witch if she'd seen other magicals acting suspiciously, but she couldn't think of any. The whole area was a bust.

"All right, into the car," Lucy said. "Let's try the next patch."

The next two areas were equally unhelpful. Buddy had a fun time sniffing out every last magical trace he could find and being rewarded with treats and pats on the head, but nothing Lucy saw led her to think that the offices Buddy singled out were anything other than abandoned.

"Last stop for now," she said as she pulled up one last time. "I'll save the long shots for tomorrow."

She got out of the vehicle, clipped Buddy's lead onto his collar, and looked around at the nearby buildings. They weren't exactly towering edifices, like the blocks big corporations liked to use, but maybe that was the point. Somewhere slightly more discreet.

Or maybe they were barking up the wrong tree, literally in the case of Buddy, who had spotted a cat running up an isolated roadside alder.

"Come on, mate." Lucy dragged him away from his attempt to chase a new friend. "Tell me where the magic is."

Buddy sniffed the air, then bent his head and started nosing the ground. His tail swayed, and a moment later he was off, taking her with him. He waddled along between the buildings, snuffling from side to side as if the whole ground was smeared with something he wanted to lick up. As they approached one of the buildings, his back and forth wanderings narrowed, and he headed for a side door.

"Hold it there, Buddy." Lucy pulled him to a halt.

Above the building's door were the remains of a sign for a bankrupt holiday firm, a big plastic orange swoosh. She pulled a card from her pocket, one of the key cards taken off Hank and his friends. A smudge at one corner, almost worn away with repeated use, was the same orange as the sign.

"I think we might have a winner." She put away the card and pulled out a biscuit for Buddy. "Good boy."

Buddy crunched the treat between his teeth. Despite the lack of a park, this day was a lot of fun. He'd sniffed all sorts of new things, and he'd eaten a lot of biscuits.

There was a coffee shop down the street, serving the staff from the offices in the area that were still active. Lucy got herself a cup of tea and took a window seat. From there she could see anyone heading for the door Buddy had picked out although the door itself was out of sight. Buddy lay on the floor by her feet, sleeping off the afternoon's excitement.

Half an hour later, her concentration was slipping, and she was starting to doubt her judgment. Then a short figure hurried past, wearing a thick hoodie despite the warm day. They were followed by two more, one with the determined stride of a dwarf. Then an elf walked past with her ears covered. All of them headed for the same building, and at least one pulled out a key card before they approached.

This was it. Magicals were gathering covertly at an empty office building, in one of the areas Hank went to, and at the center of a cluster of magical thefts. It had to be Womack's school.

"Excuse me," Lucy said as a barista walked past. "Do you know who uses that office over there?"

The barista looked out the window, and his eyes seemed to skip over the building. Lucy had to point it out a second time before he answered.

"It's a weird thing. I keep forgetting that place," the barista said. "The company that used it moved out maybe two years ago, and I guess I stopped paying attention when their staff stopped coming in."

He wandered off with a distracted expression, leaving Lucy alone with Buddy.

She reached down to pat the dog on his head. His help had made all the difference. It felt good to use his gifts, however different they might be from here.

Something clicked inside her head. She needed a case study for her management assignment, so why not this? It wasn't conventional, but she had managed a magically empowered partner while working on a project together, the project of finding the school. She had used his specialist skills, offered rewards for performance, and delivered the results she needed. Maybe the person marking the assignment wouldn't think she was taking it seriously, but she could live with that. After weeks of reading about management techniques, using a dog for her homework felt exactly as serious as the whole thing deserved.

A hideout located, an assignment planned, and she still had half a cuppa left. Today was a good day for both of them.

CHAPTER THIRTY-THREE

Night lay across LA, not the pitch dark shroud that draped the countryside, but a lacework of neon light, four million points of electric brightness linked by the illuminated sidewalks that stretched between them. Through that space of shining light and shadows, Ellis and Jackie made their way to an anonymous red door in the side of a locksmith's store.

"This seems a fine place and all," Ellis glanced down a grubby alley, "but I thought we were going to a bar?"

"Patience, pupil," Jackie said. "Haven't you ever heard of a speakeasy?"

She drew her wand and tapped three times on the door. The points she tapped were already scuffed where hundreds of other people had gone through the same routine.

A pulsing hum emerged from the door, then faded away. There was a *click*, a shutter slid open at face height, and a pair of eyes appeared. Instead of staring at Jackie and Ellis from behind the door, those eyes detached from whatever held them, rolled out through the gap and onto a narrow shelf on the front of the door. Bloodshot and glistening, they rotated independently of each other, making Ellis feel cross-eyed just looking at them. After a few moments considering their surroundings, they brought their attention to Jackie.

"Can I help you?" a voice said, and when Ellis looked down, he realized that a pair of gigantic lips had appeared in the middle of the door, adorned with brick red lipstick.

"We're here for a drink," Jackie said. "My name's Jackie. This is Ellis."

"Wait, I know you," the door said. "You're a Silver Griffin."

"Do you want to say that a little louder? I don't think people on the East Coast heard you."

"I don't have to let you in."

"Seriously, that's how you want to play this?" Jackie waved her wand. "I have authority over whether you stay on Earth. Did you think about that?"

"I'm thinking about my customers and staff, and I don't think they want to be disturbed."

"We can do this the easy way or the hard way."

"Apparently, it's going to be the clichéd way." The eyes rotated to look at Ellis, then back at Jackie. "He with you?"

"No, I thought I'd summon you in front of a random stranger."

"No need to be bitchy about it."

"There's no need for you to be obstructive. Now let us in."

"You got a warrant?"

"You've been watching too much TV. That's not how

this situation works." She waved her wand. "Last chance. Are you letting us in?"

The door sighed. "Fiiiine."

"No tipping off your customers about the fact that the Griffins are here."

"I thought you had to let them know who you are."

"I'll say it again, too much TV. Now open up before I get all Ali Baba on your ass."

The eyeballs rolled back through the shutter, which slid shut. The lips faded into the background, and the door swung open.

"Thank you kindly, ma'am." Ellis tipped an imaginary hat to the door as they passed.

"At least someone has some manners," the door said.

They walked down a set of narrow stairs into a cellar bar. Every sort of magical crowded the room. Shifters flexed and growled, Arpaks spread their wings, Kilomea bared their tusks while demanding more ale. One side of the bar had a set of steps leading up to it so that gnomes, dwarves, Willen, and other diminutive creatures could easily be seen and served. Pillars holding up the ceiling broke up the crowd, and shadowy booths provided quiet, comfortable retreats for those looking for seclusion.

"What are you drinking?" Jackie asked.

"That's mighty kind of you," Ellis said, surprised.

"Got to blend in. What do you want?"

"I'll have whatever you're having."

"Yo, bar!" Jackie leaned in past an elf nursing a martini glass. "Two tequila slammers and a couple of Buds."

"Seriously?" Ellis asked.

"What, tequila too hardcore for you?"

"That's not what I was objecting to. I figured you'd have better taste in beer."

"I don't have time to peruse the menu. At least this way you know what you're getting."

"Knowing I'm getting Bud is pretty much the problem, but I'm not gonna object when it's not my round."

"Seems a lot like you're objecting." Jackie handed him a saltshaker and a wedge of lime. "Here, get yourself set up."

Salt, tequila, and lime blazed their way across Ellis's taste buds. With that ritual out of the way, he took his beer and headed out into the crowd with Jackie at his side.

"Don't stand so far away," she cautioned. "We're trying to blend in, make it look like a date."

"I don't see that kind of connection in our future."

"Neither do I, but if you're going to be in town, I have a friend who... Wait, is that our guy in the corner booth?"

Ellis turned slightly, trying to follow her gaze without making it obvious. Sure enough, an elf with white hair and a scar down his cheek sat in the booth, along with another of his kind.

"Fits Vessfall's description," Ellis said. "I don't figure there's more than one scar-cheeked, white-haired elf in LA, do you?"

"Only one way to find out." Jackie grabbed Ellis's hand. "Come with me."

She led him to the booth. As they approached, the elves looked up impatiently.

"What?" the white-haired one said.

"Hi!" Jackie smiled and put on a bright, bubbly voice. "I'm sorry, this is going to sound, like, totally ditzy if I'm wrong, but are you Vessfall, *the* Vessfall, three times Ultimate Magical Fighting Champion? My boyfriend didn't believe me when I said it was you, did you, hon? But I've watched, like, all your matches, and you are such a legend, and like, seriously, is it really you?"

Ellis fought to keep his expression from sinking through uncertain into outright perturbed. Ultimate Magical Fighting Champion? Jackie hadn't mentioned that part of Vessfall's file.

Vessfall's face had shifted as Jackie's words washed across his ego. Pride replaced annoyance, and he gestured to an empty seat.

"I am indeed that Vessfall. And you are…"

"Silver Griffins." Jackie dropped the act and pulled out her amulet. "I have some questions about an acquaintance of yours."

Vessfall stiffened. The other elf reached inside her coat.

"Ma'am, I don't know if that's a knife or a gun you're reaching for," Ellis said. "I'll ask you kindly not to reach any further."

"I don't talk to Griffins." Vessfall scowled.

"Everyone talks to us in the end," Jackie said. "It's only a question of when."

"Are you trying to intimidate me, girl?" Vessfall stood slowly. He flexed his muscles and the seams of his shirt popped. "Have you forgotten already who I am?"

"Definitely not. I've been looking forward to the challenge."

Vessfall raised his hand, magic spinning around his fingers, and everything seemed to happen at once.

Jackie dropped her beer and lunged across the table.

Ellis flicked his wrist, launching the wand from his quick draw holster.

Vessfall roared.

The other elf's hand emerged, wearing a rune-encrusted knuckle duster.

Then the chaos began. Jackie and Vessfall grappled with each other, arms and legs flailing, magic spraying from his fingers. Ellis's first spell bounced off an invisible ward and hit someone in the crowd behind him. The second elf flung her glass at him, missed, and hit another customer. Shouting and shoving erupted all around as Ellis leapt forward, casting spells as he went.

Ellis had plenty of tricks to incapacitate an opponent. Tangles of chains and ropes. Freezing them in place. Making the surface slippery under their feet. Even magical itching powder. But every time he fired off a spell, the elf lashed out with the knuckle duster, and the runes glowed and deflected it. Magic flew in every direction, adding to the confusion in the room. Everyone hit by a spell assumed that someone near them cast it and responded with their fists or magic. Instead of a sociable crowd, the place became a brawling mass of bodies, with spells spinning off into the walls.

Jackie grabbed Vessfall and tried to pin him against the wall, but his strength overcame the advantage of her impact. He slammed her into the table, then raised a fist glowing with power. Jackie, her hand wrapped around his other wrist, brought her foot up into his abdomen and heaved. Vessfall's swing added to his momentum as she flung him over her and onto the bar floor, beneath the crowd's feet.

The other elf was out from behind the table and taking swings at Ellis. He ducked and wove, the magic of his Silver Griffin amulet absorbing the impact of a few glancing blows, but with each passing moment her weapon's runes glowed brighter, and he had a bad feeling about what would happen if they hit him.

Jackie leapt off the table and landed in a crouch next to Vessfall. He'd been kicked several times in the brawl's confusion, but now he was shoving away anyone who came near him as he pushed himself up onto one knee.

"Isn't that your bad knee?" Jackie asked. Keeping her body low, she scythed her leg around. It collided with the knee, and Vessfall howled in pain. "Hell of a match when that got broken."

Vessfall bellowed and flung himself at her, arms outstretched. Jackie launched herself back, adding a spray of magic to her agility. She flipped head over heels and landed out of reach while Vessfall slammed face-first into the floor.

Ellis kept backing away as the elf advanced on him. He shot another spell, but she ducked, and the chains rattled past to tangle around a light fitting. Then his back was against the bar, and there was nowhere left to go.

"Looks like you're out of luck." The elf swung her fist, magic shining from the runes on the knuckle duster. Ellis dodged, and her fist hit the bar, plowing through the solid wood. Beer sprayed from broken taps as she tried to pull herself loose but instead got caught on splintered ends of planks.

"Form to contain in bonds of chain," Ellis chanted.

Chains emerged from the end of his wand, finally restraining the elf.

On the other side of the room, Vessfall was trying to get to his feet. His face hurt, his shoulder was numb where it had hit the floor, and his doubly injured knee was screaming at him in the language of pain. When he was younger, he would have been straight back up and into the fight. When he was younger, he had been a champion.

"I know this is something people normally say about themselves," Jackie said as she wrenched his arms up behind his back and slapped a pair of cuffs on him, "but you're getting too old for this."

The brawl was still ongoing as Jackie and Ellis hauled their captives through the fray, up the steps, and out into the alley.

"I knew I shouldn't have let you in," the door snapped at them. "You've made a complete mess of my insides. Who's going to clear that up, I ask you?"

"Blame this one," Jackie shoved Vessfall against the wall. "He was about to assault a Silver Griffin."

"This is a setup," Vessfall growled. "You're picking on me because I'm famous."

"Famous, really? Do you know how few people on this planet know Ultimate Magical Fighting? If I were you, I'd be looking for a different way to reduce my sentence."

"Like what?"

"Like telling us where we can find Meredith Womack."

"I don't know anything about Womack."

"Really? Because I heard that the two of you met a few months back, did some business together, or at least tried to. I'm much keener to find her than I am to see you rot."

"All right, I know Womack, but I don't know where you can find her."

"Then tell me what you do know."

"She's building a big piece of mind magic, something that will make her and her home invisible to the world. The ultimate con artist's retreat."

"What else?"

"She's always using magic like that, chameleon wards, spells, and artifacts to make her marks forget anything happened. If you want to catch Womack, you'll need a way to block those."

"Anything more?"

"That's all I know, but it has to be worth something, right? You don't need to send me to Trevilsom."

"Not forever, at least."

Jackie turned to Ellis, who had the chained elf pinned against the wall with one hand and had just finished making a phone call with the other.

"Applegate's sending out a transport van," Ellis said. "From what I heard of your side, we have what we came here for. Guess you can get rid of me for the rest of the evening."

"Guess so." Jackie reluctantly smiled. "That was good work back there, the way you dealt with the fight. We never finished our beers, but once these two are gone, we should find some replacements. What do you say?"

"That sounds mighty fine, but this time no Bud."

CHAPTER THIRTY-FOUR

Applegate had booked the Griffins' fanciest new meeting room for the briefing on Meredith Womack, and he clearly expected everybody to be impressed. Lucy thought the place was all right, with its comfy chairs and the big table down the middle. Someone had even brought in cookies and coffee, though sadly no tea. Still, if anyone wanted to impress her with their big screens, they'd have to outdo Ashley's computer room, and what Applegate had couldn't compare.

"...So that's the basics," Applegate said as he came to the end of his presentation. The assembled agents and department heads nodded as they thought about what they'd heard or re-read the facts listed on the screen behind the regional manager. "Does anyone have any questions before we get into the planning stage?"

"Just one," Kelly Petrie said. "If this situation is as serious as you say, why weren't we briefed on it sooner?"

A few people murmured agreement, but Lucy wasn't the only one rolling their eyes. Every Griffin couldn't know about every case. There was simply too much going on for that.

"I understand your concern," Applegate said, "but this wasn't a single case until a few days ago. Agents Heron and Ellis each had their strands of the web to pursue, and it was at their discretion when to bring others in on their cases. Obviously, things have escalated now, so it's time."

"What you're saying is that Lucy chose not to tell us?" Kelly said sharply.

"I don't think this is helpful." Applegate waved the issue away. "Let's focus on the mission in front of us. Agent Heron, I believe you have the particulars?"

"Thank you, sir."

Lucy made her way to the front of the room. She felt like a bit of a fraud, standing up to share this information as if she'd worked it out for herself when so much of it had been Ashley's analysis. On the other hand, she was glad that her daughter didn't have to face this room and the hostility radiating from Kelly in particular.

"This is the building we're referring to as Womack Academy." She pressed a button to bring up the next slide. A photo of the unassuming office building appeared, and next to that a map of its location. "This is where Meredith Womack has been teaching a mixture of magic and crime for the past few months. We located it this week using the latest in canine detective methodology."

"You mean a dog sniffed it out?" Kelly asked disdainfully.

"Yes, a very bright dog. We hired Scooby-Doo." That drew a laugh and made Kelly sink, scowling into her seat. "Since then, we've confirmed that several dozen students are going in and out. The whole building is bound in a web of spells that are growing stronger every day and make it harder for people to notice. So far, it only affects mundanes, but if we don't stop it soon, we'll all become unable to see Womack and her school. They'll disappear from our minds, perfectly hidden.

"Even with that magic in place, a fight between us and Womack's people is likely to draw attention, especially when it takes place in such a public location. That's why we need so many agents for this raid. Some of you will maintain an extended 'never was, never will be' around the location while also keeping a perimeter to prevent escapees. The rest of us will go in, shut the school down, and arrest everyone in there."

"These are the friends you told me about?" Womack said as she walked into the back room of a toy store.

"Yep." Snivvery waved at the half-dozen trolls who were resting in a pile of stuffed toys. "I'd tell you their names, but, well, do you care?"

"Only if it matters to do the job."

"Not even slightly. I did a favor for them a while back, so they owe me, and they're easily bored. If I tell them to go cause chaos somewhere, that's exactly what they'll do."

At those words, the trolls looked up eagerly. They bared their pointed teeth, and every one had a look of excitement in their eyes.

"Perfect," Womack said. "I need a distraction. The last components of my plan are arriving today, but the Griffins are closing in. They arrested a contact of mine last night, and unless I finish my spells, it's only a matter of time before they find us. I want them very busy and very tired for the next twenty-four hours."

"Ms. Womack, I thought your plan was to teach us, to spread all that learning you're so keen on." Snivvery's voice was deadpan, but neither woman thought they were fooling each other.

"Plans within plans," Womack said. "Why would you care? You're top of the class. I'm sure you'll head on to better things than I can offer."

"I don't know. I want to see how this finishes. Then maybe I move on, or maybe I'll set up one of your franchises. If there's one thing I've learned over the last few weeks, it's that there's always a sucker looking for a way to seem smart."

Womack pondered the possibilities. She was used to working alone, but it could be helpful to have a sidekick sometimes. If she had to tolerate one, she could do a lot worse than Snivvery.

First, though, she needed to send out her distraction.

"Here." She threw a sack to the nearest troll. He opened the bag and hooted in excitement at the hoard of magic potions, sugary food, and caffeinated drinks inside. "Fill your faces, then run on down to the theme park and have some fun. Remember, I want big, I want loud, I want entertaining. The more attention you get, the more gold and loot like this will be waiting for you when you come back."

The trolls tore the bag open and rifled through its contents, cracking open energy drinks, tearing candy bars from their wrappers, and downing potions in a single gulp.

"You think they'll make it as far as Disneyland?" Snivvery asked as she and Womack walked out the door.

"You think it matters? As long as there are six giant trolls out causing chaos in LA, I'll consider this time well spent."

Back at Silver Griffin HQ, it was Ellis' turn at the front of the briefing.

"I've been chasing Womack for a while," he said. "She's slippery as a sack of eels, and she's looking to make herself even harder to find. This magic she's been building up hides her from the world. Ordinary folks don't see the building she's in anymore, and she's fixing to disappear from view completely. Even before all of this, she specialized in deception, and she's been teaching her pupils her old tricks. When we go in, you need to remember that things may not be like they seem. Watch your backs. Watch the walls. Watch out for that sneaking feeling that you've missed something because that might be your subconscious trying to show you what's real."

The door of the meeting room opened, and a messenger pigeon fluttered in. It landed on Applegate's shoulder and pecked urgently at his ear.

"I should take this," he said. "You carry on without me."

As Applegate left, Jackie got up from her seat.

"Hiding behind magic is Womack's big strength, but it's also how we can hurt her," Jackie said. "She's a witch who relies on avoiding confrontation, one who can't take any of you in a straight-up fight. There might be some thugs in her class, but the boss herself is soft if she's caught out in the open. If we can cut through the illusions and expose her, this will be an easy win, but that's a big if."

Lucy nodded. She admired Jackie's confidence, but she had seen how powerfully Womack's illusion affected people in her neighborhood, and it seemed like that magic was getting stronger. They would have to be careful not to let anything distract them once they got close.

"Assignments for the raid are as follows," Jackie said. "Perimeter team will be—"

"Hold everything!" Applegate said as he burst back through the door. "We have an emergency down by Disneyland, a group of rogue trolls causing absolute carnage. I need everyone to head down there for containment and clean up."

"But Womack—"

"Will have to wait."

"That ain't a good idea," Ellis cautioned. "If she finishes this spell Vessfall told us about we'll never catch her because we'll never know that she and her base exist. They'll be gone, like that." He snapped his fingers. "From what Lucy saw, it's nearly a done deal already."

"That's a lot of ifs and maybes when I know for a fact that these trolls are causing carnage now." As other wizards and witches rushed from the room, Applegate looked thoughtfully at Lucy, Jackie, and Ellis. "I can spare you three to keep an eye on the place, intervene if something big happens, but that's it."

He hurried off, leaving only the three of them behind.

"Keep an eye on the place." Ellis kicked the table leg. "It

won't do us a damn bit of good. We'll be killing time while she vanishes into the air."

"Then we go in," Jackie said. "We're allowed to intervene if something big happens, and this is big."

"Three of us against her whole crime school?" Ellis raised an eyebrow. "I'm not saying no, but I don't like those odds."

"Not only the three of us." Lucy pulled out her phone. "It's time to call in the little guns."

CHAPTER THIRTY-FIVE

Lucy rallied the troops around the corner from the Womack Academy. In an ideal world, she would have gone in with a whole office's worth of Silver Griffins at her back, but if she had to have a substitute, her family and the Underfoot Brigade were the best anyone could ever want.

"Is everyone ready to go in?" she asked.

"Go in where?" Kix looked around in confusion. "What are we doing here again?"

"Going to shut down the magic school."

"What magic school?"

"Don't worry," Twylan said, "I'll show you."

Lucy frowned. Kix wasn't the only one struggling to keep the mission in her head. The magic Womack had cast was growing in strength, making it harder for anyone to remember that there was a mission to fulfill. This was their last chance.

"Dylan, Eddie, Siltor, I need you to hold the perimeter in case any mundane people come near," Lucy said. "Siltor and Dylan, use illusions to send them away. Eddie, turn into an animal nobody wants to get close to. That should drive them off."

Eddie turned into a fat, flea-ridden rat and started scurrying around under the others' feet. This seemed like a really fun game.

"Ashley, Octo can climb up the building, right?"

"Yes, Mom."

"Then send him up to the roof and keep an eye on the camera feeds. I want to know if Womack tries to get out that way."

"Got it."

"I can go up there too." Leontine flexed his new prosthetic wing. "Then it's not only a robot blocking the exit."

"Good idea. Everyone else, we don't have time for a complex plan, so we'll go in en masse. I have enough key cards to use all three doors. I'll lead one group, Jackie leads another, Ellis the third. Watch out for each other in there. If someone you're with starts looking confused or uncertain, cast a counterspell on them. It's our best chance to cut through Womack's magic. Everybody ready?"

They all nodded.

"Then let's go."

They ran up to the building, and Lucy led her team to a side door. She had Charlie and Twylan with her, as well as several more of the teens from the tunnels. Everyone wore a determined expression.

Lucy swiped the key card through the lock, and swung the door open. They ran in and found themselves in a long corridor with a series of featureless doors. Nothing would have told her that this wasn't simply one more office block.

"Which way?" Twlyan asked.

"I don't know," Lucy admitted. "It could be any of them."

"Or none of them," Charlie said. "Look at those doors at the end. They're exactly like the ones here. It's like when programmers copy the same image over and over in a video game."

He waved his wand and chanted a spell. The walls shimmered like the air over a hot road, then a section at the end melted away, revealing the bottom of a staircase.

"If they hid it, they don't want us to see it," Lucy said. "Up that way."

They dashed up the stairs and emerged onto another corridor. This time, it was occupied. A mismatched band of magicals faced them, elves, dwarfs, and wizards standing side by side.

Lucy launched a tangle of magical nets at the students. Most of them dodged clear or countered the spell with their magic, but a dwarf got caught up and dragged to the floor.

Spells shot through the air: fire and water, chains and nets, staggering blasts of power and shields to hold them off. Some of the students didn't have fighting spells of their own and instead ran at the attackers with baseball bats or raised fists.

An elf swung a punch at Lucy. She dodged aside, caught his arm, and twisted him around, driving his face into the wall. A flick of her wand summoned a thick layer of glue that held him in place, struggling and shouting but unable to get back to the fight.

Two of the students shoved Charlie through a doorway and cut him off from the rest. He looked around for help and instead saw an old computer sitting in a corner, wires trailing in every direction.

"Tangle and trip," he called while waving his wand.

The wires snaked across the floor and wrapped around the legs of the students advancing on him. One fell to the floor, where the cables coiled themselves tightly around her. The other one kept his balance but had to turn his attention to getting his legs free. As he waved his wand frantically back and forth, trying to summon the magic he needed, Charlie strode up and punched him out cold.

In the corridor, Twylan looked around in alarm. The other Underfoot volunteers were getting distracted. The whole building was pulsing with magic, its power like the pull of the moon on the sea, dragging Twylan's magic back and forth in great waves. At least her power was holding back the effects of the spell, keeping her mind clear. It had almost overcome the others, their gazes growing distant as the building around them faded into a haze of confused memories.

She cast a counterspell, and they came back to reality in time to fight off a fresh assault by Womack's students. As long as they were fighting, whether with fists or spells, they would be in the moment. If the spell grew much stronger, even that might not help, and they would be left helpless.

They had to get through while they still could, but the corridor ahead was crowded with opponents.

Twylan drew a deep breath and summoned all her power. Instead of controlling it as she was teaching Dylan to do, she unleashed it. A raw wave of force rushed down the corridor, smashing magicals aside.

"Lucy," Twylan shouted, "go through now, while you can!"

Lucy dashed down the corridor, past the dazed and bruised students, past an abandoned office, and up another flight of stairs. In the corridor behind her, Twylan slumped against the wall, the magic almost gone from her eyes. A dwarf pushed himself to his feet and advanced angrily on her.

"You're gonna regret that," he growled.

Charlie stepped out into the corridor with computer leads slithering like snakes behind him.

"Not while I'm still standing, she won't," he said.

Outside the building, Eddie was having a great time running back and forth as a rat, scaring off anyone who came too close. Then an exterminator's van pulled up, and a man in overalls got out. While Eddie scampered for cover, Dylan slid his wand into his pocket and hurried to the vehicle.

"Is something the matter?" he asked.

"Heard there was a rat infestation near an office building here," the exterminator said. "Although I can't remember which one. Is that weird?"

He looked at his clipboard, then glanced around, his eyes sliding off Womack's building as if it wasn't there. Most people would have given up beneath the power of the spell, but professional determination held the man in place.

"Rats here?" Dylan shook his head. "I don't think so. We have an office cat. He deals with them. Isn't that right?"

Eddie, now in feline form, emerged from behind a dumpster and rubbed himself against the exterminator's legs.

"Yeah, that…that sounds right." The exterminator scratched Eddie between the ears. "Cats, rats, all that." He looked confused again for a moment, then shrugged. "No idea why I'm here anyway."

He got into his van and drove off.

On the third floor of the office building, Lucy found what looked like a training room. A couple of scarred mannequins, dressed in thrift store clothes and decorated with magical symbols, stood in the middle with empty seats all around them. A door hung open on the far side.

As she dashed across the room, there was a swishing sound, and something grabbed her arm. As she twisted, a mannequin slapped her with its plastic hand while the other dummy reached out to grab her. Their hands were hard and cold, their faces blankly inhuman.

"Displodo!" Lucy exclaimed, shoving her wand at the first dummy's chest.

The mannequin exploded, showering Lucy in pieces of charred cotton and melted plastic. An arm stuck for a moment to the wall, then fell to the floor with a *thud*.

The second dummy grabbed Lucy by the throat, holding her up with hard hands and surprising strength. She gasped and waved her wand but couldn't get the words of the spell out. She squirmed and kicked, but the mannequin didn't feel pain and didn't care about the negligible damage she was doing. It kept squeezing, following the orders its creator had given.

Jackie charged into the room and slammed into the mannequin from behind. All three of them fell on the floor, and the dummy's head rolled off, but it kept moving, rising into a fighting pose with fists raised. Lucy and Jackie scrambled to their feet, wands raised.

"I'll deal with this," Jackie said. "You keep going."

Lucy sprinted out the far door and up another set of stairs. The walls were becoming blurry, like the hazy details of a half-lost memory. She could feel her concentration fading, her steps growing slower as her sense of purpose evaporated. Even her ability to see the building would soon be lost. She would forget all of this and walk away.

She stopped and rubbed her eyes, then slapped herself, the sharp shock bringing her back to reality.

"No need for that," said a low voice.

A Willen stood in a doorway, arms hanging loose by her sides, eyes spinning hypnotically.

"Just forget it all," Snivvery said, using her natural power to accentuate the bigger spell all around them. "Step away. There's nothing of interest here, and there are other things you should do."

"Yes…" Lucy said, her mind wandering. "I need to cook dinner, file my cases, pick the kids up from…from…" She snapped back to reality. "From right outside this building, because they're here too."

She raised her wand. Snivvery drew back through the doorway, but Lucy was after her.

Snivvery's hand twitched, and a knife appeared there, where none had been before. She flung it straight at Lucy, who ducked, and the blade slammed into the door.

Another one appeared between Snivvery's fingers. "I have all sorts of things hidden up my sleeves. You should leave before I find the grenade."

"I'm not going anywhere," Lucy countered. "Not until I get to Womack."

"Ten out of ten for effort, but I don't think that'll get you a passing grade."

Snivvery produced another knife, apparently from thin air, and raised them both ready to throw.

"Attractionibus magneticis," Lucy chanted.

The knives leapt from Snivvery's hands and *clanged* into each other, then fell to the floor.

"Neat trick," Snivvery said. "Got any more like it?"

Her eyes twitched for a moment to look over Lucy's shoulder. Lucy spun, but there was no one there. She looked back to see Snivvery running away, but as the Willen dashed for a fire exit, Lucy launched a spell.

"Glacio!"

Ice formed around Snivvery, freezing her in place.

"I'll be back for you later." Lucy headed for a final set of stairs. "As long as I remember this."

She emerged through a fire escape onto the roof of the building. It was flat, the sort that would usually be home to pigeons, but today it was very different. The surface was covered in paint, ink scratches, and scorch marks, creating a network of magical connections. There were artifacts and images where the lines intersected, each of them a connecting point in a powerful net of interlinked spells.

Leontine stood to one side, eyes glazed and mouth hanging open, unable to focus on anything, while Octo the robot prodded him with a spidery leg. In the middle of the roof, holding a lighter and a wax hand, was Meredith Womack.

"Agent Heron." She set the lighter's flame to the wax

hand's wicks. "So this is you at last. I was afraid we might meet."

Thick oily smoke trickled from the wax hand as it burned. A soft smell drifted across the rooftop, and Lucy's mind started to drift with it. She looked up at the clouds and smiled at the shapes she saw there.

"Look," she said. "That one's like Buddy."

She had left Buddy at home, hadn't she? He probably needed a walk now. She should go home for him. This place wasn't important anyway. If it had been, she would have remembered why she was here.

Her wand throbbed in her hand, a reminder of the powerful magic she had been wielding. Magic to protect other people. Magic to keep the world safe.

She forced herself back around to face the woman in the middle of the roof.

"I know you," Lucy said. "You're…"

She couldn't remember, but she did remember that it was important. This witch had done bad things. She was dangerous. She had to be stopped.

Lucy forced herself across the rooftop with shaking steps. Her body and mind both wanted to turn, to walk away and never think about this place or this woman again. But she couldn't. She mustn't. She had to keep going.

Why did she have to keep going?

She had almost reached the other woman, who looked at her with a little surprise and even more amusement.

"My, you *are* strong," the woman said as she set the burning hand in place on the last intersection. "But not strong enough. The spell is complete. It's over. I won."

Most of Lucy was fading away. It was like going to

sleep. Her mind drifted off into another realm, the one where connections shifted and memories were lost—the realm of dreams.

However, a small part of her remained, a part that could never let go, not when people she loved were in danger. That part stepped into the dream realm, then stepped away, leaving the rest of Lucy behind. That strong part of her flowed through her wand out into the world.

Womack stared in shock as a second Lucy, ghostly but determined, appeared next to the first.

"That's amazing," Womack whispered. "I don't suppose you'd teach me how?"

The new Lucy stamped on the wax hand, smashing it to pieces and putting out the flames.

With its central connection destroyed, the spell snapped. Stray strands of magic flapped away in every direction. Symbols on the rooftop blazed brightly, then went out. For a moment, as reality returned, Lucy stared at Womack through two pairs of eyes. Then the two Lucys slammed back together, making her head spin and her stomach churn.

Lucy bent over, desperately trying not to be sick. The world around her seemed more solid than it ever had, the building more real. It was overwhelming, this sudden rush of sensation.

Footsteps clattered across the rooftop as Womack dashed for the edge. "Next time, Agent Heron," she called and grabbed the top of the fire escape.

"No." Ellis emerged from the stairwell. "You don't get away this time." He flicked his wand, and a handcuff appeared around Womack's wrist, chaining her to the fire escape.

"Oh, come on," she cried, rattling the cuffs. "You can do better than that."

"We don't need to, sunshine," Lucy said. "We won."

CHAPTER THIRTY-SIX

Lucy sat outside Applegate's office, watching the chaos that had descended on the Silver Griffins' headquarters.

Two dozen agents were grappling with the captured trolls, using every trick of magic and manhandling to keep them under control while they tried to drive them into the holding cells. One of the trolls had broken free and was swinging from a light fitting, screeching and laughing under the influence of a massive caffeine and sugar high. Another one had grown monstrously tall and fallen over, smashing three desks. Eight agents were pinning it to the floor while Kelly Petrie tried to wrap it in enough magical chains to prevent an escape.

Meanwhile, other Griffins were processing Womack's students. Snivvery had thawed out enough to be slapped in handcuffs and was sitting next to her teacher at the back of the room, water dripping from her fur. When she and Womack looked at each other, it was with bitter anger and disappointment. Neither one wanted to accept that they had done anything to lead to their arrest.

The Underfoot Brigade stood guard around the captives from the school. After having their minds played with by Womack's spell, they weren't going to let her get a second chance at freedom.

"Trevilsom transport's gonna be busy." Ellis took a seat next to Lucy.

"Will you be part of that?" she asked.

"No, thank goodness." He rubbed his eyes. "My brain's so fried from the spells on that place that I need to sleep for the best part of a week."

"If your head's hurting, I know a good magical doctor."

"That's mighty kind, but my job here's finished. I'm due on the next flight out of town. Gotta go hunt a dwarf gunsmith in Texas."

"Sarah will be disappointed."

"Really?" A smile fought its way across his face. "In that case, I'll keep an eye out for cases that might bring me this way. It's not a bad town you've got here, wouldn't mind another look around."

Jackie walked over carrying a tray of cardboard coffee cups. "Here you go. Tea for the foreigner and black coffee for our guest."

"That's mighty kind," Ellis said. "Next one's on me."

Jackie snorted. "Yeah right. We'll probably never see you again."

"You're probably gonna say good riddance, huh?"

"I wouldn't go quite that far. Not anymore."

Applegate emerged from his office. His tie was crooked, and sweat soaked the collar of his shirt. The trip out to deal with the trolls was the most fieldwork anyone had seen him do in years, and the strain had taken its toll.

"I've spoken to the warden at Trevilsom," he said. "Obviously, they're happy that we've rounded up this lot, but they're going to need time to sort out cells and align the transport portal. Apparently, today was a maintenance day."

"What does that mean for us?" Lucy asked.

"It means we have an office full of trolls until tomorrow unless you want to put them in the holding cells."

"Oh no. We need Womack locked up as tight as possible as soon as possible. That lass is trouble."

"And you brought her down. Congratulations, all of you, on a job well done."

"We couldn't have done it alone." Lucy was glad to hear their efforts recognized, but she would never be a glory hog.

"Ah yes, I gather we're indebted to your family again."

"Not only them. There's someone you should meet."

Lucy hurried across the room to where the Underfoot Brigade stood. She took Twylan by the arm. "Come meet my boss."

"Me?" Twylan asked. "Why?"

"Because we couldn't have succeeded today without you. Now come on."

Lucy led the young woman across the office, past a troll still trying to break free from Kelly's constraints.

"This is Twylan," Lucy said when she reached Applegate. "She helped track down Womack's lair and cleared the way for me to arrest her. Twylan, this is our regional manager, Roger Applegate."

"Congratulations, young lady." Applegate shook

Twylan's hand. "Not many teenagers could achieve what you did."

"Thank you." Twylan blushed. The magic flickered a little brighter in her eyes. "I wanted to help."

"Twylan is one of the smartest young people I've met," Lucy said, "and a powerful witch. If she's interested, I think we should start preparing her for recruitment into the Griffins."

"Me?" Twylan blinked in surprise, and for a moment only shadows of her bright magic showed.

"She is a little young," Applegate said. "And the, um…" He pointed at his eyes.

"We don't need everyone to look perfectly human," Lucy said. "We do need the best talent we can get if we're going to face more people like Womack."

"Well then." Applegate nodded. "We can't recruit you yet, young lady, but I could talk you through the sorts of things you'd need to learn if you want to become a Silver Griffin one day."

"Can I think about it?"

"Of course." Applegate handed Twylan his card. "Call me when you're ready."

From across the office, Leontine called Twylan. She hurried off, clutching the business card.

"Speaking of learning," Applegate said. "I have the results from that management training course." He looked at Kelly, who was standing triumphant over the chained troll and raised his voice. "Agent Petrie, do you have a moment?"

Kelly walked over, straightening her suit as she went. She slid her wand into her pocket and shot Lucy a sidelong glare, then nodded respectfully at Applegate.

"Can I help you with something, sir?" she asked.

"The management training course." Applegate pulled a piece of paper from his pocket. "Got the results for both of you."

Lucy tensed. She wanted to tell herself that she didn't care about this. She was a Silver Griffin first and foremost. None of this management stuff mattered. That was why she had written an assignment about taking Buddy out for a magic-hunting walk.

She knew she was kidding herself. She'd put time and effort into the course, and it could make the difference between whether she one day became Kelly's boss or Kelly one day became hers. Those were wildly different futures, and one of them was a lot more comfortable.

"The two of you were top of your class." Applegate brandished the piece of paper. "You've done this department proud."

"Which of us came first?" Kelly said. "I only ask because the tutor was so complimentary about my assignments."

"It was Agent Heron," Appplegate said. "Apparently, she really impressed the examiners with an unorthodox approach and innovative thinking. Congratulations, Lucy, and of course to you too, Kelly."

Lucy struggled not to laugh as she watched Kelly fake a smile. Lucy had wanted to do well, and she would have been happy being in the top two. Kelly had wanted to win.

"All things considered, you two have earned the rest of the day off," Applegate said. "Go get some rest. I'll see you bright and early tomorrow."

"Hey, what about me?" Jackie asked.

"Sorry, Agent Kowal, but someone has to process all these perps."

Feeling a little guilty and a lot relieved, Lucy left her friend behind, grabbed her bag, and headed for reception, where her family waited. Charlie sat on the floor with Eddie, helping him make towers with the receptionist's stationery while Dylan read a history book and Ashley ran some checks on Octo.

"Mommy!" Eddie ran over and hugged Lucy's leg. She picked him up and carried him to the others.

"You're getting big," she said. "Not sure I can carry you much longer."

In response, the air around Eddie rippled, and he turned into a mouse.

"Okay, maybe you'll be light enough for a while yet."

Lucy leaned against Charlie. She was exhausted, but she had her family with her, and that made everything better.

"It's been a long day for all of us," Charlie said. "Why don't we head home and order in for dinner? Nobody wants the work of cooking tonight."

"Octo could cook," Ashley said, "if I write it a new program."

"Let's save the experiments for another night, sweetheart," Lucy said.

"Can we get Chinese?" Dylan asked.

"I want Thai," Ashley said.

Eddie turned human again long enough to shout "Pizza!"

"We'll decide on the way home," Lucy said. "Get your things together, and we can go."

Ashley screwed a plate back in place on Octo while Charlie and Eddie tidied up their construction site.

The receptionist's phone buzzed. He answered it and listened for a moment before looking up at Lucy.

"Agent Heron, Dodger Stadium's on your patch, right? We've had a report of magical smog attacking wildlife near there. Would you be able to go and have a look?"

"Sorry, lad, but I'm done for the day." Lucy took Charlie's hand and headed for the door. "I'm going home to spend time with this lot."

"Well, do you know who else we could send? Everyone seems really busy right now."

"Send one of the new guys. Tell them to think of it as a learning experience."

Magical smog is killing plants around L.A. Is it accidental or something more devious at play? Lucy and her family are on the case in ONE MOM ARMY.

Recipe for Double Chocolate Muffins

I mean, who can get enough chocolate and ever since Cocoa Puffs, even chocolate at breakfast is okay. I still remember drinking that chocolate milk that was left at the bottom of the bowl.

So, why not double chocolate muffins? A few notes – I have Grapeseed oil here because it works better (and leaves out soy that way – canola is usually a mixture of oils and one of them is soy, and 'vegetable' oil is soy oil). And you can substitute yogurt for the sour cream if you want, but not the low fat kind. Fat matters in baking.

Also, when stirring together the ingredients, don't over do it. A few lumps are not only fine, they'll work in your favor.

First, preheat the oven to 375 and in honor of Lucy Heron – that's 190 Celsius.

Ingredients:

- 2 c all purpose flour
- 1 c granulated sugar
- ½ c cocoa powder
- 1 ½ t baking soda
- ½ t salt
- 2 eggs beaten
- 1 t vanilla
- ½ c milk
- ½ c Grapeseed oil
- 2/3 c sour cream or yogurt
- 2 c semisweet chocolate chips (I like the little ones, but you do you)

Combine all dry ingredients (except those chips).

In a separate bowl, mix together the oil, milk and sugar. Next, add the beaten eggs and vanilla and stir well. Add the sour cream or yogurt and stir till barely combined. Add the dry ingredients slowly and stir till there's still a few lumps remaining.

Spoon mixture into cupcake tin lined with papers (I have some flashy gold ones in my pantry) to just below the top. Makes about 2 dozen.

If you didn't eat all the remaining chips somewhere in the process (no judgment, I've been known to do the same), sprinkle what remains on top.

Bake at 375 for 15 to 18 minutes. A toothpick or knife inserted in the center should come out with a few crumbs but no shmears.

Get sneak peeks, exclusive giveaways, behind the scenes content, and more. PLUS you'll be notified of special **one day only fan pricing** on new releases.

Sign up today to get free stories.

Visit: https://marthacarr.com/read-free-stories/

AUTHOR NOTES - MARTHA CARR
MARCH 5, 2021

Last weekend I was channeling my nine year old self. I took a mono print making class at a local gallery. Just five of us spread out over a large art room with paper, big presses, tons of colorful ink, and bags of leaves, fuzzy materials, sponges shaped like dinosaurs, bubble wrap, mylar – you get the idea.

The goal was to ink up a large piece of plastic, throw on different objects and run the whole thing through the press.

Out of the small group, I was the only amateur. Everyone else was there to create something worth hanging on a wall. I was interested in seeing what kind of impression the bubble wrap would make.

At first, I had the weirdest reaction because I realized I was also the only one lacking a 'vision' of what I wanted to create. For about a half a minute I tried to come up with something but thank God another instinct kicked in and I thought, screw it. Let's have some fun.

A little bright blue there, some green, maybe a little

orange. Let's try a cutout of a house and some trees but not in the usual positions. What if they were falling all over the paper instead?

After each run through the fifty pounds of pressure on the hand-cranked press, I peeled back the paper to see the surprise and was never disappointed – because I had no expectations. That kid thing.

Since I had no idea what it could, or worse, *should* look like, I was thrilled with what was.

Colors blending into each other, splatter appearing in unexpected places, the sound of bubble wrap exploding under the pressure and echoing inside the press. Ridiculous fun.

All of this was possible because somewhere along the way I stopped caring how I looked to other people. It's like finding the key to your own birdcage.

The teacher, Alex clapped and oohed and aahed over every new layer I added to the paper. We even took a tiny dried up, flattened lizard she found behind a table and inked it up and stuck it on the paper. What came out was a perfect rendition of not just the outline of a lizard, but every little vertebra inside of it. Very cool. My inner kid was wide-eyed with wonder.

It wasn't long before a strange thing happened in the room. The young woman across the room sighed and said she wished she could just let go too. She looked back at what she had already made and muttered to herself, "I think I can," wandering back to her table to try putting something randomly on the paper.

The other artists squinted and pursed their lips and meandered back to their areas, pulling out more things to just try. Soon there were colorful explosions everywhere. No two the same and all of them so interesting. It felt like summer camp again.

At the end of the two days the teacher looked at me and smiled. "I have never seen anyone lean in so much to trying anything. It was amazing how many layers of images you got on your works."

I smiled and thought, *when did I change, exactly?*

I have spent more of my life overthinking everything but eventually, and fortunately, I wore myself out and sought another way. Over time, I learned to trust in something bigger and just let go. It's that simple and that hard.

My goal all along was to go back to that little kid again but this time, stay here.

When I wasn't looking, just like most things in life, I got to that place. Maybe quarantine had something to do with it. All that time to reflect. Maybe it's years of writing that is its own form of meditation. Maybe it was just the willingness to try without expectation. In the end, it doesn't matter. I wonder what I will get to try next. More adventures to follow.

Thank you for taking the time to both read this story and these author notes as well!

I have to admit I'm a little scared...kinda.

I am pushing myself to learn a new way of creating stories in 3D (specifically, Unreal), and having to deal with all new technology (AGAIN!) in my life is daunting.

I look at YouTube videos about learning Unreal for Cinematography and see the hundreds of little menu choices and just want to give up.

I'm fifty...<<mumble mumble>> for @#%@# sake! My mind screams that I should be satisfied with the success of the stories I have created and be done.

I'm not.

So, this last weekend I was learning about computer parts, including the Nvidia GTX 3090 24Gb video card, the AMD Ryzen 5950X, and the fact that it is pin-identical to the same motherboards that use earlier Ryzen cards. This is important because these parts mentioned are almost impossible to purchase.

It seems every game player and the thousands of crypto-currency players have bought the things, pushing the street price for the card to $3,000.

My wallet had a heart attack.

I am a professed Apple fan. Almost fanboy, but not quite. I owe many years of my professional career to Windows, and as far as I can tell, the best operating system to run Unreal is Windows.

So, I (eventually) bought an Alienware system with the right video card but not the best AMD Ryzen option. When you buy the whole computer, you aren't stuck with the street price for the video card, and I'm too damned old to want to build my own.

I did that back in my 20s and 30s, but now I can afford to tell "them" to come to my house and fix it. I bought that privilege, too. Every privilege has a price.

Back to learning and being scared.

So, I played with a few tools over the years and realized three things. First, the learning curve for me would be very high. Second, working on a scene (at the time) required a LOT of patience, which is an attribute I have never had a sufficient amount of, and third, seeing the results was SLOOOOWWWWWWW.

The tools are now there to solve most of the issues. I have a person in the company who can help me past the hardest learning hurdles. We have pre-built actions for rigged 3d characters and/or we can buy a suit to make them. Finally, the new video card makes the waiting problem (for the most part) a concern for the past.

Now, the last hesitation is, *am I too old to learn something new*? Will I end my days working on books and stories and just be too worn out to want to play in 3D?

Is this a young person's game?

I don't know. But I'm willing to try.

As my collaborator would say, "More adventures to follow!"

Ad Aeternitatem,

Michael Anderle

Solve a murder, save her mother, and stop the apocalypse?

What would you do when elves ask you to investigate a prince's murder and you didn't even know elves, or magic, was real?

Meet Leira Berens, Austin homicide detective who's good at what she does – track down the bad guys and lock them away.

Which is why the elves want her to solve this murder – fast. It's not just about tracking down the killer and bringing them to justice. It's about saving the world!

If you're looking for a heroine who prefers fighting to flirting, check out The Leira Chronicles today!

AVAILABLE ON AMAZON AND IN KINDLE UNLIMITED!

OTHER SERIES IN THE ORICERAN
UNIVERSE

THE LEIRA CHRONICLES

SOUL STONE MAGE

THE KACY CHRONICLES

MIDWEST MAGIC CHRONICLES

THE FAIRHAVEN CHRONICLES

I FEAR NO EVIL

THE DANIEL CODEX SERIES

SCHOOL OF NECESSARY MAGIC

SCHOOL OF NECESSARY MAGIC: RAINE CAMPBELL

ALISON BROWNSTONE

FEDERAL AGENTS OF MAGIC

SCIONS OF MAGIC

THE UNBELIEVABLE MR. BROWNSTONE

DWARF BOUNTY HUNTER

MAGIC CITY CHRONICLES

ACADEMY OF NECESSARY MAGIC

OTHER BOOKS BY JUDITH BERENS

OTHER BOOKS BY MARTHA CARR

JOIN THE ORICERAN UNIVERSE FAN GROUP ON
FACEBOOK!

BOOKS BY MICHAEL ANDERLE

Sign up for the LMBPN email list to be notified of new releases and special deals!

https://lmbpn.com/email/

For a complete list of books by Michael Anderle, please visit:

www.lmbpn.com/ma-books/

CONNECT WITH THE AUTHORS

Martha Carr Social

Website: http://www.marthacarr.com

Facebook: https://www.facebook.com/
groups/MarthaCarrFans/

Michael Anderle Social

Website: http://lmbpn.com

Email List: http://lmbpn.com/email/

Social Media:

https://www.facebook.com/LMBPNPublishing

https://twitter.com/MichaelAnderle

https://www.instagram.com/lmbpn_publishing/

https://www.bookbub.com/authors/michael-anderle

www.ingramcontent.com/pod-product-compliance
Lightning Source LLC
Chambersburg PA
CBHW050508110726
47899CB00005B/1370